Conflicting Hearts

Conflicting Hearts

by

J. D. Burrows

Disclaimer

This work is not intended as a substitute for any advice that may be given by a mental health professional, such as a therapist or psychiatrist. If you are a victim of childhood sexual abuse, please be aware that this book may trigger flashbacks, memories and/or upsetting emotions.

Author's Note

The occurrence of childhood sexual abuse portrayed in this book is not fiction. It is the author's true-life experience.

Acknowledgements

Thank you to the following businesses who granted permission to reference their establishments in this work.

Stephanie Inn
2740 South Pacific
Cannon Beach, Oregon 97110
http://www.stephanie-inn.com

Portland City Grill
Unico US Bank Tower/30th Floor
111 SW 5th Avenue
Portland, Oregon 97204
www.portlandcitygrill.com

Dedication

To every child who has experienced the horrors of sexual abuse, may you find healing, hope, and the love you deserve.

TABLE OF CONTENTS

Chapter 1

A FATED OCCURRENCE

It is eight o'clock in the morning. I squeeze my lips together in frustration and rest my right hand on top of the steering wheel, repeatedly tapping my fingers from pinky to index finger. As I look at my nails that sorely need a manicure, I wonder why I don't tap my fingers the other way, from index finger to pinky. I try, but my brain refuses to obey. I'm obviously bored.

Beep. Beep. A blaring horn behind me causes me to glance in my rearview mirror. The irate driver shoots me an angry glare and raises his hands. I glance forward and note that the traffic has moved. *Thirty feet and you need to beep at me, you creep?* I accelerate toward the bumper of the snazzy roadster ahead of me and come to another stop. The traffic is going absolutely nowhere.

I flip on the radio station and punch the buttons, one after another, searching for a traffic report. Finally, I hear the news. *"The Sunset Highway is backed up at Sylvan Hill due to a three car accident. Only one lane is open . . ."*

"Crap," I blurt in frustration. This is not a good start to my day.

A quick glance in my rearview mirror tells me Mr. Hurry-It-Up is as frustrated as I am. It's time to break the law. I shove my hand into my purse and retrieve my phone. I glance around to make sure no cops are nearby to give me a ticket for driving while talking on my cell. Of course, idling isn't driving, mind you, but if anyone would be ticketed, it would be me. Funny, but everyone else is on the phone too. I hit the speed dial and push the speaker button.

"Kennedy Advertising Agency, this is Julie."

"Julie? This is Rachel. I'm stuck in traffic, and I don't think I'm going to make it to work on time. Can you let the boss know?"

"You caught in that accident on the freeway?"

"Yeah, and it's a bugger. I should be there before my nine a.m. meeting."

"All right, I'll let Mr. Stewart know you're running late."

"Thanks," I reply and end the call. Okay, that's taken care of, so I drop my phone back in my purse.

Beep. Beep. Beep. The guy behind me lays on the horn again. I turn my head around and glare at his rude face, before checking through my front windshield. After I turn my head forward again, I see why he's cursing me. The traffic is moving. I accelerate and am surprised I'm actually rolling along at twenty-five miles per hour. It appears another lane has opened, easing the gridlock.

As I pass the three vehicles off to the side of the road that caused the backup, I see the police cars with their flashing overheads. My head cocks to the right to take a quick glance. Wow, what a mess of jumbled steel. Nobody appears injured, so why does everybody have to gawk at accidents? Of course, I'm being judgmental and doing the same thing.

The next I know, I turn my head forward and *bam*! The traffic has come to a quick halt again, and I've just rear-ended the car ahead of me. My airbag goes off and slaps me in the face, stopping my heart from the shock.

"Oh, God, no," I cry out. Devastated, I place my forehead on the steering wheel and feel like banging it repeatedly. Inwardly, I say a thousand curses, afraid to look at the damage. I don't have the courage to gaze at my latest screw-up. A sinking, accident-sick feeling clutches my stomach. *Shit, shit, shit!* I whine inside my scatterbrain head. My next expletive rant is interrupted by a *tap-tap-tap* on the glass.

I slowly raise my head and notice a tall man, with dark hair, peering down at me through my driver's side window. The car ahead is empty, and I assume this is the guy I creamed. I push the button, and it rolls down.

"Please, don't yell at me," I beg, looking up at him. I'm on the verge of tears.

"I'm not going to yell at you," he calmly replies. "I saw your head against the steering wheel and was concerned that you might have been injured."

Wow, that's a first. I look at the damage to his car and cringe. His trunk is bent and popped open. The hood on my car is crinkled like an accordion.

"I'm okay," I answer timidly. "Are you okay?"

His narrowed blue eyes look at me

intently, and I wonder if he's going to sue. Crap, everybody who gets rear-ended sues. It's a given.

"I'm fine. Just a minor fender bender. Perhaps we should pull off to the shoulder and exchange insurance information. We're holding up traffic."

"Oh, okay," I say, watching him walk away and get back into his car. I finally take the time to examine my victim. He looks around my age, tall, dark hair, dressed in an expensive navy-colored, three-piece business suit. *Maybe he doesn't need my insurance money,* I think to myself.

As I pull my crunched car over to the right side, I hear the front bumper rub against the left tire. Steam is hissing from underneath the hood. Damn, I really did a job on my junker. My poor twelve year-old, foreign make looks like it's had its last day on the road. I glance at his beautiful car and cringe. Not only is his trunk smashed, but the bumper is falling off on the right side.

After we pull over to the shoulder, cars start moving past us. I sheepishly look in the visor mirror and check my looks. Why, I have no idea, except already I feel intimidated by the man in the suit who is back, standing on the passenger side of my car, tapping on the window. I hit the button and roll it down.

"Yes?"

"You should get out on this side rather than on the driver's. It's too dangerous."

"Dangerous?"

I look out my window and see how close I'm parked to the lane. He's right. If I open my door, I'm going to lose it. *Crap.* Thank goodness I wore a pantsuit to work rather than a skirt and blouse. In a very unladylike manner, I swing my right leg over the protruding gear shift, slide my butt into the passenger seat, and pull my left leg over feeling like a pretzel. I unlock the door, and he opens it for me. *Good lord, who is this guy?* I ponder inwardly.

"Here, let me help you," he says, offering me his hand.

"No, I'm fine," I protest, as I wiggle my way out of the seat and stand up outside the car. My hand shoves a piece of hair out of my eyes, and I try to compose myself. The scent of the man's cologne wafts toward my nose. He takes a step back toward the concrete barrier giving me room to maneuver.

"Are you sure that you're okay, ma'am?" He wrinkles his brow and gives me the once over, as if he's looking for broken bones or blood.

"Yes, I'm okay, but I should be asking you that question. Look what I did to your car!" I've crashed into a dark blue British made roadster. Dang, what a shame! I'd kill me, if I were him.

"Nothing that can't be fixed," he assures me in a composed and even tone.

"But what about you? Did I wrench your neck and shoulders?" I wince after the words leave my mouth. Why am I encouraging a lawsuit?

"Well, for now, I'm okay. I think my car took it harder than I did."

"I'm sorry," I blurt out. "I was gawking at the accident off to the side, cursing the traffic, and then I rammed your bumper. It's entirely my fault." I remember the warning on my insurance card not to admit fault. Stupid, I *am* at fault, and my insurance rates are going to skyrocket.

"We should exchange information," he says, giving me a somber look.

For a moment, I make a closer inspection of the driver and curse myself for running into him. Damn, he's one decent-looking man. At least I have morning eye-candy to soothe my wounded ego, if nothing else.

"Let me grab my purse." I lean over inside my car, feeling embarrassed that my ass is in the air, and snatch it off the floor. My head comes up for air, and I see the steam hissing through my hood.

"Oh, God, I think I'm going to need a tow," I moan.

"Yes, it looks as if you've cracked your radiator, I'm afraid," he says, stroking his chin.

I frown over his astute observation and glance over at his car, wondering if he can drive off with a hanging bumper.

"Excuse me," I say, squeezing between him and the freeway barrier. The close quarters of the shoulder cause me to brush against his body, giving him the familiar boob graze. *Why didn't you just ask him to move?* I chide myself.

He towers over my five-foot, four-inch frame and watches me like a hawk with his dark eyes. His lashes are so thick that he looks as if he's wearing eye liner. The more I stare into them, the more I realize he's a natural hunk. His piercing gaze makes me nervous, and I hope that I didn't rear-end a serial killer. You never know.

I plop my ten-pound purse on top of the trunk and start rifling through the contents. After finding my wallet, I flip through the multiple cards I carry that give me discounts throughout the city. Somewhere between the grocery store and the pet store I find my insurance card.

"Here it is." I breathe in relief, as I pull it out and hand it over to him.

"Driver's license?" he asks coolly.

"Oh, sorry." I locate it and pass it to him. Immediately, I notice he hasn't pulled any of his cards out, but I've bared my horrible license photo, address, height, weight, age, color of my eyes, and insurance company to this complete stranger. He peruses my driver's license attentively and then grins.

"Nice picture."

"Oh, sure," I say. "You're trying to make me feel better." My eyes narrow, and I scowl at him.

He chuckles and then reaches inside of his vest pocket and retrieves a small, black notepad. Quickly, he flips it open, grabs a fancy pen from inside, too, and places my information and his pad on the trunk of my car. I'm fascinated, wondering who he is, as his cologne rides upon the passing breeze, swirling around me like a toxic drug. It's been too long since I've inhaled the scent of a man. His hair is thick and dark, and I have the urge to run my fingers through it.

"Rachel Ann Hayward," he slowly drawls, as he pens my name down in perfect script. He jots down the numbered address and my apartment unit, and recites the rest out loud. "S.W. Barnes Road, Portland, Oregon 97229. Date of birth May 25, 1982." He pauses, and I know why. It dawns on him what I already know.

"It's your birthday today?" His smile fades, and he looks at me with a pitiful stare.

Hastily, I turn my gaze away, shrug my shoulders and nod "yes" acknowledging the perfect start of my day turning thirty.

"Apparently, the big three-o was meant to be a memorable one. It's downhill from here on out," I reply, trying not to look at him. I keep my eyes on the impressive pen instead.

"I doubt that," he says sweetly. "It's only the beginning, I assure you."

What's that supposed to mean? I wonder, scrunching my brow. *Is he a fortune teller?*

He finishes penning the remainder of my information and then hands me back my driver's license and insurance card.

"Now yours?" My eyebrows are raised, in case he thinks I'm going to let him off. Suddenly, I see a policeman walking up from the accident behind us.

"Is anyone hurt?"

The cop takes the usual take-charge stance. Mr. Cutesy answers.

"No officer, everything is fine. We're just exchanging information now."

The police officer takes a quick look at our damage, scowls at me, and then nods at my victim.

"All right then, if there are no injuries, I'll leave you two." He turns around and walks back toward the other pileup.

"Uh, license and insurance," I remind him, holding out my hand.

"Sure thing," he says, shoving his hand into his inside jacket pocket and retrieving a slim, brown leather wallet. With his long fingers, he pulls out his driver's license and insurance card, which look brand new. Mine, on the other hand, looks as if it went through the wash.

I tilt my head so I can see the inside of

his wallet. To my chagrin, each card is neatly situated in the slots, and I notice the first three are in alphabetical order. I suspect the others are too. He quickly closes it up in front of my snooping nose. Curiosity always gets the best of me, and I am overwhelmingly fascinated by this guy. He wears an expensive suit, his hair doesn't have a strand out of place, and his nails actually look manicured. I conclude he's a neat freak and some high-powered business executive who works downtown.

"Thank you," I mumble. I snatch his license and insurance card, and then put them on the trunk of my car. He's quietly watching me, almost as if I'm his morning entertainment. I shove my hand into the black hole that is my purse and search for a piece of paper and something to write with. Finding an old receipt and a pen with a smidgen of ink left at the tip, I quickly jot down his information, taking note of his life points.

Ian A. Richards, age 32, Skyline Drive, Portland, Oregon and realize he doesn't live that far away from me. I glance at his fancy insurance card. He's not in the friendly hands of my insurance company. Instead, he's got the buck with the antlers.

"So, you have the insurance company with the deer picture," I announce in stupidity.

"Bull elk," he replies with a smart-ass grin.

His face looks as if he's sporting the hunter of the year award and instantly I wonder if he has a gun. I eye his smug attitude up and down and then fly one off myself.

"Wow, as nicely as you're dressed, in your three-piece suit, I sure hope you're not an attorney or I'm screwed."

Immediately, I laugh at my sense of humor and scribble the rest of his information down on the back my prescription receipt. I should have asked him for a piece of paper from his little black notebook. He didn't offer one either, so strike against him.

"I am, as a matter of fact," he unexpectedly declares, interrupting my thoughts. He cocks his head to the side and sports an arrogant smile. His hand slips into that inside pocket, which apparently carries everything he needs, and whips out a business card, handing it to me. I gawk at it and then read his name aloud in disbelief.

"Ian A. Richards, Attorney at Law."

Damn it! I scream in my head. This day is *not* going well.

"You have got to be kidding me." Suddenly, I feel the blood drain from my face as I pale to the color of the concrete barrier behind me. "I can't believe I just rear-ended an attorney, of all people." I bring my hand to my head and hold it, as if it's going to help or something.

"I'm a corporate attorney, not a litigation attorney, if that makes you feel any better."

"That's supposed to make me feel better?" I look into his eyes, which look playful and not mad. "I bet you know a few bright litigation attorneys anyway."

"I do." A painful grimace replaces his smile, and he reaches his hand back to his neck and rubs it with a groan.

Oh, damn. He's going to sue my ass, and I hope my insurance company's hands are large enough. He sees my horrified face and then stops his tease.

"I have no intention of suing you, Miss Hayward," he says, flashing a grin as he removes his hand.

"God, I hope not, but I'm sure if your

neck starts to ache, my insurance will cover whatever you need." There go my cheap premiums. I'll be categorized as a risk on the road.

"Here." I give him back his driver's license and insurance card. "I am really sorry," I whine, while throwing him a remorseful look that screams for pity. I look over at my car, which obviously isn't going anywhere on its own accord.

"I guess I should call for a tow."

"Please, let me," he says. He flips out his cell phone, does a quick contact search, and hits speed dial. The next I know he's summoned a tow truck to haul my car off the freeway and tells the guy to charge his account.

"Someone will be here within the next half hour, if they can squeeze through traffic," he confidently states.

"Wow, that's really nice of you, but I do have towing coverage through my insurance," I tell him, digging through my wallet looking for the card again.

"It's on me," he insists.

He seems determined, so I forgo the search. "What about your car?"

"Hum, well, let me see," he says,

walking over to the back end. He plants his feet at a wide stance and examines the damage for a few moments. "It should be drivable to the repair shop," he says, after stooping down and peeking under the bumper. He stands upright, pushes open the crunched trunk and then leans over fishing around for something inside. The next I know, he's sporting a roll of duct tape in his hand.

"The cure for the world," he notes, as he rips a long strip off and begins wrapping his bumper. After a couple of minutes unrolling and tearing tape, he has the bumper secured, as well as his trunk.

"Well, that should hold," he announces with pride.

Impressive. I stare at him and secretly gush. I've run into a stud on wheels. As my tongue hangs out of my mouth, I hear the tow truck pull up behind my car. He guns the monster truck once, turns it off and then opens the door. A man in a dirty white shirt and blue jeans wobbles toward me. He walks over, scratching the unruly hair on his head and surveys the damage to my hood.

"Where to, ma'am?" He sounds as if he has a wad of chewing tobacco in his mouth.

"Where to what?" I sound like a dumb blonde.

"Where do you want me to tow it?"

My mind draws a blank. I don't know where to tow it. Should I have it dragged back to my apartment? It's not like I have a list of body shops in my head.

"I'm . . . I'm not sure," I answer with a befuddled look on my face.

"Look, lady," he says, exasperated. "I can either tow it to the yard and you can pay storage fees or I can tow it—"

"Tow it to Johnson's Auto Body on Canyon Road," the attorney pipes up. "That's near the lady's home and should be a convenient location. They're reputable and should do a proper job."

"Fine with me," he says, walking back to his truck. He starts fiddling with chains and gears, and whatever they do to haul cars away.

I turn and look at Mr. Richards, grateful for his help. "I feel like the proverbial helpless woman. I'm not really." I lie through my bashful smile. With a gentle, comforting tone, he puts me at ease.

"That's quite all right, Miss Hayward. Automobile accidents have a tendency to leave us in a bit of a haze."

"You coming with me, ma'am?"

The driver is now scratching his beer belly and looking at me. Does the man have bugs? The idea of sitting next to him from here to the body shop does not appeal whatsoever. My nose wrinkles.

"I'll take her," Mr. Nice Guy offers.

"What?" I brandish a startled glance and look into his dark eyes, which scare me a bit.

"It's your birthday. Hey, it's the least I can do." His smile sends me vibes.

"Oh, I couldn't," I promptly answer, horrified over the thought of sitting in his car next to him. The chance he's a serial killer still exists. He did brandish a roll of duct tape.

"Surely, I must be keeping you from work," I remind him.

"Is this keeping *you* from work?" He furrows his brow.

I glance at my watch mortified over the time. "Oh, God, I'm late for a meeting now."

"Were you on your way downtown?"

"Yes, Second and Main."

"Well, that's three blocks from my firm's office."

"But what about my car?" I glance over

at the tow truck driver, who now looks peeved over my conversational exchange with the law man.

"He can drop off your car, and you can phone the body shop when you get to work and make arrangements for repairs. Would that be convenient?"

He's undeniably eager to convince me to come with him. I see in his eyes a distinct kindness, and foolishly I want to relent. Mr. Richards is jingling the keys in his hand; the tow truck driver is glowering at me as he waits for my answer.

Rationally, I try to think this out. He does have a business card, so maybe he is legit. I weigh my chances looking back and forth at two strangers, who both could rape and strangle me at a moment's notice. If I have to die, I choose the clean-cut attorney to do me in.

"All right then."

A winning smile curls his lips. He walks to his car and opens the door for me. I can't remember the last time anyone bothered. For a brief moment, I glance at him, and like an obedient little girl, I crawl inside. He gently closes the door and waits for traffic to clear before jumping in the driver's seat. A car whooshes by his side.

"I wouldn't advise that tactic," he says, putting the key into the ignition.

Quickly, I snatch the seatbelt and buckle myself into his snazzy car. A moment later we're back in traffic, and I'm riding in the cockpit of a roadster probably worth over fifty grand. I glance over my shoulder and see my car worth twenty-four hundred that is being pulled up on the tow truck bed. The poor thing needs a hug, and so do I.

"I'm ashamed," I admit aloud. "I'm taking advantage of your kindness, and you should be mad at me."

"Why, for heaven's sake?" He glances over at me with a surprised look upon his face. "It was just an accident. They happen."

"A stupid one on my part. I should have been looking where I was going."

"Perhaps, but frankly I think it might be a fated occurrence."

Huh, fated? What's that supposed to mean? I glare at him over his bizarre comment. A grin, which looks far too mischievous, spreads across his face. Now I'm really uneasy.

"So where do you work? What's at Second and Main?" he suddenly asks.

I feel uncomfortable over the question, but answer anyway. "Ah, Kennedy Advertising Agency."

"I'm impressed," he says. "That's a large and prestigious organization. What do you do there?"

He's impressed? Wait until he hears of my stellar career. "Administrative Assistant," I mumble under my breath, feeling like the extremely dumb secretary that I am. He's probably a Harvard law graduate, and I'm a high school graduate—the vast difference between us looms like the Grand Canyon.

"Frankly, I don't know what I'd do without my assistant," he sincerely expresses. "I'd be lost. Admirable job that doesn't get enough credit."

I'm in a car with a freak, or he's pulling my leg to make an impression. I've worked at a law firm before and know the pecking level. An assistant is at the bottom of the scum pile, and there is no fraternizing between the attorneys and staff.

The traffic crawls down the freeway, and I'm wondering how long I'll be in the car with Mr. Perfect sitting next to me on my left. I look out the window, and for a minute get lost in my thoughts. Hopefully, he's a decent driver, because I feel as if I have no control over my destiny when I'm not behind the steering wheel. Of course, my ability to care for myself has suffered a tremendous blow this morning.

"So, what are your plans to celebrate your birthday after work tonight?"

His out-of-the-blue question catches me off guard. "Plans? I have no plans. It's business as usual," I nervously answer, clutching my purse.

"And what's business as usual, Rachel?"

Oh, now we're on a first name basis? I don't like his prying. "Well, tonight, I'll probably stop at a restaurant on the way home, get a high carb carryout dinner for comfort food, go home, hug my cat, and find some British soap opera series on cable."

"Not exactly what I would call a memorable birthday," he swiftly responds in a critical tone. "Your thirtieth should be a milestone celebration. Don't you have any friends that want to take you out for drinks or dinner?"

"Not really. I have work acquaintances, but everyone has a life after five. I hate to intrude." Being a fifth wheel is worse than being single and alone, but he probably doesn't know that. He's quiet for a moment and then comes back with his next question.

"What about family?"

Now, he's annoying the hell out of me. I swing my head to the left and glance at him again. His eyes are narrowed as if he's worried about me. Why does this stranger give a damn how I celebrate my birthday? With a tone of irritation, I give him a snappy answer.

"I have no family, except a brother two thousand miles away who never keeps in touch. My parents are dead."

Swiftly, I look out the passenger window, stifling the urge to cry. I stick my fingertip between my teeth and start chewing on my nail. The freaking traffic won't move fast enough so I can get out of the car.

Finally, he takes the City Center exit and weaves through downtown to Main Street. I see my building approaching off to the right. The light turns red, so I quickly grab the opportunity.

"This is fine. I can walk from here."

His car comes to a halt, and I grab the door handle and swing the escape hatch open next to the curb. I jump out as if I'm on fire, lower my head, and catch a glimpse of the astonishment on his face.

"Thanks for the ride, and, again, I'm very sorry for the accident."

I gently close the door and walk quickly to the entrance of the building, duck inside, and heave a relieved breath after taking a ride with a complete stranger. My mother would have scolded me for sure. *Sorry*, I talk to her in my head as if she can hear me. *But, God, he was adorable, Mom.*

Chapter 2

I take the elevator to the tenth floor thinking about which comfort food to stuff myself with when I get home tonight. Suddenly, I'm reminded I need a rental car. The first order of business is to call my insurance company and report the accident. Afterward, I need to check with the body shop and see if my clunker has been delivered.

The elevator door opens, and I sprint to my desk. Oh, great, the usual "come get a donut to celebrate Rachel's birthday" email has gone out department wide. Already, the pastry box on the corner of my desk is three quarters empty. Crumbs and powdered sugar are sprinkled everywhere on my desktop, and I've missed all the well-wishes. *Whatever, like it matters*, I inwardly gripe.

Julie runs up to my desk. "Rachel, where have you been? Mr. Stewart is spitting mad you missed the meeting. He pulled in Kathy in from the Marketing Department to take the minutes.”

“I got into an accident,” I moan, while shoving my purse into my bottom desk drawer.

“Accident?” She brings her hand to her mouth. “Oh, my gosh, what happened?”

“I rear-ended some lawyer in a fancy sports car, if you can believe that. I guess I should be thankful it wasn’t a cop.”

“Are you okay?”

“Yes, but my car isn’t. They had to tow it away.”

“What a way to start your birthday,” she says, giving me a sorry look of empathy.

I shrug my shoulders. “C’est la vie. It’s just another day as far as I’m concerned.”

“Hey, Rachel, happy birthday.” Stephan, our mail clerk, rolls up the basket with the morning delivery. He picks up a donut and stuffs it into his mouth. “Hope you have a happy one.”

I can barely understand him as he chews the tasty fried grease. I reach over, choose one of the leftover donuts, and shove the whole thing into my mouth too.

“Thank you,” I mumble, anticipating the

incoming sugar high. Before I can swallow the mass of dough stuck to my tongue, my boss is standing at my desk.

"Where have you been?" He creases his bushy eyebrows together and scowls at me with his brown eyes.

Julie, the coward, hastily retreats leaving me alone to fend for myself. As fast as I can, I push the pastry down my throat.

"Accident," I mutter. "I got in an accident."

"I thought you were caught in traffic last I heard."

"Well, yes, but afterward I got in an accident."

"Next time, call if you can't make the meeting."

"Yes, sir. Sorry, sir." He returns to his office and closes the door without a happy birthday well-wish, or I hope you weren't hurt comment. As usual, there goes another male that could give a damn. *Creep*. I give him the Rachel evil eye.

I sit down at my desk, rev up my computer, and squeeze in a few quick calls to my insurance company. Apparently, I can't get a rental until the morning, which means it's public transportation to get home. I shudder at the thought of the stinky bus, two transfers, and the three-block walk from the bus stop in the dark. This is not going well, and I will have to skip my fancy takeout dinner on the way home. Looks like I'll have to settle for delivered pizza.

After that business, I immediately call the body shop and give them my insurance information. They want me to drop by and sign some papers before they start work, so another task I need to take care of first thing in the morning. I'm angry at myself for being so stupid and not watching where I was going! Now, I'm paying for it, like I always pay in life for all my dumb-ass mistakes.

The day progresses, as usual, until three o'clock arrives when I get a phone call from the receptionist, Melanie, at the front desk.

"There's a delivery for you, Rachel."

"All right," I acknowledge and hang up. Immediately, I figure it's some package being couriered to my boss, which is the usual reason I get calls to come fetch. As I arrive at the reception desk, I see a large bouquet of red roses on the corner.

"Wow, some lucky girl," I say, gawking at the flowers. I peer over the reception counter looking for an envelope or package for my boss. Melanie looks at me cockeyed.

"I would say so, they're for you."

Rapidly, I stand up straight and drop my jaw. "You've got to be kidding me?" I squawk.

She leans her elbows on the desk and sighs wistfully. "Looks as if you have a secret admirer."

"I sincerely doubt that." I quickly dismiss her conclusion. "Maybe my brother had a pang of guilt after twenty-five years of ignoring me."

The suspense is killing me, so I grab the card and open it. My heart leaps into my throat when I recognize the neat-freak's handwriting.

"Miss Hayward, no woman should spend her thirtieth birthday alone. Let me take you out for dinner and drinks after work to celebrate. If you refuse, you'll be hearing from my personal injury attorney."

He signs it "Ian Richards" in impressive script and then adds RSVP and his phone number underneath.

"Unbelievable," I mumble, shaking my head in disbelief.

"Who sent them?" Melanie pries.

"If I told you, you wouldn't believe it."

My hand grabs the bottom of the vase, which looks like crystal and not glass, and holds a dozen long-stemmed red roses, surrounded with baby's breath and decorative ferns. The fragrance is overwhelming. I'm grinning like a fool from ear to ear, because I really can't remember the last time I received roses from a man.

Hopefully, my cat won't eat these, I think to myself. I don't keep live plants in the house for fear he will. As I'm heading back to my desk, I'm trying to think where I can put the flowers out of reach from Whiskers.

As I walk into the cubicle world of my department, all the female heads follow me with their eyes. Julie jumps up from her chair and tags along behind me to my desk.

"Gosh, pretty. Who sent those?"

"My victim," I say impassively, trying to hide my giddiness.

"Victim?" She buries her nose in one of the blooms and inhales.

"Yes, the guy I rear-ended this morning."

Her eyes widen in surprise. "Wow, you must have made an impression on him."

I shake my head in doubt. "No, he's just feeling sorry for me, because I started my birthday off on the wrong foot." Purposely I fail to mention the dinner and drinks invitation, because she'll give me advice if I do.

The blooms look spectacular on the corner of my desk. I decide to leave them here at the office rather than take them home. At least I won't worry about Whiskers overindulging on some toxic plant and me coming home to find him dead by the front door. I scrunch my nose over the thought, because I'm such a freaking worrywart about everything.

It's three-thirty, and five o'clock is fast approaching. He's probably waiting for my phone call. After sliding open my bottom desk drawer, I fish my cell out of my purse. Discreetly, I take the gift card and walk over to a private employee lounge area, which is out of range of everyone's hearing.

My stomach flutters like a butterfly. I dial his number and notice I've pushed one of the numbers wrong. Damn, I'm so freaking nervous, my brain won't work. I repeatedly blink a few times to get my vision squared away so I can see straight. Afterward, I try again and meticulously tap the numbers on my shiny cell phone screen. I bring the phone to my ear, hear it ring, and he immediately answers.

"Ian Richards," he says, upbeat and cheerful.

The lump in my throat won't let me say anything. A few seconds pass, and I hear him again.

"Hello? Anybody there?"

"It's me," I squeak out, sounding like a mouse.

"Me who?" I hear a chuckle in his voice as if he already knows 'me who.'

"Rachel." The pitch in my voice is still high.

"Well, hello there," he drawls in a relaxed tone. His voice reminds me of black velvet, and I see his handsome face in my mind and turn to putty.

I draw in a breath and control myself. "Thank you for the flowers, Mr. Richards."

"You're very welcome, Rachel. Are the roses to your liking?" He sounds so sweet and sincere.

"Yes, but you shouldn't have."

"Why not?"

"Because, I don't really know you, and I killed your fancy car this morning."

"Well, you know the rear end of my car, the interior of my car, the contents of my trunk, my driver's license number, address, height, weight, color of my eyes, and location of my employment. I would say that you do know *some* things about me."

I try and stifle a girlish giggle, but it's no use. *Why am I having this conversation with this man?* I ask myself.

"So, what about dinner, Miss Hayward? Can I pick you up at five?"

"I don't do dinner out," I reply in a sheepish voice.

"Why not?"

"Because." My eyes close. I'm such a ninny.

"I'm not sure I understand. Can you explain the 'because' statement?"

The reason is childish and silly, but I might as well tell him the truth. Maybe he'll go away. "I get nervous when I'm with strangers, and I can't eat. And if I do eat when I'm nervous, I get sick to my stomach. So I made a pact with myself never to eat out with strangers. Saves the hassle."

He pauses for a few moments as if he's digesting my stupid explanation. "Then how about drinks?"

"You're not giving up are you, Mr. Richards." I state it as a fact and not a question.

"Well, I don't want to pressure you into anything."

Oh, yes, you do, I think warily to myself.

"Do you need to pick up a rental car after work?" He continues his questions.

"No, I couldn't get one until tomorrow morning."

"Well, then how will you get home?"

"Bus."

"Have one drink with me, and then I'll drive you home."

Boy, this guy is pushy. I hesitate and then continue. "How do I know you're not an attorney during the day and a serial killer at night and on weekends?" My tone is dead-serious. "You did have duct tape in your trunk."

I'm not joking, and his breathing gets heavier at the other end. Maybe he is a serial killer, and he's thinking how to do me in even now because I've annoyed the hell out of him.

"You'll have to trust me that I'm not." His voice is calm and unnervingly even.

Trust. Oh, sure. A concept that for me doesn't exist, my brain reminds me. "It's hard for me to trust," I admit, clearing my throat.

"Look, Miss Hayward," he says, slightly annoyed. "I have no intention of harming you whatsoever. I felt sorry that you were spending your birthday alone. Since we met during unpleasant circumstances, I just thought I'd offer you a chance to celebrate. Nothing more."

I've offended him. Guilt washes over me and anxiety gnaws at my stomach. I hate it when I've annoyed people, especially when they are trying to be nice. It's not my intention to make him dislike me. Rejection hurts, even from strangers. Perhaps I'm reading way too much into this, like I usually do, so I relent.

"Okay, then."

"Five o'clock? I'll meet you in the lobby of your building?" He sounds as if he's about to spring out into a chorus of Hallelujah.

"Okay." I'm feeling the usual deer in the headlight syndrome. I can't think of anything to say, because my brain is frozen. He gets what he wants, and I can't say no.

"Okay, five o'clock in the lobby," I repeat.

"See you then," he replies and hangs up.

Immediately, I feel like I'm on the verge

of a panic attack. I hate doing things I don't want to do. Now I'm mad at myself for giving in to his offer and want to throw up.

I wander back to my desk clutching my phone with a death grip. *I don't want to do this*, I moan again to myself, but now I'm committed. *Stand him up*, the cowardly little voice inside suggests. *No, I can't*, I dismiss the taunt. *He'll sue me if I do.*

For the next hour I can hardly work, stewing over what's ahead. Time ticks toward the hour of doom. At quarter to five, I run into the ladies' room and powder my nose. My dull blonde hair is in disarray. Thank goodness I find a brush in the bottom of my purse. I try to untangle the strands, but I don't have any hairspray to make it stay. A quick freshening of my lipstick, a mint to suck on the way down to my rendezvous, and I think I'm ready—for what, I have no idea.

As the elevator descends to the ground floor, so does my self-esteem. Why is this man insisting on taking me out for a drink on my birthday? He's way out of my league, and I question his motives. I'm beginning to wonder if he thinks I'll sleep with him so he won't sue me.

When the elevator door opens, my brick

wall is stacked high. After inhaling deep breath, I turn the corner and enter the lobby. He's standing by the front door with his hands in his pockets. For a minute, I think he looks worried and uneasy too. Maybe he's having second thoughts. It helps with my jitters.

I walk toward him, and he turns around at the sound of my heels clicking across the lobby floor. A smile spreads across his face, and he suddenly looks relieved.

"Rachel," he says, flashing a smile. "I'm glad you're here."

I stop a few feet away and release a coy grin myself. "Did you think I'd stand you up?"

He tilts his head and glances at the floor. "Oh, the thought crossed my mind."

"It crossed mine too," I admit to my shame. "But I'm here."

"Yes, you are," he says with a smirk.

He gazes intently at me, roving his eyes up and down my frame. Is he undressing me in his mind or something? I'm a bit miffed.

"So, what's next?" I eye the revolving door, wishing I could make a quick escape.

"I thought we'd have a drink down the street at a small Italian restaurant that I like.

They have a cozy bar where we can talk, if you're sure you don't want anything to eat."

"I'm sure," I say, feeling my stomach growling. I can't eat next to this man, or I'll be running to the ladies' room every five minutes. Nervous heebie-jeebies and humiliation come in all forms when dealing with my anxieties. It's not worth the risk.

He walks alongside of me and makes no attempt to touch, for which I'm thankful. I try and give him the benefit of the doubt, that this is a friendly birthday drink and nothing more. *I can do this,* I tell myself, as he holds the door open for me to enter. A hostess quickly greets us.

"Table for two?" she asks, grabbing the menus and standing at attention.

"No, just drinks," he replies. He sounds disappointed.

He nods toward the bar entrance and leads me into the dark lounge. Immediately, I see the romantic surroundings. The easy-listening music is playing low, small candles illuminate the center of the tables, and a dark mahogany bar with an ornate mirror and liquor takes up a long wall.

Ian, whose name I've been trying to get used to, chooses a table off in the corner and pulls out a chair for me. All this polite masculine treatment feels bizarre. I obediently slip myself onto the seat and try to act natural. My hands are sweating, and my heart is in my throat.

He sits down across from me, and a waitress quickly approaches to take our orders.

"What can I get you?" The server asks me first.

"Uh, Coke," I respond, looking up at her hovering over us.

"No wine or maybe a mixed drink?" His eyes are wide with surprise.

Alcohol will make me turn red as a beet. I'm already self-conscious as it is, and I don't need to make myself any hotter. Especially around him, as I melt into his mesmerizing gaze.

"No, Coke, is fine."

"Okay," he says, turning his head toward the waitress. "Coke for the lady, and a Bud for me."

He's a beer drinker? I thought for sure that he'd be drinking some expensive wine that has a name I can't pronounce. The waitress puts two white napkins on the table, and scurries off to get our orders.

"Don't you drink alcohol?"

"Um, sometimes." *Not when I'm on anti-depressants*, I think to myself, but I'm not going to tell him that.

"Interesting," he replies.

Instantly, I think he's disappointed that he can't get me drunk, so he can get in my pants.

"I've never been much of a drinker. I don't like beer or the taste of hard alcohol. A Merlot once in a while is okay, but I buy the cheap brands. You know, the $3.99 bottle specials at the grocery store." He laughs, and I wonder what's so funny—the fact that I don't drink or my $3.99 cheapo comment.

The waitress returns with his beer and my pop. As soon as he takes the glass in his hand, Ian lifts it toward me. His dark and expressive eyes flash me a sincere look that just about melts the ice in my glass.

"Happy thirtieth birthday, Rachel Ann Hayward. May you have many more."

My mouth falls open. I'm flabbergasted. His glass is extended toward me, and he wants me to clink it in return. Nobody has *ever* toasted me on my birthday, and I'm red-faced over his kind gesture.

Regardless, I raise my glass in my shaky

hand and quickly give it that one-time clink and take a sip through the straw. It tastes fantastic. The cold liquid slips down my throat helping to move the lump that's been there for the last fifteen minutes.

The usual speechless mode takes over as I look into his blue eyes. Suddenly, I'm thinking thoughts I shouldn't be—like what he looks like without that suit. The dark atmosphere and the romantic background music play havoc upon my female psyche. He watches me intently in return, while he takes another sip of his frothy beer.

"Thank you for the toast. That was nice," I blurt out.

"Hey, you're thirty. Great time to be alive. I think the thirties are the best years."

"Why?"

He lowers his head and looks inside of his beer glass as if he's looking for the answer, then shrugs his shoulders.

"Oh, I don't know about you, but I feel like I understand my life, where I've been, where I'm going, and what I want."

His eyes darken into a sexy stare, and I'm dumbfounded that I'm picking up vibes from the guy that I rear-ended this morning. Is he my birthday present from heaven or something? I smile at the thought and then slap my foolish, wandering mind back in place.

"I'm not quite sure that I feel like you do."

"How do you feel about being thirty?" He leans forward.

Lonely, pathetic, loser, doomed to die an old maid.

"Oh, I don't know. Unsettled, I guess is the only word I can think of at the moment." I take a long sip through my straw and soak up the sugar in the glass.

"How so?"

"You mean unsettled?"

"Yeah. Sounds like you haven't found what you're looking for in life."

Well, that's obvious. Look at the lack of a ring on my left hand, I think to myself.

I suddenly wonder why he's not married. Of course, I'm assuming he's not married, because I don't see a ring, but that doesn't necessary mean a hill of beans these days. After all, he's thirty-two years old, smoking hot, and probably has plenty of money. If he's unattached, maybe he has a girlfriend or maybe he's gay. *God, I hope I got that wrong,* I silently muse for my sake.

"Do you have a boyfriend?"

Whoa! I flinch, wondering if he's reading my musings over him. "Nope," I say, curling my lips in a circle and smacking them together.

He reaches over and grabs my left hand and thumbs my ring finger. "Nothing there, so I'm guessing you're not married either."

"Nope." I take a sip of Coke and look at him. I'm sure he figured that out this morning. My tongue is twisted and tied at the end, and I'm back to a one-word conversation.

"You?" I gulp.

"Nope," he answers, smacking his lips, too, sporting a grin.

We both laugh, and then I realize he's still holding my hand. Suddenly, I feel uncomfortable. Very gently, I pull it away and grab my Coke glass to cool off. I'm scared.

"You sure you don't want dinner?"

He looks over his shoulder into the inviting restaurant. The aroma of food is tempting. My stomach growls, and I'm afraid he's heard it. I cough to cover up the sound.

"Uh, no, that's okay. No food." My mouth is drooling, but I know it will be a disaster if I agree to dine with him.

Ian takes a sip of beer and glances around the bar. He suddenly seems awkward and ill at ease, and I wonder why. Perhaps he thinks my spurning his dinner invitation means that I'm not interested in him. The way I feel now, I certainly don't want to leave that message, especially if he's interested in me. Then again, maybe he's figuring out he's not that into me. I wish I'd stop trying to analyze everything. It's exhausting.

"So, tell me about your job." I grin with a bit of enthusiasm to see if I can bring him back. "Do you like what you do?"

He returns his gaze and parts his mouth with a small smile. Once again, he looks into his magic glass of beer for the words. I'm surprised that I'm sensing a bit of shyness, and it makes me feel more relaxed.

"Yes, I like it. Hate the time I have to put in, but that's law firms."

"Do you keep long hours?" I try and sound interested.

"Yeah, sometimes fifty to sixty a week, maybe more on important deals."

"Gosh, when do you have time to unwind and have a life?"

"Well, I don't have much of one right now, but I don't have anything else to occupy my time."

"Yeah, me either," I admit.

"One of these days, I'd like to change jobs and work as an in-house counsel at a large corporation. Usually, those types of positions are a little easier on the hours."

"Oh, are you looking?"

"Not seriously."

He takes a sip of beer and keeps looking directly into my eyes. I wonder what's going on underneath that thick head of hair that I'd love to run my fingers through. For some reason, I think he's reading my thoughts again, when a suggestive smile curls his lips. No, he's thinking about sex, I quickly conclude. *Men,* I inwardly grumble. Every twenty seconds, or is it every twenty minutes, they're thinking about screwing someone?

Of course, I should talk. It's on my mind constantly. There are times I think I'm a nymphomaniac, but since I haven't had a good lay in over five years that probably doesn't qualify, or maybe it does. My thoughts are running amuck, and I'd wish he would say something.

"So, what do you do for fun?" He breaks the awkward silence.

"Uh, fun? What do you mean fun?" I sound like I don't know the meaning of the word, and I don't. *Think of something*, I urge my blank mind.

"You know, hobbies. How do you spend your time on weekends? Things like that."

"Oh, catch up with life. Go grocery shopping, to the bank, get an oil change. I take care of the things I don't have time to do during working hours."

He shakes his head and sports a half-frown. "No, I mean *fun* and relaxation, Rachel."

Boy, this guy is persistent, but I like the way my name sounds when he speaks it. I think for a moment and then answer.

"There are things I'd like to do, but I don't because I'm alone. You know, take a hike down the Columbia Gorge, go camping at the beach, and travel overseas." I drop my gaze into my dwindling Coke glass, searching for the next words. I'm as guilty as him now.

"I'm careful, though, about doing things by myself as a single woman, like hiking. It can be dangerous." I'm feeling like a rascal, so I look him straight in the eye. "You never know when you'll run into a serial killer in the Pacific Northwest."

He lowers his head and snorts a laugh. Then Ian's eyes turn dark, and he gives me a startling gaze that scares the crap out of me. His mouth opens, and a sexy drawl leaves his lips, which sends shivers up my spine.

"That's probably wise, Miss Hayward, because you *never* know."

His hand reaches across the table. He swallows mine in his broad palm. It's warm—very warm. Hot, in fact, like my body from his touch. I feel my neck burst out in red blotches, and my cheeks flush.

"Sounds as if you need a strong male to protect you and take you hiking. Mind if I apply for the job?"

"Huh?" I blubber, with my eyes bulging out of my head. Is he asking me out? "Uh, I don't know what to . . . what to say," I stammer.

"Well, what are you doing this Saturday? How about I pick you up, and we take a hike."

I giggle. "Take a hike. That sounds funny." Now I am acting like a total nervous ditz. "Let me think about it." My eyes are pleading for him to back off. "It's only Monday, and you never know what the week will bring."

"Okay, I'll let you think about it. If you say no, I reserve the right to ask again."

"Or what, you'll hire a personal injury attorney? That was extremely funny, by the way."

"Well, Rachel, being turned down by a beautiful girl like yourself could cause any man personal injury, I would think."

He speaks the words with such heartfelt earnestness, I actually feel flattered. Once again, I'm back to the thought that he wants to get in my pants. Compliments are an excellent way to get in there, and maybe he senses my vulnerabilities.

"You're embarrassing me," I whisper and lower my head to the table.

"You should learn to take a compliment, Rachel. I tell it like I see it."

I shove the straw in my mouth and suck, but the bottom of the glass just gives that empty slurp sound.

"Want another?" He waves the waitress over to our table.

"Better not. I think I should be going home." I can't drink another if he's driving, or I'll need to stop and pee somewhere between downtown and home.

"So soon?"

A flash of disappointment spreads across his face. He wants me to stay. I want to stay. My fears tell me to go.

"Yes, my cat . . . he's probably hungry."

"Okay, then. You're still going to let me drive you home, right?"

"Sure."

"Beginning to trust me?" He sounds anxious for me to do just that.

His hand squeezes mine. I had forgotten he was still holding it. For some odd reason, it felt as if we blended together as one. I'm disappointed when he pulls away and goes fishing for his wallet to pay the tab.

For the next few minutes, I'm off somewhere in my mind, wandering around in a daze. The world around me diminishes into a blur. I know I'm walking with him, and I feel his hand holding mine, guiding me down the street. A moment later, we're in the concrete basement of some garage, and I hear the beep-beep of his security system on his car and see the latches pop up on the doors. His bumper is still wrapped in tape.

"You didn't get a loaner yet?"

"Tomorrow, I'll have one."

I glance at the damage that I've done to his lovely car, and the sense of mortification returns. If I had watched what I was doing, I wouldn't be here now—with him—the perfect specimen of manhood, who is far too good to be with a girl like me. Of course, I could be prejudging him solely based on his smoking looks and kindness. He could be a monster underneath, just like the rest. A woman never knows. My half smile fades into a frown as the memories of former brutes flood my mind.

"You okay?" he asks, as he opens the car door for me.

"I'm a bit tired." Hasty lies always hide the feelings. I can't tell him the truth for heaven's sake. We've just met.

The journey home is quiet. He appears immersed in his own thoughts, but he's driving straight toward where I live. "I should give you directions," I offer, a bit surprised he hasn't asked.

"No, that's okay. I checked on the Internet and mapped it out," he says nonchalantly.

Ingenious man, I think to myself with a tad of suspicion. I decide to check the web for information on him when I get home.

Surprisingly, I feel comfortable with his driving. I don't usually like the passenger seat. That out-of-control feeling sweeps over me. I look at the dashboard and see he's not speeding. He's following the car ahead at a safe distance. He's an excellent driver. It's probably the perfection part in him that I am sensing.

While I'm thinking about it, some car speeds by him and cuts in front. It startles me, and I grab the arm rest. He doesn't flinch. Now, I'm thoroughly impressed. Not a trace of road rage tendency stirs him whatsoever.

"That was a close one." He glances over at me with a concerned look.

"Yeah. Crazy drivers," I moan with self-righteousness.

"There are a few, that's for sure." He smirks.

"Probably not the thing to be saying after my own faux pas of this morning."

Now he's grinning from ear to ear. He turns his head quickly and winks at me, then looks back at the road. I relax in my seat for the remainder of the way home.

Ian pulls up to my apartment complex

and magically arrives in front of the exact building. He finds a visitor-only parking spot, turns off the car, and reaches over to pat my hand.

"Let me walk you to the door."

"Uh, no, that's okay." I feel compelled to refuse his offer, afraid he's going to want an invitation to come in.

"Just to the door," he says, opening his and climbing out.

He comes around and opens my door and then offers his hand for me to take. I look into his sincere, kind eyes and release my fate into his palm. It's unusual for someone to take care of me with such thoughtfulness. I don't know how to respond.

After I'm out, he releases my hand, and I start walking toward my apartment. "I'm on the third floor," I tell him, taking the first step. I practically run upstairs, and he follows behind me. The door to Apartment 306 is there, and I hesitate before putting the key into the lock. I turn and look at him watching me.

"Ian, thank you for making my birthday a memorable one. I don't think I'll forget this day, thanks to my inability to pay attention to the road ahead of me." I'm captivated by his sympathetic eyes. Admiration threatens to drown my cautious heart. Immediately, I try to suppress the urge to like him—really like him.

"No, problem, Rachel. Frankly, I'm glad we ran into each other." He chuckles and changes his sentence. "I mean *you* ran into me."

He reaches out and touches the tip of my nose with his index finger. I flinch over his cute antics.

"Thanks again." I push the key into my lock and shove open the door.

"Saturday," he asks, sounding like a little boy. "Are we on for a hike?"

The longing in his eyes touches me. "I'll call and let you know, okay?" It's all I can offer at the moment without feeling pressured.

"Okay. You have my number. Call me." His face is clearly etched in disappointment.

He turns and heads toward the stairs and climbs down the first six and stands on the landing for a brief second. "Goodnight."

"Night." I wave goodbye and smile.

A moment later, I'm in my apartment. I lock the door and slide my back down to the floor, until my rear hits the throw rug. The thought of spending time with him is overwhelming. I feel drained in so many ways, I can't number them.

Confusion swirls through my mind, mixed with the fear. I'm not sure what I should do about his invitation. Finally, my pent-up emotions from the day expel in tears. For the next ten minutes, I'm lost in a crying jag I cannot stop, because of the kind respect Ian Richards has shown me. I know I don't deserve it, but it felt so wonderful it makes me want more.

Chapter 3

A RELUCTANT ACCEPTANCE

I wake up Tuesday with my usual morning depression, after a restless night's sleep. Attorney blue-eyes kept showing up when I closed my eyelids. He's hard to eradicate, and now I have four days to decide whether I want to accept his offer or not.

After climbing out of bed and showering, I'm reminded that I need to catch the bus to the body shop a few miles away to sign papers and pick up a rental. Already, I'm behind at work, which adds more stress to my day. I reach for my prescription and down my morning anti-depressant. Tonight at seven o'clock I'll take another.

Three months ago, I had fallen back into the dumps. It's been a constant battle being on and off medication since I was a teenager. I feel happy, and then I feel awful. When I think I've got the depression beat, I go off the pills and feel cheerful for a few months. Then stress, loneliness, and heartache take their toll again, and I'm calling my doctor begging for the return of the purple-colored pill.

I'm to the point in my life that I'm thinking of making this a permanent arrangement. We're old friends by now. I don't know what else to do, because I need to function so I can work and take care of myself. There's nobody else to do it for me.

As soon as that thought crosses my mind, I think of Ian Richards. It's far too tempting to believe that a handsome and successful man would find an interest in me, especially on a long-term basis. I'm not sure if I accept his story that he wants to be friends. We're not on the same playing field. Another twang of distrust hits me as I try to figure out his motives for wanting to take me on a hike.

It doesn't take long for the alone-in-the-woods thought to resurface and the notorious serial killers of the Pacific Northwest to haunt my mind. I can see it now—my poor bones with the flesh picked off by ravens will make headlines in the Oregonian newspaper—unidentified skeletal remains found on Larch Mountain by a hiker.

If I do go with Ian, then I am choosing a trail that I know is heavily travelled. Perhaps I should check his backpack to make sure he hasn't brought any duct tape. The irrational worries keep prancing through my mind from rape to murder. I have four days to figure this out. At the rate I'm going, I'll make myself sick by then and won't be able to go.

After climbing into my economy rental, I drive to work and park in the structure next to our building. I'm early enough not to get a lecture, so I head upstairs to my desk and am greeted by the red roses that look as fresh as the day before. They make me smile. I shove my nose into a bloom and inhale the scent reminding myself how delightful it feels to receive a fresh bouquet. I should give him credit for that, at least.

"Hey, Rachel!" Julie greets me. "The roses still look fabulous. Did you thank your victim?"

I smile and feel the urge to share. "Yeah, we had a drink after work last night."

"No!" She plops herself in the chair next to my desk and leans forward. "Tell me, what happened?"

"I ordered a Coke, he had a Bud, and we

just talked." I try to make light of it, then added the rest. "Then he drove me home."

"Wow, did he come in and you guys . . . you know . . . .?"

"Gosh, do you think I'm bonkers?" I squawk at her in disbelief. "I hardly know the man. No, I didn't invite him in."

"Are you going to see him again?"

Now the questions are annoying me. Why do I share when I know that people are going to poke and pry even more? There's a reason I'm private, and this is it—Julie Rogers with her big nose. If I tell her everything, soon the whole office will know of my personal life before the noon hour. Afterward, in the months that follow, everyone will line up at my desk telling me what to do next.

"I'm not sure," I say, turning my head away. I push the power button on my computer and wait for the software welcome sign. Maybe she'll get the hint her welcome has ended.

"Well, let me know if anything comes of it," she says, with a tad bit of disappointment in her voice. She rises from the chair and heads over to her home-sweet-cubicle.

As I wait for the computer, I glance at

the picture of my cat stuck to my cube's wall with a push pin. Whiskers, my life. My eyes turn toward the flowers, and I imagine a picture of Ian, with six-pack abs, sitting in a silver frame, adorning the corner of my desk. Now, wouldn't that be something? I'd never get any work done.

At last, the computer is up. The clock has rolled over to eight a.m. It's time to get to work and leave my fantasies behind somewhere in my mind. Already, I know that concentration is going to be difficult today. When I'm down, I can't focus, and work is painful. Mr. Stewart has filled my incoming box to the top. He's probably trying to pay me back for being late yesterday.

"Time to earn my $14.68 hourly wage," I mutter under my breath. I grab the first piece of paper and get at it.

The week has shown me no mercy by making each day fly by toward my decision point. He hasn't called me, and I'm assuming he picked up the hint that I don't like to be pressured. I feel guilty that I haven't called, but I've thought it out carefully what I want to say.

Late Thursday afternoon, I decide to take the leap. Beforehand, I write down each point that I want to get across. Otherwise, I'll freeze in my thought process and forget everything. I want to hike at Multnomah Falls. The place is crawling with people this time of the year, and the trails are packed with visitors. There are bathrooms nearby, in case I lose it, and places I can scream if I need to be rescued. Of course, it's a long drop to the bottom falls should he decide to push me from the top, but I know I'm stretching the imagination with that lame thought. My pathetic paranoia tendencies make absolutely no sense.

I get up and walk over to the employee lounge again and dial his number. It rings and then goes straight to voice mail.

"You've reached Ian Richards. I'm away from my desk at the moment or on the other line. Please leave a message, and I'll return your call as soon as possible. Thank you, and have a pleasant day."

I pull the phone away from my ear, drop my mouth open, and look at it as if I just visited an alternate universe. Why is this guy so nice?

Beep. I hear it and then bring the phone

back up to my ear and freeze for a second. "Uh, Ian? It's me, Rachel. I'm calling about Saturday." I leave my number and hang up.

My stomach is nauseated, and I feel my heart flutter. My usual physical reactions raise their ugly head, because my mind can't handle an ounce of stress. *I hate myself*, I complain, and walk back to my desk.

I keep checking the time as it slips by, wondering why he hasn't called. Perhaps he's with a client, in a meeting, or didn't come into work because his neck is out of whack. It's possible. Four o'clock arrives, then four-thirty. Maybe he's changed his mind—that's more probable. He's thought about his invitation and wants to back out. I wouldn't be surprised.

My cell phone starts to vibrate on my desk top. I jolt and glance at the caller ID that reads Anderson & Wyatt Law Firm. It's him. I pick the phone up, rise from my seat, and answer it as I'm walking toward the employee lounge.

"Hello?"

"Rachel, it's Ian."

"Hi, Ian," I answer unemotionally. I try not to sound too anxious.

"I'm glad you called. I was getting

worried there that you wouldn't." He definitely sounds anxious.

"Oh, it's just been a busy week."

"Yeah, me too. Put in a couple of long hours the past few evenings."

"Sorry," I say, feeling genuinely bad this guy has to work so much.

"Have you decided about Saturday?"

"Yes."

"So?"

"Okay, I'll go under certain conditions."

"Name them."

"Can we hike at Multnomah Falls? You know, to the top? Haven't done that in years, and I think it would be fun."

"Yeah, sure. You up for the steep climb?"

I hadn't thought about that. It's a killer walk, that's for sure. "If we go slow, and you promise not to laugh at me when I need to stop and catch my breath."

"Deal. What time you want me to pick you up?"

"Oh, I don't know. Nine o'clock sound okay to you? We should get there about ten."

"Sounds fantastic. Want to do breakfast beforehand?"

"Uh, no," I say emphatically. The rascal

chuckles.

"Okay, I get it. I'll pack some snacks in my backpack just in case."

"Okay." I already know I'm going to refuse them.

"Well, thanks for calling, Rachel, and I look forward to our hike. See you Saturday morning."

"Okay."

My nose wrinkles in embarrassment over the same word I've said three sentences in a row. He's going to think I'm pretty dumb if all I can articulate is okay . . . okay . . . okay.

"Bye," he says, sounding pleased with himself.

"Bye." The call ends. I lean against the wall and catch my breath. This whole thing is pure torture.

I walk back to my desk and think about him for a few more minutes. It dawns on me that I haven't done an Internet search on this guy. Quickly, I glance around the office, and everybody is busy. My boss has left for the day, so I click on the web explorer. It pops up, and I head straight for the search box and type in "Ian Richards Attorney at Law." A few seconds later, a massive laundry list of information fills the page. My hand clutches the mouse, and I inhale a surprised breath.

His law firm comes up first, along with other search results such as professional organizations, Oregon State Bar Association, a former law firm he worked at, and a page on the same social media site that I use.

It's impossible not to giggle with glee over that discovery. I click on that first and groan in disappointment. He's got all his information locked down—his wall, his pictures. Damn. I click on "About" and there's not much there either, but I do see his relationship status. It says "Divorced."

I lean back in my chair. "You sly dog, you," I mumble under my breath. "Left that little tidbit out." My own guilt pokes me. *You didn't tell him that you were married before either. Yeah, yeah, I know. I'll cross that bridge when I come to it,* I rag on my conscience.

My eyes go back up the search results, and I click on his law firm information. A picture of him pops up. He's dressed in a pinstriped, dark-gray suit, white shirt, and black tie with diagonal gray stripes. I salivate over his good looks.

Next, I scroll down to his credentials. There it is . . . Harvard Law. *Oh, great, I feel like such a dummy now*, I moan in disappointment. The rest of the information goes on with details about his practice area and expertise.

As I keep clicking on search results, it's obvious that he's well educated and respected. I wonder about his family. Perhaps they're rich. He probably makes a six-figure income every year, and I'm reminded of my own pittance of a salary and multiple credit card debts. The more I read, the more depressed I become. The dichotomy between the two of us builds a broad chasm in my mind. I'll never be able to breach it, especially when he gets to know me.

Quickly, I exit the Internet. My eyes start to water as I ponder my worthless life. I notice the time. One more trip to the ladies' room before heading home, and then I'm going to stuff my face with ice cream and hug my cat. I need comfort and assurance from something, even if it's a ball of fur.

Thanks to my online snooping, I'm in the doldrums as I drive home. The feeling of hopelessness smothers me. Saturday will no doubt turn out disastrous, and our acquaintance will come to a swift end. The voices in my head taunt me.

Nothing good ever happens to you. You're such a loser.

Yeah, yeah, I know, I acknowledge them in return. I believe every word they've told me for twenty-five years and always have. Why should anything change now? It never does.

Chapter 4

TAKING A HIKE

The morning dawns, and I try to find courage to face the day. I eat an early breakfast high in protein, so I don't succumb to the need for food until later. Strangely, I'm not feeling as nervous as I thought I would be. In fact, I feel excited to be doing something besides staying home alone.

I dress in my best jeans, pink tee shirt, and grab a light jacket. The weather is clear and sunny today with a high of seventy-five degrees. Perfect for hiking the Columbia River Gorge, except as usual, it's a bit breezy from the east winds.

My long, blonde hair is freshly washed and pulled back in a ponytail that I weave through the back of my pink baseball cap. Apparently, I'm into pink today. I try not to overdo the makeup and definitely forgo any perfume. Otherwise, I'll be a target for every bee from here to Idaho.

After riffling through my dresser drawer, I find my waist pouch. I stuff it with my keys, wallet, tube of lipstick, small comb, a couple of tissues, and breath mints. I think that covers all the bases.

The anticipated knock comes at the door. For a moment, I hesitate to answer and make sure it's him by taking a peek through the peep hole. Sure enough, it is. He has his head down, and I wonder what he's thinking about.

My delay causes him to knock again, so I relent and answer. My heart leaps into my throat. God, he's a hunk even out of a suit. He's wearing a Blazer team tee shirt, which lets a few chest hairs peek over the top, and blue jeans with a matching jacket. I glance at his feet and see top-of-the-line hiking boots.

"Hi," he says, sporting a smile that flashes his pearly-white teeth.

"Hi." I keep my mouth shut and grin. He's contagious in a strange way—all that positive energy, laced with manners and kindness.

"You, uh, want to come in for a second? I need to grab my jacket and stuff."

"Sure," he says, walking in and closing

the door. He glances around my apartment. "Nice place."

It's obvious he's just saying that to be polite, but I try to accept the comment. "Yeah, works for me. Been here about five years now."

"Wow, long time."

"Rent is cheap. Neighbors are quiet. That's important."

"Sure is."

He stands there and watches my movements. I grab my waist satchel and my jacket. "Well, guess that's all I need."

Ian opens the door for me, and I lock it. Once again, time stops, and I'm off somewhere in my thoughts as I gleefully bounce down the steps and stop.

"Where's your car? I don't see any duct tape."

He laughs. "Over there. It's a rental." He walks toward a huge sport-utility vehicle.

"Wow, your insurance sure put you up in a nice ride."

"Well, I'm paying extra. I was hoping we'd take this little trip, so I wanted something enjoyable for the drive."

When he opens the door, the new car smell hits me in the face, and the leather seats feel fantastic. *I can do this*, I tell myself. He closes the door for me and climbs in on the other side. Over the visor, he grabs a pair of expensive sunglasses and puts them on. The engine starts up, and the next I know, we're gliding down the street.

"Nice," I say, as I check out all the great gadgets on the dashboard.

"You get a rental too?" He turns his head and glances at me.

"Yeah, Ford Focus. It's okay. Sits kind of low to the ground. I like being up high like this."

"My roadster sure hugs the road. This thing feels like a truck to me, but it's a nice rig."

I'm not very talkative as I struggle with my nerves that are now raising their ugly heads. It's one thing to think I can do something; it's another to sit next to a man like him and think I can pull it off. It's obvious that I'm in way over my head. He is quiet as well, as he heads east down the freeway toward the gorge. It's been so long since I've been there, I feel excited to get back.

"Are you taking the freeway all the way to the falls, or the scenic route?" My question hopes to influence his decision.

"Which do you prefer, scenic or freeway? Either way is okay with me."

"It would be really nice if we could do the scenic. I hope you don't mind," I meekly ask, hoping he'll agree.

"No, absolutely not. Whatever you'd like."

He's being very agreeable, and I'm glad. A few minutes later, Ian approaches the exit across the Sandy River. I'm surprised he knows exactly which route to take. It's exciting to be back on the old scenic highway. I can't wait to reach Crown Point and see the view.

"How long has it been since you been out this way?" He turns his head and gives me a quick glance.

My excitement must be filling the vehicle. "Oh, probably a few years. I used to drive out here once in a while by myself, but then I eventually stopped coming when I moved over on the west side of town. Hate doing things alone."

"Yeah, I know what you mean."

Purposely I turn and look at him, because he's gone quiet on me again. He seems to be thinking about something. For some odd reason, I wonder if it's his ex-wife, but it's too early to bring up the subject, so I let it pass.

The road twists and turns back and forth and through a couple of small bergs. Then he starts the winding descent down the narrow two-lane highway that hugs the cliff. The SUV seems frightfully large in the tiny lane. The road has been paved over several times, because the asphalt buckles and cracks like it's going to give way down the cliff one of these days. Ian takes it slow, and then pulls into to a parking space when we reach the visitor center.

"Let's get out and let the wind blow in our hair for a minute."

I can feel the wind buffeting the car. God I love it here. The sky is clear, the Columbia River is blue with whitecaps, and the air is fresh and clean. Now that I'm used to it, I wait for him to open my door, and I jump out.

"Thanks." I flash him a nervous smile. Surprisingly, he grabs my hand.

"I better hang onto you so you don't blow away."

The warmth of his palm against mine feels heavenly. The winds must be at least forty miles per hour. As we walk into it, loose clothing snaps back and forth on our body. I pull down my baseball cap tight, so it doesn't go flying off. His hair is blowing in every direction, and I notice how thick it is. He takes me over to the side of the stone barrier, and we stop and look out over the river. Ian lets go of my hand, and I grab the railing.

"Gosh, it's pretty." I gush like a stupid tourist.

"Have you lived in Oregon long?"

"Uh, about eleven years. I was born and raised in the Midwest and came out here in my early twenties."

"How come?"

The question leads us both to a door I'm not ready to open regarding my ex-spouse. I look at him and lock my jaw. Thankfully, he sees hesitation in my eyes.

"You don't need to tell me why," he says. "Hey, look, an eagle." He lifts his hand and points to a bird circling overhead.

I tilt my head back and look at the magnificent fowl. He is so close that we can see his white-feathered head. The bird is riding the current of the wind, gliding in splendor.

"Ian?"

"Yeah," he says, turning to look at me.

"Thanks."

"For what?"

"For bringing me here. I seriously needed this—definitely been hibernating way too long."

He gets a twinkle in his eyes. "No problem," he says, slipping his arm around my waist and pulling me in for a hug toward his side. I'm a bit surprised over his actions, since he's acting like he's more interested than being a hiking buddy. He holds me like that for few minutes as we both stand there and get lost in the scenery. Finally, he suggests we leave.

"You ready to climb to the top of the falls?"

"Ready."

"Let's go then." We walk back to the car, and before I know it, we're weaving back and forth on the winding path. The trees have overgrown like a canopy across the road. The ferns are abundant in the woods, and thankfully the traffic is pretty light. I sit and look out the window as we pass all the places I remember and the various waterfalls that cascade down Larch Mountain to my right.

"So pretty," I mumble.

"Yeah, it is."

Another mile we start entering into the Multnomah Falls parking lot. It is not as crowded as I thought it would be, but it's still early in the morning. The falls drop five hundred and forty-two feet into a pool, which overflows into another drop of sixty-nine feet. I can hear the roar of the water inside the car. It's one of my favorite places, with a visiting center, restaurant, gift shop, and trails that lead to the lower and upper falls.

Ian finds a place to park, and I'm bursting inside with excitement. *Why don't I come here more often?* It doesn't take long to answer my own question—memories and the pain associated with a rotten marriage. I glance over at Ian and hope I can make a treasured memory to erase the unpleasant.

We both jump out of the car. He grabs his backpack and slings it over his shoulder. "I brought water for both of us and a few munchies in case we get hungry."

"Water, thanks for thinking of that." I feel pretty stupid that I didn't think of it myself. The trek to the top is a long climb. I'll be dying for something to drink once up there.

"Wow, what a day. Couldn't ask for better weather," he says, tilting his head and looking up at the falls.

"Yeah, I know."

He holds out his hand to me with a smile on his face and nods his head toward the steps ahead. "Come on, let's get at it."

I look at his hand and pause for a moment. *Trust him*, I tell myself sternly. It's a beautiful moment. I want to cry, but I quickly lower my eyes to the stone steps and grab his hand. He gives me a little tug and off we go.

"It's been some time since I've been here too," he admits.

"Are you from Oregon originally?"

"No, California. Born and raised in the Bay area."

"Oh, and then you went east to Harvard?" *Damn it*, I inwardly balk and scrunch my shoulders. He's going to know I've been checking up on him.

He immediately halts his steps, turns and looks at me with narrowed eyes. "Did you search my name on the web or something to make sure I'm not a serial killer?" I can tell he's not mad, but playful.

"Ah, yeah, something like that," I reply

with a wry glance.

He shakes his head at me. "Probably a smart thing I didn't stuff a roll of duct tape into my backpack."

Ian swiftly pulls me onward, tightly holding my hand. We start the climb. He hasn't answered my question yet. "So, back to my question—you went east to Harvard?"

"Yes, I went to Stanford University and then off to Harvard Law School."

"Wow," I say, starting to huff through my words as my legs strain on the incline. "I went to Redford High in Michigan, and only took twenty hours at a community college. Definitely not as smart as you."

"Hey, there are a lot of dumb-asses that come out of Harvard. Education doesn't necessarily mean you're a better person," he says emphatically. He glances over at me. "Don't feel intimidated around me, Rachel, about my education. It's not that big of a deal, believe me."

I'm amazed there is not an observable trace of arrogance about him. There must be something wrong with this guy somewhere! I'm so intrigued that I want to find it, so that I can feel better about myself. Sick thought, but true.

Ian drops my hand and starts to climb faster ahead of me. I'm beginning to have trouble keeping up with him on the asphalt path that meanders back and forth. At last we reach the bridge, which spans the lower falls. The tallest waterfall looms in front of us, and the shortest drops behind us into the pool below. It's still early enough in the year that the runoff is heavy. The sound of pounding water fills my ears.

I'm panting like a dog, while I let the invigorating spray touch my face. After staring into the pattern of the cascading falls, I look for the apparition.

"Have you ever seen the Indian princess ghost in the water?" I wonder if he knows the legend.

"You mean the princess that jumped from the top of the falls?" He tilts his head back and looks upward.

"Yeah, the sacrifice lover story. Kind of a sappy one, actually," I reply in a sarcastic voice. He looks surprised over my statement, and then gazes back into the water as if he's waiting for her to appear.

"No, I've never seen her ghostly figure. Have you?"

"No. Probably because I'm not much of a

romantic about legends and all that. Find them hard to believe." My face turns sour, but I don't care.

"Not a fairytale girl then, huh?"

"You kidding? Every prince I've ever met turned out to be a frog."

I let go of the railing and walk away. My comment probably bugged him, but I don't want to talk about it. A slight irritation over my past rotten love life will spoil the moment, if I do. Swiftly, I turn around and walk backward a few steps and look at him standing there gawking at me with a dumfounded look upon his face.

"Come on, I'll race you to the top, Harvard man," I tease him. "Let's see what you got."

"Deal," he says, taking a giant stride toward me with a determined expression.

We start the climb up the side of the mountain together on the dirt and rock path. Immediately, I curse myself for not being in better shape. The strain on my calf muscles is killing me, and I'm huffing like an old sailor. By the time we make it halfway up the climb, it's beginning to get embarrassing.

"Need to rest?"

He stops for a minute and looks at me.

My face is sweating. Great, now my makeup will run. "Whew! I'm a bit out of it," I admit. "Just a minute to catch my breath."

Another couple passes on the right. They're climbing at an insane speed, but they both look buff and in shape.

"Do you work out?" I huff, trying to regain my strength. No doubt, he's got six-pack abs underneath his tee shirt.

"Yeah, sometimes. Here, let me get you some water."

He swings his backpack off his shoulder, unzips it, and pulls out a bottled water. Like the gentleman he is, he doesn't just hand it to me. Instead, he untwists the white top and then places it in my outstretched hand.

I bring it to my lips and gulp a few times to let the fresh water run down my throat. "Thanks a lot. I needed that." I put the cap back on, and he takes it back.

"I'll put it in the pack so you don't have to carry it. Just let me know when you want some."

Why does he think of everything? I'm beginning to wonder what woman in her right mind would let a guy like this go. I feel ashamed that I'm not as thoughtful to others as he is.

After another half hour of a grueling climb, we reach the top. The view is spectacular, and we stand on the platform and peer over the side at the long drop. The air is crisp and clean. I let out a contented sigh over how much I miss precious moments like these. All I do is stay within my apartment like a hermit, and it's beginning to take its toll on my life. I've got to get out more.

Ian is quiet, as if he's pondering life too. I don't say much of anything, because frankly I'm afraid to speak. It's better to be relaxed, enjoy the sight, and let things progress naturally—whatever that means.

"Yeah, it's been way too long since I've been up here," he says broodingly. I wonder if his own memories are swirling around his head.

"Me too."

"I like to hike some of the other trails down the gorge. Hopefully, we can do this again some time." His tone changes as he appears to shrug off the private musings.

"I'd like that, but I think I better get in shape first." I stretch my aching back with a moan.

Suddenly, he turns and looks at me with

his warm blue eyes, studying every aspect of my face. The attention makes me feel uncomfortable, so I turn my head forward and stare down at the cascading water.

"You're very pretty." He gives me a little shoulder-to-shoulder nudge.

"It's the altitude," I respond. "The oxygen depletion is affecting your thought process." He looks displeased that I can't take the compliment.

"So, you want to hike up farther to the next falls or have you had enough?"

"Wow, that's another half hour or so, isn't it?" The thought makes my feet pound.

"Yeah, about that."

"I don't know." I grimace. "I'm spent right now. Do you mind if we try that on another day?"

"No, not at all."

After a few more silent minutes of taking in the scenery, I breathe a deep sigh.

"Want to go?" he asks, probably sensing my fatigue.

"Sure, but let's take it slow."

We turn around and start heading back down the steep trail. While we're descending the mountain, I'm really starting to hurt. My legs have turned into marshmallow, and one of my knees wants to buckle every tenth step.

Ian is being patient—more than patient with me, actually. Finally, the klutz in me rules, and my right foot slips on a rock in the path. The next I know, I'm falling backward about to land on my butt. I let out a harrowing shriek of terror, thinking I'm going to fall off the edge and splat on the rocks three hundred feet below. Ian quickly rises to the challenge and grabs me on my way down.

"Whoa! I got you," he says, grabbing my upper arms and holding onto me tight. He sets me back up on my feet, and I'm trembling from the near splat.

"You okay?" He genuinely sounds concerned.

Ian slowly turns me around so that I'm facing him. We're nose to nose. Our bodies are touching front to front. This is not good, or maybe it is good. He doesn't say a thing, except to look at me with a smoldering gaze. A second later, he lazily moves his eyes toward my lips.

I'm frozen. I look at him with half anticipation and half panic. He's going to kiss me; I know it. His intentions are clearly expressed in his blue eyes, which have turned a shade darker. I'm losing it. Hurriedly, I remind him of his words to fend off the advance.

"Uh, I thought you wanted to be just friends?"

A look of admiration sweeps across his face. He gently brings his hand up to my forehead and brushes a few strands of hair out of my eyes. Ian is silent, but it's obvious he is thinking this through. It's driving me crazy being close to his body.

"You want more?" I whisper, trying to get him to say something.

"Do you?"

He answers with a question. It's annoying. "I asked you first," I reply, not cracking a smile or giving away my heart pounding in my chest. I can't look at him any longer. I close my eyes, and silently ask God, who I've ignored for years, to help me.

Then I feel the warmth of his breath approach. He circles my lips with his and gives me a long, tender kiss. *Sweet Jesus. He tastes so delicious!* I hope the breath mint I popped in my mouth a half hour ago is still working. Eventually, he pulls away, and I open my eyes.

"Does that answer your question?" His

voice is deep and sexy.

I nod my head. My ability to speak has vanished. What does he expect? I haven't been kissed in more years than I care to remember. The closest I've come to a smooch is a lick from my cat and his sandpaper tongue.

"Now, what's your answer, Rachel? Do you want to be more than friends and see where this goes?"

I'm not ready for this, and I know it. Old fears shroud me in doubt as he gently holds me. Yes, I want him. Who wouldn't want him? Handsome, strong, intelligent, kind, and the list goes on. I can't believe, though, that anyone like *him* would want *me*. Maybe he wants in my pants, and he's trying to figure out if I'm an easy lay. That's it.

"It frightens me," I whisper.

"Why?" His eyes narrow.

"Just does."

"I like you, Rachel, a lot. You probably get that by now." He smiles. "The moment you lifted your head off that steering wheel and turned and looked at me, something clicked inside. Can't explain it."

"I like you, too, Ian. Does this mean you want to date me or something?"

He grins. "Yeah, something like that," he says, giving me an endearing look, which melts my heart. "Come on, let's get back to the car."

He turns me around, and I inhale a deep breath. *Yes! This guy wants to date me*, I scream inside with glee. A silly grin plasters across my face and stays there the entire way down the mountain until my cheeks hurt. God, this really can't be happening to me.

Even though I feel elated, my fears are standing by the sidelines ready to snatch the emotion away. I wish they'd back off and take my insecurities with them. My smile fades by the time we make it back to the SUV, and a foreboding feeling grabs my tummy.

"You want to get a bite to eat in the lodge?" He's standing by the car door hesitating.

It's the dine-with-him offer again. I glance at the lodge and the memories inside. It's been so long since I've sat inside the stone walled and wooden beam restaurant.

"Okay, maybe a Coke and a bowl of soup." If I don't have anything solid, I might make it home. Ian looks as if he's won the lottery, because I agreed to eat with him. We climb the stairs and a hostess greets us.

"Would you like a table by the window?"

I see there's an empty table by my favorite spot, and immediately I blurt out my preference. "How about the table by the fireplace?"

"Yes, of course," she answers. We're escorted there, and Ian pulls out a chair for me. He waits for me to be seated before he takes his. The menus are put in front of us, and I remember their good brewed coffee.

"Would you like anything to drink?" the hostess asks.

"Coffee."

"Same for me," Ian replies.

At last we're alone and looking at each other across the table. "Nice place. Too bad the weather is too warm for a fire," he says, glancing over at the empty hearth filled with ashes.

"I know. This used to be my favorite table when we drove down here on fall and winter mornings for breakfast." I let the word "we" slip out of my mouth, and immediately I regret the personal leak.

"We who?" He gives me a curious glance.

He picked up on that slip fast. I look at

him, and my heart pounds in my chest. He kisses me, tells me that he wants to date me, and now I have to start my true confessions. I might as well get it over with, because he has some confessions of his own.

"My ex-husband," I say in a low voice, while my eyes shift over to the empty hearth so I don't have to see the look on his face. Before he can reply, the hostess pops back with our drinks. Thankfully, I have a few more moments to collect my thoughts.

After stirring in the cream and taking a sip of coffee, I raise my eyes to look at his face. I'm surprised he's staring into his own cup, swirling the spoon around in aimless circles. He's either digesting my confession, or deciding whether to spill the beans about his past.

He lays the spoon down and then looks at me. There is a recognizable sadness in his eyes, which throws me for a loop.

"I have an ex too. An ex-wife, that is—Susan."

Susan. I wish he would have never dropped her name into my head. Nevertheless, Ian looks embarrassed as hell, as if he just revealed the biggest failure of his life. The miserable look on his face makes me feel sorry for him, so I make light of it.

"Yeah, I know. I saw your marital status on your social media page." I smirk, and then lower my lips to the coffee cup and take a sip.

"Boy, you've really done your homework." He leans back in his chair and crosses his arms. "Did you run a background check on me, too, to make sure I have no outstanding warrants?" His eyes are gleaming at me, filled with mischievous intent.

"Not yet, but the thought crossed my mind."

He relaxes and sits forward. "Okay, that's out of the way," he says. "What next?"

"That's enough confessions for one day," I say emphatically. I have my own dark secrets stuffed behind a closed door, and I don't know if I'll ever let them out to this perfect male specimen.

"Can I at least ask how long it's been? I mean since your divorce," he inquires in a low voice.

He has the right to know if I'm on the rebound, so I tell him the truth. "Five years."

"Wow, that's a long time. Have you

dated since then?"

This is certainly going to sound like a lie, but it's the sad, awful truth. "Not really. Just once or twice for a few nights out here and there." His eyes widen in surprise. "I never found anybody I liked." *Or someone I could trust*, I honestly confess to myself.

"Do you ever see your ex-husband?"

"No, thank God, nor do I want to. He lives out of state." I think to myself, *okay tit-for-tat*. "How about you?"

"Three and sometimes."

"Define sometimes."

He glances down at his coffee cup for a moment and then looks back up at me. "Our paths cross in our jobs."

"You mean she's an attorney too?"

"Yes."

Oh, great. His ex-wife probably looks classy, makes tons of money, and is smart as hell. Maybe they met at Harvard. "Okay," I mumble.

"Does that bother you?"

"You over her?" I pry.

"Yes. You over him?" he quickly asks in return.

"Yes."

"Well, if that's the case, I don't see any

problem with us . . ."

"Can I take your order now?" The waitress stands by our table with her pad in hand, and I haven't even opened the menu yet.

"Not quite," Ian replies. "Can we have a few more minutes?"

"Sure, I'll come back later." She leaves, and he reaches over and touches my hand. "As I was saying, I don't see any problem with us dating. Do you?"

Only that my self-esteem is in the toilet, I have bizarre needs, and I know you'll leave me one day, my mind quickly rants.

"No." I might as well enjoy it while it lasts. Maybe I'll get laid.

The menus get read, I order soup, and barely sip a fourth of it. Ian doesn't comment on my lack of appetite, thankfully. Since my hand shakes every time I lift the spoon to my mouth, he's probably picked up on the fact I'm petrified to be eating in front of him. I hate my nerves and lack of confidence.

We have superficial conversation about nothing substantial. Before we leave, I make a quick visit to the ladies' room to collect myself, check my makeup, and go before the long ride home.

Ian takes the freeway back, rather than the scenic route, and returns me home mid-afternoon. After he pulls into a parking spot, he turns off the SUV and looks at me.

"When can I see you again?"

"Whenever you like. I think my calendar is wide open." It's not exactly like I have dates penned in for every day.

"How about tomorrow? You go to church or anything in the morning?"

"Who me? I used to, but not anymore."

"Yeah, me too." He hesitates and then offers a suggestion. "Well, how about we take a drive to the coast tomorrow?"

Wow, gorge one day, coast the next? Now I'm singing praises in my head. I'm starving for a chance to walk the beach.

"Yeah, that sounds great," I say in a perky tone.

"Cannon Beach okay?"

"Perfect."

"Pick you up at nine a.m.?"

"Perfect."

He's smiling from ear to ear, and I'm suddenly overwhelmed by the fact that I get to spend more time with him. Guess things turned out okay, and I haven't scared him off yet.

"Thanks for today. I had a lovely time."

"Yeah, me too. Let me walk you up to your apartment."

He jumps out of the car, opens my door, and grabs my hand. We walk together up the stairs, and he stops. The usual question looms in my brain, do I invite him in or not? I don't want to, because I need a break to process our time together and prepare for tomorrow.

"Mind if I kiss you?" His blues eyes beg.

"No," I sheepishly reply.

He puts his arms around me and draws me close into his firm torso. My body responds to his touch, and suddenly I'm mush. It's been too long since I've felt the embrace of a man. I literally want to sob in his arms because I'm being held, but I control myself. After another sweet and tender kiss, he looks at me adoringly.

"So glad you ran into me. See you tomorrow."

With that, he turns and trots down the steps and out of sight. Suddenly, the absence of his presence is painful. The tears I held in a moment ago, sting my eyes. I insert the key into the lock and disappear into my solitary cave to be the pathetic Rachel once again.

Chapter 5

A TIME TO SNOOP

Whiskers wanders out of the bedroom, meows and flashes me an about-time-you-got-home look of disdain. I pick him up and cradle him in my arms, rub his belly until he purrs, and then give him a kiss on his black nose. He's my rescued cat, who rescued me—for the most part.

The taste of Ian's kiss lingers on my lips, and I remember his warm arms around me. It's been so long since I've received a tender touch, I still cannot process the act with clarity. I love the feel of a man's embrace, yet at the same time my alter ego wants to push him away. He's invading my space. It's a carefully planned and well-built line of defense that follows me like a protective bubble wherever I go. When breached, I feel uncomfortable, threatened, and unnerved. There is so much I want out of life, but I possess so little courage that I cannot make myself believe that anything worthy awaits me in this relationship long-term.

After spending a few minutes sulking around the house, I turn on my computer and sit down. Windows comes to life. I connect to the Internet, and click on my page to see if I have any pseudo-friend comments. I look at my four hundred and eighty-two friends, most of whom I've never met face-to-face. I think only twenty-five people I actually know. The others are pictures of smiling faces or false identities. My own consists of some nineteenth century painter's portrait of some beautiful woman. I hate my photo, and this makes me feel better about myself.

The first thing I notice is a new friend request, so I click on it. Ian Richards wants to be friends. My heart skips a beat, and I stare at the CONFIRM or IGNORE button. I could ignore it, but then I'm dying of curiosity about his locked-down domain. Surely, it will reveal more about this interesting man. There will be pictures of him, family, and friends I can peruse, quirky statements, and who knows what else. With trepidation, I hit CONFIRM.

The picture he uses as his header is a

scene of the ocean. It looks so peaceful. I hope to God his pictures aren't locked down, but before I get a chance to peek around, I see the red notice of "1" on the top of my page. Dang! He's posted on my wall already.

"Had a terrific time today. Looking forward to seeing you tomorrow. Now go ahead and snoop all you want, while I snoop over you!"

I chuckle at his snoop comment. He knows darn well I'm going to read every entry and check out every picture. Before I do, I write a comment underneath his.

"I'm looking forward to the snoop."

Suddenly, it dawns on me that he's probably reading all of my entries and looking at my pictures. I close my eyes and cringe. Like a computer doing a check disk, my brain tries to remember what I've been posting on my timeline for the last year.

Of course, there have been a few off-colored comments. I've posted a few pictures of hot models with six-pack abs. Moaned about a doctor or dentist appointment. Most of my friends do the same. Then I remember a few photos of myself, and I wince. There are some seriously lousy ones of me in years past where I was overweight and more depressed than I am now. He's going to die when he sees those goodies.

Since it's too late to start deleting pictures left and right, I leave it and pop on over to his page. I hit the picture album link, and suddenly my tongue hangs out of my mouth. There's a couple of him on the beach, without a shirt, and damn does he look hot. He's tan, toned, buffed, and scrubbed, and everything else a woman could want. I open the picture, right click, and save it on my computer. *Me bad*, I think to myself, but I don't care. I need visuals.

His other pictures appear to be with friends or family, and I can't tell who is who. His page is as neat as his wallet. His friends are kept at a minimum of one hundred and twenty-three. Nothing uncouth is written in any of his comments, which are few and far between. Everything is perky and upbeat. I hate him already.

I check out all his friends, but don't see any marked as family. They're probably too sophisticated to be on a social media site. The perfect life, perfect family, and perfect past—he possesses everything I don't. The whole comparison stings me, and the usual loser feeling is back with a vengeance. I know when he finds out everything about me, my heart is going to be broken into a thousand pieces. Suddenly, I want to pick up the phone and call tomorrow off.

After a few more torturous minutes, I leave my computer and walk into the bedroom and lie down on my bed. I curl my knees up to my chest and bring my arms across my breasts. My head lowers to the pillow and my eyes close. The feelings of dread and fear push me into the mattress like heavy weights upon my body. My chest constricts, and the familiar sense as if I'm suffocating takes over. I'm a mess again as I struggle with self-doubt, and my eyes well with tears.

"Why am I doing this?" I scold myself aloud. I know why. It's because I want to believe someone can love me, but I can't believe. I've never known unconditional love from a man. Frankly, I don't even know if such a thing exists.

Do men genuinely love? No, I've convinced myself that they don't. They just want sex and have no emotions. The male race consists of lust-driven robots that want to screw. All I know is that I'm never good enough, and when Ian discovers my secrets, he'll leave me after he's gotten what he wants. There's no way around it.

My head sinks deeper into the pillow. I want to sleep, so I don't have to think. When I sleep there's no pain, no thinking, no chiding myself for being a failure, no memory, and no voices in my head to haunt me, unless nightmares return. It's a place where I can retreat and cease to exist, as long as I don't dream about the man with no face. I take a deep breath and wait for darkness to arrive.

-·❈·-

The telephone rings and awakens me out of a sound sleep. I sit up in bed startled and try to clear my fuzzy thoughts. It continues to ring, so I get up and run to the kitchen to answer it. The caller ID shows it's my brother, and I wonder what he wants.

"Hello?"

"Hey, sis!"

His voice sounds like I'm his loving sister that he talks to every day. Usually, he calls when he's drunk to tell me how much he loves me. Other than that, I never hear from him.

"Yeah, Bob, what's up?" I sound

annoyed.

"Did I wake you or something? You sound groggy."

"As a matter of fact, you did."

"Oh, sorry. I wanted to let you know I was coming out to Oregon this fall for a conference, and I was wondering if I could stay at your place."

The idea of having my brother here suddenly gives me shivers down my spine.

"If the conference is downtown, you'd be better off staying at a hotel. The commute from where I live is a killer." There, I've warned him off, so now maybe he'll bug off.

"Well, I just thought . . ."

"Bob, I haven't seen you since dad died, and now you want to stay with me?"

"Okay, I get it," he says, annoyed. "I thought I'd make the effort."

"Well, it's a bit late for that!" The anger explodes inside of me, and I slam down the telephone receiver.

"Damn you!" I scream at the telephone as if he can hear me. Tomorrow, I'll probably be sorry that I was so mean to him, but we've never been close.

I'm feeling cranky, so I go back to my computer to see if maybe Ian has visited my page again. I open it and have email. Let it be him, I think to myself. I click the mouse and it is.

"Hey, you got a home phone number? I forgot to ask."

I smile, type the number, and hit send. As soon as I get up, the phone rings again. I run back to the kitchen, look at the caller ID, and see that it's blocked. "Shit," I mumble, staring at it. I'm afraid it might be Bob again, but then it could be Ian. The phone keeps ringing, and I know my voice mail is going to pick it up, or they're going to hang up.

Swiftly, I pick up the receiver and answer with a hesitant, "Hello?"

"Hey, Rachel, it's Ian."

"Oh, God, I'm glad it's you."

"Yeah?"

"Yeah, but I almost didn't pick up because the number was blocked."

"Oh, crap," he says apologetically. "I didn't mean to do that; just forgot to undo the block. Sorry."

"No, that's okay. A few minutes ago, I hung up from an unpleasant call, and I didn't want a repeat performance."

"Someone bugging you?" I hear concern in his voice.

"Well, not really. Just family stuff."

"Oh, okay."

"So what's up?" I'm immensely curious as to why he's called.

"I was thinking about you."

My mind squeals like a teenager. "Me too. Uh, I mean me thinking about you."

"Listen, I saw the weather report tonight. It might rain tomorrow afternoon at the coast. Still want to go?"

"Hey, we're Oregonians. We can do rain."

He laughs. "Okay, I just wanted to check."

"I'll pack a jacket and whatever, but I have to hear the waves and walk the beach."

"Well, we should be there early enough. The rain isn't expected until afternoon."

"Okay, thanks, Ian."

"Hey, no problem. See you in the morning. Bye."

"Bye." I hang up and beam like a light bulb. Gosh, he's so nice. I want to dream that this will work, but I don't know if I have it in me.

I glance at the clock, and it's time for my purple pill again. Thank God for feigned happiness in a drug. Otherwise, I'd probably be six feet under pushing up daisies.

Chapter 6

PASTS REVEALED

My night turns out to be a fitful one. I wake up several times through the evening, tossing and turning. Dreams for the most part are unmemorable, which I know means I didn't get enough REM sleep to be worth a darn. When I wake up, the dark circles under my eyes prove it. I look like death.

After a shower, I carefully put on makeup and dry my hair. When all is done, I look at myself and sigh. It's not what I want to see. My ex-husband's demeaning voice from the past runs through my mind like a ticker tape.

Look at you, you're pathetic. Who would want you?

My facial expression confirms to me that I still believe every word he uttered during our married life. It's time to suppress the pain and insecurities before Ian arrives at my door.

I walk over to my bedroom window and pull up the blinds. The sky is gray, and it's overcast but dry. It appears the weather report was right, but I don't mind if I get drenched from head to toe. I need the ocean, and a kind man is going to take me there.

My backpack is laying on the kitchen table, and I recheck the items I gathered the night before.

Lipstick – check
Hairbrush – check
Breath mints – check
Wallet – check
Cell phone – check
Small throw – check

The throw is probably never going to be used; but in case we decide to sit on the beach, we won't be plopping down in sand. I'm conjuring up visions of us embracing and smooching under the gray skies. It will be wonderful to lounge on the beach and listen to the waves together.

According to my outdoor thermometer stuck to my window, the morning temperature is about sixty-five. It will be at least ten degrees cooler by the ocean, so I grab my heavy jacket. Before Ian arrives, I run into the bathroom and put my pink baseball cap on, and pull my ponytail through the hole in the back. I turn my head from left to right and check out how I look. Not much can be done. The damage is already there.

I hear the faint knock at my door, so I dive over and open it. "Come on in," I invite him with a smile on my face. "I'm just gathering a few last items."

He walks in, and Whiskers wanders out of the bedroom. The cat takes one look at his long legs and decides to coil himself around his calves like a snake.

"Ian, meet Whiskers. Whiskers, meet Ian."

"Hey, Whisk."

He bends over and picks up the cat. I'm flabbergasted. Ian holds the fuzz ball upside down in his arms and starts stroking his belly, like I do. Why am I not surprised my cat is a traitor?

"He prefers men," I tell Ian. "He tolerates me." I can hear my cat purring in high gear. His eyes look like he's drugged.

"Do you have a cat?" Since Ian is so adept at tummy petting, I can't help but wonder.

"No. Wish I had a pet, but it wouldn't be fair. Work too many hours to take care of one." He lowers Whiskers to the floor. "I think you've had enough." My jacket is draped over my arm, and my backpack is hanging from my right shoulder. "Ready," I announce, grinning from ear to ear.

"Here, let me carry that for you," he offers, taking my pack.

I want to protest with, "no I can handle it," but he melts me with his nonchalant, gallant behavior. It's engrained in him, and I wonder if there's a mean bone in the man's body.

With my protest stifled in the back of my throat, we head on out. The SUV makes for a smooth ride down Sunset Highway westward toward the coast, and I feel like a giddy little girl. The first few miles we are both silent. Ian is driving with a pensive look upon his face, and I'm looking out the window at the passing scenery. To break the awkward silence, I ask him an off-the-wall question.

"Is Cannon Beach your favorite spot along the Oregon coast?"

"Yeah, you could say that," he replies, with a sly grin that I wonder about. "What about you?"

"Yeah, I like it. I enjoy it anywhere the waves crash against the rocky shoreline."

"I'm a sand man, myself."

"That sounds funny." I chuckle. "The rocks are what I love, especially on a rough day. I can stand and watch the ocean for hours on end."

"Well, if you want, we can drive up Ecola Park, and you can peer over the edge."

"Yeah, that would be nice."

For the next mile, we revert to silence. He looks as if he's deep in thought, and I'm calculating how far we are into the hour and a half trip. As we start climbing the coastal range and make it on the other side of the tunnel that cuts through the mountain, he decides to take the lid off of things.

"Do you mind me asking what happened with you and your ex?" He pauses for a moment and rearranges his question. "I mean why did the marriage end?"

Ian turns his head and gives me a quick glance, no doubt to determine if I'm reacting to his intrusion into my private life. I ponder for a moment how to respond.

"Tell you what, I'll tell you why my marriage ended, if you share why about yours."

He cocks his head to the right and rubs the back of his neck with his right hand. It's obvious that he's uncomfortable. "Fair enough," he half-heartedly responds. "You go first."

"Oh, thanks," I sarcastically reply, while noting the relieved look on his face. I don't belabor my response and get right to the point. "I got married at twenty. My ex was seven years my senior. He swept me off my feet, and three months later, like an idiot, I became his wife."

"Whoa, that was quick," he blurts out in surprise.

"Unfortunately, I quickly discovered that I wed a man with a violent temper. For the next four years of my life, I struggled to find the courage to leave, while he systematically abused me." As my confession reaches his ears, I notice Ian's grip on the steering wheel tighten. His swift reaction to my words surprises me.

"Rachel, did he hit you?" He takes his eyes off the road and glances at me with an appalled look. Shamefully, I tell him the truth.

"Once, early in our marriage, because he said I mouthed off at him. He punched me in the arm and left a bruise." I wring my hands together remembering the hurtful moment. Poor Ian's face cringes.

"There's no excuse for men who hit women," he growls with a sneer.

"Afterward, it escalated to verbal abuse, which I think is more painful than the other. Although, when he got mad, he threatened me with a raised, clenched fist."

"Why did you stay with the creep?" Ian's voice is deep and angry, as he glances over at me with a quizzical look.

I begin to feel he's climbing my walls of protection. Desperately, I try to find the right answer that won't make me sound like an idiotic loser for staying. Should I tell him the real truth? Gee, Ian, there's this thing about me, and I can't say no to abuse. As an alternative, I wonder whether I should skirt the fact and blame it on another issue. I project the blame elsewhere.

"I was going to church at the time, and the denomination I was in was pretty strict about divorce. In the pastor's eyes, it was akin to blasphemy. So I stayed in the marriage, lest I be ostracized for leaving him and not submitting to my husband, like I was taught."

"Did the pastor advocate that you were obligated to remain in that kind of abusive situation?"

"Well, not in so many words," I say. My ignorance is about to flash like a neon light. "I was afraid to expose my husband for what he was behind closed doors. Frankly, I didn't know if anyone would believe me, let alone side with me."

Ian shakes his head. "Gosh, Rachel, I'm sorry that you went through that." His voice is more sympathetic than it is angry.

"Live and learn, but it did turn me against the church, unfortunately. I think my theology got all screwed up because of it."

It's hard to admit I'm a backslidden divorcee. The guilt from religious teaching adds to my sense of sinfulness over my dark desires. Every day I'm afraid of God's punishment. I never feel good enough, even for God's love. My eyes water when Ian continues the questioning.

"So what happened that you finally did leave?"

My mouth blows out a puff of air before continuing the tale of woe. "A counselor helped me to do it. I didn't have the courage, and she helped me find the strength to walk away."

"Good for her or him," he says, sighing in relief.

"Her."

"Did you file or he?"

"I did, and he didn't contest it."

"Well, at least that part of your life is over and buried."

My head turns, and I gaze at Ian with profound sadness. His conclusion is far from the truth. Every insult, every belittlement, and every time my husband yelled at me, felt as if he picked up a hammer and drove a sharp, painful nail into my soul. By the time I left, my self-esteem had been damaged beyond repair. I wanted to die.

My counselor helped me to remove the nails one by one, but all it did was leave gaping holes in the fabric of my heart. I can remember her advice. "Even though he said those things about you, doesn't make them true."

Her pie-in-the-sky statement did nothing to help me, because by that time my brain had accepted every word as fact. How can you change what you believe, when there is no one in your life to tell you that you have value? When I divorced him, I was emotionally bankrupt. The account had been overdrawn, and no deposits of kindness were being made by anyone else to fill the void in my soul.

Ian returns my sad gaze, and I see a curious look upon his face as if he's wondering about my sanity. I swiftly avert my eyes and look out the windshield at the road. Then I throw the ball back into his court.

"So, you next. What happened in your marriage?" I hear him draw in a breath and look to see that his mouth has turned into a hard line. It's obvious that his revelation will not be an easy one either.

"I met Susan at Harvard. We dated while in college and before graduation from law school, we married."

"Sounds like you took longer than I did to make that decision."

"A couple of years, yes."

Wise man, I think to myself. "Then what?"

"After we wed, we wanted to relocate out west. Portland felt more attractive than Seattle, so we both found jobs in firms out here, purchased a house, and then spent the next few years drifting apart."

It's hard for me to imagine why any woman would not stay close to Ian. I try to wrap my head around his ex-wife, but can't. I press for more. "Why did you drift apart? Was it you or her?"

"Susan is extremely career-minded, more so than I am. With our crazy schedules and overtime, we rarely saw each other. The marriage grew stale pretty fast."

"Sorry," I say, void of any comforting words.

"That's life, I guess. One day I came home, and she shoved divorce papers in my face telling me that it was over."

"Was there another guy or something?"

"Yeah," he answers with a frown. "Apparently, I had become a bore, and her new male companion was more outgoing and adventurous." Ian clenches his jaw as he continues. "It was devastating to learn of her unfaithfulness. She confessed she had been seeing him for three months behind my back."

"Damn," I reply. "Did she have . . . ." My words trail off, afraid to ask if she had screwed his competition.

Ian affirms my assumption with a nod of his head. I am dismayed. How could she do that to him? His face is filled with painful memories. It's difficult not to wonder if he still loves her, even though yesterday he said he didn't. He could have lied. While I'm thinking about it, my mouth blurts out my pondering thought.

"Do you still love her?" I try to sound concerned, rather than accusatory.

He's quiet for nearly a minute and then turns his head and looks at me. I'm aghast over the smoldering gaze he throws my way. It practically melts me into the leather seat. His gorgeous blue eyes communicate something totally unexpected. Timidly, I squirm and my breath hitches in my throat.

"What do you think?" he drawls in that deep velvet voice of his.

What a loaded question! This man definitely wants in my pants. He pulls his eyes back to the road. Thank God he did. If I had been driving, we would have been wrapped around a tree.

"Um, probably not." I gulp.

"Definitely not," he quickly replies. "Susan has moved on, and that's exactly what I'm doing now."

Ian reaches over and grabs my clammy hand, which is resting in my lap. He gives it a gentle squeeze, and then pats me on the leg. A moment later, his attention is back on the road.

"Wish I could kiss you." He wickedly smirks.

"Me too."

I look out the window and see the mileage sign alongside the road—twenty-six miles to Cannon Beach. God, I can't wait to get this guy in the sand and attack his mouth.

Chapter 7

PINCH ME

The wind blows into my face, and I close my eyes and tilt my head back. Ian is behind me somewhere. For the moment, I'm lost in the atmosphere that captures my soul. It's cool—in fact it's cold. I zip up my jacket to my neck and pull my hood over my baseball cap. When I open my eyes again, I'm greeted with the white, foamy waves of the Pacific Ocean pounding the shore. Out in the distance are dark storm clouds. It won't be long before the rain arrives.

Suddenly, I feel Ian behind me. He slips both of his arms around my waist and pulls me back into him. He lowers his head to the right side of my face and gives me a peck on the cheek.

"Bit chilly," he says, tightening his grip upon my midsection. My eyes remain fixed on the horizon until I'm suddenly aware of an erection pressing against my derrière. I don't know whether to run, cry, or laugh. It's been so long since I've felt the need of a male against my body, I'm not sure how to react.

"Yes, it is, but I don't care." I tug away from him, and he releases me. When I turn around, I can see heat in his eyes, but a slight frown on his face.

"Race you to Haystack Rock." I tease him with a wink and find my footing on the hard sand where the waves play games getting me wet.

"You're on," he says, and off he goes, flying ahead of me.

"Hey, you!" I yell at the top of my lungs. He doesn't stop. Before I know it, I'm out of breath, and I've caught up to him. The tide is coming in, and the waves are getting higher and more frequent.

"Okay, I concede, you won," I admit.

He flashes a smile. "Looks like the rain is coming sooner than later," he says, looking at the clouds out on the horizon.

I try and ignore the threat.

"Do you want to keep walking down the shore?" Ian grabs my cold hand and holds it tight.

"Yes, and then find a place in the sand to sit. I brought a little blanket," I announce, patting my backpack.

"Okay," he says, drifting off in a weird way. He has a strange look on his face, but I shrug it off.

We start strolling down the beach, heading into the oncoming wind. The waves are pounding the shore with a roar. I'm in a fantasyland, where nothing hurts me and nature tenderly caresses my wounded soul. After a few minutes, I spot a perfect spot by a large driftwood log that has rolled up on the beach.

"How about we sit over there," I suggest, pointing in the direction of where I want to head.

"Looks good."

Ian grabs my hand and pulls me through the sand I'm now struggling to walk in. With every step that I sink, I can feel my shoes filling up with the beach.

We reach the log, and I throw down my backpack and fish out the old blanket. It's big enough for two. I set up camp, plop down, and Ian follows suit. He slips his arm around me and tugs me close. When I look up at him, he's staring into my eyes with a smile that tells me that he wants more. A moment later, his lips give me another sweet kiss.

His mouth is always tender and not invasive. I wonder if he even knows how to French kiss, because I haven't once felt his tongue. The reserved behavior surprises me, because he's not as aggressive as I secretly hoped. Maybe, he's taking it slow. When I think about it, that's probably wise because I'm an easy lay, and I'm not going to brandish that poor quality of my character. At least not yet, I smirk inside.

"God, I so love it here," I breathe out in complete satisfaction. I don't care that the wind is pounding my face, or that I feel a chill from the cold sand underneath the blanket. It's been far too long since I've visited the coast, and I chide myself for not leaving my cave more often.

Ian is quiet, and I watch him stare out at the horizon as if he's deep in thought. We leave each other to our musings until I feel a drop of rain splat on my cheek.

"Don't tell me that was a raindrop." I pout, as another pelts me on my nose.

"Afraid so, sweets."

"Damn!" I growl. Next I know, the

heavens open up, and it's a torrential downpour. Oregon weather is as unpredictable as my period. I don't want to leave this lovely moment, but I'm afraid we have no choice.

"Geesh!" I complain, as the rain begins to fall harder.

Ian stands up and pulls me to my feet. "Give me your hand, and let's run for cover."

I quickly stuff my damp blanket into my backpack, and we sprint down the beach, back toward the public parking where we left the SUV. By the time we arrive, we're soaked to the bone. The rain continues to pelt us both as we jump into the SUV. We slam shut the doors, and I quickly glance over at Ian. His hair is drenched, and he looks as sexy as hell with his dripping locks.

"I know a place we can go to dry out," he announces.

He places the key into the ignition, pulls onto Hemlock Street, and heads south down the coastline. We leave the outskirts of town behind. A minute or two later, he turns right down a street that heads back toward the ocean. I glance over at him, wondering where we're going. His face is expressionless, but there's a mischievous glimmer in his eyes.

"Where are we headed?" I'm thoroughly confused now.

He smirks like a roguish teenager. "My beach house."

"Your what?" The words fly out of my mouth as he pulls into the driveway of a beautiful home that sits smack dab on the ocean front. I'm stunned.

"It's my house, Rachel. Come inside and let's get you warmed up."

Panic floods through my veins, along with anticipation of what getting me warmed up insinuates. If he touches me, I'm toast.

He helps me out of the car, leads me to the front door, and fiddles with his keys until he finds the right one. It fits in the lock, and the next I know I've been ushered into his home in Cannon Beach. God, talk about a dream come true! My wide eyes gawk at my surroundings, while he takes my wet jacket. He kicks his shoes off, and stomps his feet to get rid of the sand.

"Leave your shoes at the door, and I'll go light a fire."

I look inside where he's headed and see a magnificent stone fireplace on the right. Walls of windows from the floor to the cathedral ceiling look out over the stormy

Pacific Ocean. The interior is decorated throughout in warm earth tones. It is so gorgeous that I want to cry.

After removing my shoes and wet socks, I brush the sand off my toes and leave a pile of dirt at the front entrance. I feel awful for messing up his house. For a brief moment, I'm frozen as I take in my surroundings, and then I slowly shuffle my way into the interior.

Off to the right is a staircase that leads to what appears to be a bedroom loft upstairs. I gulp. To the left is a kitchen and dining area, and another bedroom. I see a desk and computer inside, and figure it's his home office. Straight ahead, Ian strikes a match to the kindling. A moment later, it pops and cracks as the fire catches and starts to burn. He turns and looks at me like a mischievous little boy that got his hand caught in the cookie jar.

"This is home for me, for the most part, Rachel. I only have a small apartment in town, much like your own. I work so much, all I do is sleep there, but when I want to live and relax, I come here during the weekend and on my days off."

"Oh, my God," I breathe, in secret

jealousy. "You're so fortunate, Ian."

"Oh, I don't look at it that way, really." He seems embarrassed and looks over at the fire. "Yes, it's gratifying to be here on the ocean, but it's no fun being here alone."

I'm chilled to the bone, and my lower lip is quivering.

"We have to get you out of those clothes and throw them in the dryer. Your lips are blue." He looks at me for a moment. "I suppose you don't have anything to change into," he says, with a knowing smirk across his face.

"No, I hadn't planned on this detour," I reply. He nods toward the bedroom upstairs.

"You'll find a robe behind the door in the bathroom. Go take those things off, and throw them down to me. I'll put them in the dryer."

I'm petrified of what is upstairs. He sees my hesitation. My feet are planted in cement, and I can't move.

"Listen, Rachel, I'm not going to take advantage of the situation, I promise."

Ian reaches over and strokes the side of my cheek with the palm of his hand. His eyes look sincere. The fire is warm, and I'm cold.

"Okay," I reply, answering with my

favorite acquiescent word.

I trot up the stairs, and turn around to see the view from the railing. His bedroom looks over the massive great room below, straight to the ocean. Behind me is a large king-size bed, covered in multiple throw pillows and a brown satin comforter. I see a door to the right and assume it's his bathroom, so I head in that direction. Sure enough there's a robe hanging where he said it would be.

Hurriedly, I hide and start stripping. I'm shivering. When I look into the mirror, I see that my lips are blue. I glance about the bathroom, but don't touch anything. My panties and bra are dry enough to keep on, so I wrap his robe around me and tie it tight.

"Hey, toss me your clothes," he yells up at me.

My arms wrap around the pile, and I walk to the railing. He's looking up at me with his head tilted back. "Here you go." I let them fly down to his feet. Ian picks them up, and then disappears toward the kitchen, where I'm assuming there is a utility room somewhere with a washer and dryer.

I don't descend the stairs right away, but stand at the railing and get lost in the view through the floor to ceiling windows. It must be spectacular when the winter storms roll in. I close my eyes and imagine us together on the floor in front of a roaring fire, with the sound of rain pelting the windows and the roar of the waves outside. I can't think of anything more that I'd love to experience. Maybe I will in a few minutes. My heart rate increases over the thought, as I make my way downstairs to bask in the unique fairytale backdrop.

"Your clothes are in the dryer," he announces, giving me a grin. "I'm going upstairs to change. Be right back."

The fire beckons me to approach. The warmth is filling the room. I'm thinking that it's ingenious, as the hot air will rise to warm the loft upstairs. A large, brown couch faces the fireplace, and I plop myself on it. My nose catches the smell of coffee brewing in the kitchen. Before I know it, he's back in loose sweat pants and a tight tee shirt.

"I should have given you a pair of these," he says, looking at me enticingly in his bathrobe.

"Oh, I'm okay. It's warm." The robe is way too large for me, and I feel like I'm caught in his perpetual embrace. I'm enjoying the secure feeling of being wrapped in something he owns.

"You want a cup of coffee?"

"Oh, God, yes," I reply, jumping to my feet and following him into the kitchen to snoop around. "Wow, nice." He remains casual while I ogle.

"Cream? Sugar?" He fills my mug to the top.

"Just cream."

The refrigerator door opens, and there's plenty of food inside. I surmise he must come here every weekend, and suddenly I feel terrible. He should have been here yesterday, relaxing, but instead he spent it with me.

Ian looks at home and calm. My eyes rove over his toned, bare arms. He definitely lifts weights with those biceps. His taut chest, underneath his tight tee, teases the hell out of me. The law man looks smoking hot. Thank God, his sweat pants are loose. I eye the dangling string that I would like to loosen, so I can peek behind the curtain.

He clears his throat as his eyes catch me during my examination of his goods. I can see he's pleased with my exploration, but suddenly I'm blushing like a school girl. I take the cup and lower my gaze into the brew. "Sorry," I mumble. I hear him chuckle under his breath.

We sit down on the couch and start sipping the coffee, staring at the fire together. The rain continues to fall in a steady stream, and I look at the clock above the mantel. It's only just noon, so we don't have to drive back to the city yet. As I sip the warm drink, my mind wanders. He's already flopped one arm over my shoulder, while he holds his cup in the other.

"Did you own this place when you were married?" I'm curious, of course.

He tilts his head down. I've hit a sore spot, and I wince, sorry that I asked the question. I can tell he honestly doesn't want to answer it, but he does anyway. He looks at me with that same sad, screwed-up look.

"Yes."

I feel disappointed, because now my mind runs to his bed upstairs imagining the two of them together. The romance of it all sort of takes a step back, because I bet there are memories underneath that brown comforter.

"Yeah, I gave her the house in town, and I took this one in the divorce. She didn't care," he says, pulling his mouth to one side.

"Susan doesn't enjoy being here."

"Oh." It sounds strange to me, until he explains.

"She's more of the city lights, city-type girl. I'm more of the laid back, get-me-out-of-the-city-type guy. It was a substantial difference between us."

My favorite one word comment pops out between my lips. "Okay." I don't know what's okay about it, because suddenly I feel terribly sorry for Ian.

"You hungry?" He changes the subject and forces a grin.

"Um, a little."

We head off to the kitchen, and for the next few hours I feel like the two of us are playing house together. I enjoy the fantasy, and he seems comfortable with it as well. We eat a sandwich, talk, sit by the fire, watch the storm, a little television, and relax until the hours slip away. He's being a perfect gentleman, for which I'm happy and disappointed all at the same time.

When the clock reaches five, I feel like he's getting antsy. Maybe he wants to get back to Portland, and I don't blame him. The drive back will be miserable in the rain. Before we go, I really want an intimate moment.

"Kiss me." I invite him with a sassy expression.

He looks surprised over my request. A small, sexy smile brightens his face. My body goes limp as I see him coming toward my lips. I don't know whether it's the coffee, the fire, or the storm outside, but something ignites between the two of us.

The tongue that's been hiding bursts forth with a thrust into my mouth that turns me hotter than the embers in the fireplace. If he keeps this up, I'm going to lose it.

I soon discover he's a freaking good kisser, once he gets going and loosens up. Beside his tongue, which thrusts deep into my mouth, he has a way of sucking my lower lip that drives me nuts. It's such a turn on, that I'm aching.

One of his warm hands finds my bare leg underneath the robe and slips up and down my inner thigh, stroking me tenderly. I moan over his touch. All I can think of is his long fingers and where I'd love to feel them in the next few minutes. It doesn't take but another moment for the red flags to start waving between the two of us yelling "warning, warning, warning."

Suddenly, he stops sucking my mouth, and lets me come up for a breath of air. I realize that I'm desperately clutching him and panting.

"God, Rachel, this isn't good," he puffs, out of breath. I can't help but notice the erection looming in his sweat pants.

"What's not good?" I ask innocently, looking at him like I don't know what is going on.

"I told you that I wouldn't take advantage of you, but all I want to do is strip that robe off and devour you here and now. It's too soon."

He stands up and runs his fingers through his hair, and then turns back and looks at me. I know it's too soon. If we start this trip down sex lane, there's no turning back. We've been together what, three times? Of course, what does that matter to me? In three months, I could be his wife—if I had my way. Besides, I'm easy, and I know it.

"You want to do this?" I can see in his eyes that he wants to. Of course he does, he's a man. I hesitate. He looks at me. My body is wet and aching as I imagine every muscle underneath that damn, tight tee shirt he's got on. Indiscreetly, I wonder how big the joy stick is in his pants.

Then it hits me. "I . . . I . . ." Words are escaping my brain. I look at him square in the eye and blurt out my confession. "Ian, I haven't had sexual relations with a man for over five years. I'm so starved for affection and touch that I don't know if I can say no to your offer." I don't want him to think I'm a slut, but it's the truth—I'm ravenous inside.

He stands there staring at me. I know he's contemplating the cost. *Make the decision for me!* I scream in my heart. *I'll do whatever you say. Just tell me.*

"It's been a while for me too, Rachel."

"If I say yes, you won't think less of me, will you?" Fear fills my eyes.

"God, no," he says, flashing me an adoring look of desire.

Next I know, he grabs my hand and pulls me to my feet. I don't even have time to think about anything else, because I'm climbing the stairs to his loft. I'm suddenly lost in raw manhood and female desire. The robe is gone before I know it, his hands are all over me, and his tongue is in my mouth.

"I'm not on any birth control," I urgently tell him.

"That's okay, I'm prepared."

He starts in on me again, and all I can do is moan like a fool over the feeling of being touched again. I want to cry. I want to laugh. I want to faint. Every emotion courses through my body as he relentlessly feels my flesh. My breasts are captivated by his touch, and my mouth is filled with his sweet taste.

I'm so overwhelmed that I keep my eyes tightly shut. A few moments pass, and I realize he's stripping off his clothes. I hear the rustle of a condom packet, and then he's back at it, exploring my body.

"You're beautiful," he whispers into my ear.

He unhooks my bra, shimmies down my panties, and then pulls me against his naked and warm flesh. My knees buckle beneath me, and he holds me upright.

"No woman should go without tenderness and touch for that long, Rachel," he says, as he gently lays me upon the bed.

He touches me quickly with his fingers and discovers I'm wet and waiting. I'm lost in craving, and my mind flows to dark places. The door to my imagination is flung open, and then I'm consumed with visions of Ian.

He's so hungry, that he quickly parts my

legs and slowly slips his penis inside of me. I gasp at being stretched by a man when I've been closed and unwanted for so long. It's overpowering, and I start to whimper.

"Rachel," he says, stopping. "Am I hurting you?"

I shake my head. "It feels wonderful."

He begins his slow progression of love making. It's sweet, too sweet. Inside my mind I beg him, *Ian, hurt me. I want you to hurt me. Please.* It's what I truly want, not sweet, but rough, painful, and wild sex.

The demons of my mind pull me behind the dark door. *Ask him to hurt you. Beg him to hurt you,* they tell me. *Imagine him hurting you,* they growl. Ian keeps tenderly trying to bring me to an orgasm, and I know he's at the brink. I want one so bad, but I can't do it—not like this!

"It's okay, Ian, go ahead."

He knows what I mean, and suddenly he bursts inside of my body. I lie underneath him and leave my dark desires behind in the closet and close the door.

Tearfully, I explain my lies. "I'm sorry that I couldn't . . ." I don't want him to feel like a failure.

He pulls himself out of me. "Hey, open

your eyes and look at me," he says sweetly. I do. "Is there something I can do to help you?"

"No," I say. "It's not you, Ian. It's me because it's been too long since I've done this."

He looks devastated, as if he's taken advantage of me and given me nothing in return. "It's okay, really," I say, touching the side of his face with the palm of my hand. All the while I know I can't tell him why. Not now. Not like this. Maybe never. I'll do what I always do. I'll go home, fondle myself, and come in the darkness of my desires that I'm too ashamed to share with another human being.

Chapter 8

PENITENCE GONE WRONG

When I arrive at work on Monday morning, I'm reminded of Ian. My poor roses are slowly dying, and I can't help but wonder if this flash-fire introduction with the law man is about to suffer a quick death. It's time to throw them out, because the petals are falling and making a mess on my desk.

I pick up the vase and walk to the employee lounge, where the large, green compost container resides. I open the lid, pull out the dead flowers, and drop them into the bottom. It saddens me, so I retain one dead rose and decide to press it between the pages of a book when I get home. After I wash the vase out, I take it back to my desk. I'm not about to leave a crystal vase underneath the sink for someone else's enjoyment.

Feeling in the dumps, I plop on my chair

and turn on the computer. With my letter opener in hand, I start slitting the morning mail open and reliving the weekend in my mind. I have much to think about, because the last two days have, for the most part, been a heavenly whirlwind. I reposition my butt, because I'm embarrassed to admit that I'm actually sore from my previous night's activities. Five years of no sex definitely made it a bit uncomfortable.

Our drive home from Cannon Beach turned out to be pretty quiet. I think we were both in shock after our unexpected romp on top of the satin comforter. Ian looked mortified, and I didn't know how to console the poor man. His ego was either suffering from not being able to bring me to an orgasm, or he was sorry he lost it and dragged me to the loft.

To be honest, I was glad that he did. My slut in the closet has no moral compass anyway, so I felt no guilt over letting him in my pants. Of course, I predicted he wanted in there all along, and then encouraged him to enter. As fast as he did me, it was obvious he hadn't had any in a while either. I wasn't surprised he shot it off so fast and left me hanging.

As I think about it, a smile spreads across my face just remembering the heat of his embrace and that I actually had sex. The dark door in my mind, where all of my secrets are kept, flies open and fear stares me in the face. I'm in no mood to be taunted, so I imagine banging the door in the demon's face and focusing upon work.

My computer boots up, and I quickly check my personal email and social page. It's my usual morning routine of cheating on company hours by using the Internet. Mr. Stewart doesn't get in until eight thirty, so it gives me a half hour to fool around unnoticed. I enter and see I have mail. I scrunch my nose afraid to look who it's from. As soon as I click it, Ian's name pops up.

I was right. He's sorry, mortified, filled with remorse for taking advantage of me when he said he wouldn't. The guy has a conscience like none other. It amazes me that the mold for a decent man hasn't been thrown away after all. Unfortunately, it doesn't get used enough.

After reading the doleful, remorseful email over and over, I don't know what to say. He's probably staring at his page even now. I note the time he sent it—three o'clock in the morning. "Poor soul," I say aloud. I hope he didn't lose any sleep over it.

Perhaps I should console him. What I really should do is to tell him to walk away from me, because I've got a hell of a lot of baggage he knows nothing about. Then my mind drifts to fantasyland, and I see us living together happily ever after. *Yeah, sure*, I chide myself. I click on REPLY and type a quick note.

"Nothing to forgive, Ian. I'm a grown woman, and I could have said no."

Boy, was that a flat-out lie. When did I last say no? There hasn't been a time since I was five years old. The truth slaps me in the face hard enough to sting my eyes with tears. *You're such a slut*, I chide myself.

I tap my fingers across the keyboard trying to think of what to say next. "I had a wonderful time this weekend. Let's not spoil it with remorse." I hit SEND and exit. I've got to leave this behind, because my emotions are in my throat. People are arriving at work, filling up their cubicles, and life goes on as it always does—in pain.

The day progresses as usual, and I try to fill my mind with work rather than with Ian.

It's hard to do, because at three o'clock I get another call from reception about a delivery. Instantly, my gut tells me that it's not an envelope from a courier.

I hesitantly get up from my desk, walk toward reception, and slowly lift my eyes to the top of the counter. There it is, another huge bouquet of flowers—this time pink carnations. He's figured out my favorite girly color. This guy is serious, or he's just an apologetic sod who can't get over his failures.

"Looks like your admirer is at it again," Melanie grins. Her face is filled with jealousy. I take the card, and sure enough it's from Ian.

"Thanks for the great weekend, sweets. Next time, I'll control myself."

All I can do is shake my head. The problem is he's ignited the hunger in me for him, and I'll never let him control himself. I can see the red caution signs ahead. Hopefully, my emotional ambulance is on alert.

When I get back to my desk, I grab my cell and walk over into the employee lounge. I've got to get his number in my speed dial, because trying to push the right ones doesn't work when my hands shake. It rings, and I hear his velvet voice.

"Ian Richards."

"What are you doing?" I question him with a tight jaw.

"Uh, talking to you?"

"No, the flowers. You didn't have to do that."

"Yeah, I did. Made me feel better. It's my penance for taking advantage of you when I said that I wouldn't. Also, I wanted to let you know how much I still like you the morning after."

Someone walks by, and I lower my voice to a whisper. "You made me feel wonderful yesterday, Ian. You don't need to buy me flowers."

"I didn't make you *feel* wonderful enough," he says, with his voice laced in distress.

"Get over it, *sweets*." I enunciate his little endearment. "I thoroughly enjoyed the moment."

He doesn't say anything, and the end of the line goes deadly quiet. For a moment, I think we've been disconnected. Then I hear him sigh and whisper into the receiver. "Next time, it will be better. I promise."

Now the cat has got my tongue. I don't know what to say. A myriad of emotions are buzzing about my head like angry bees.

"I've got to go. My boss wants me. Talk to you later."

"Rachel . . ."

I hear his voice, but I end the call. I'm sick inside over the anticipation of next time. The poor man thinks he can't perform, and it's me who is unable to respond. He'll never get an orgasm out of me with his tenderness, and the idea of how I'd ever be able to tell him that I need more, frightens me to death.

—·❋·—

Home sweet apartment greets me at five o'clock, along with my purring cat. I haven't heard any more from Ian, and frankly, I'm glad. I need a break from the roller coaster of emotions spiraling around and around in my brain. I'm exhausted just thinking about it.

I put a high-calorie frozen dinner into the microwave and hit start. There's an old bottle of wine in the fridge, and I need a drink, but it's pill time again in a few hours. Alcohol and purple don't mix.

After dinner, I stare at the telephone and suddenly wish he'd call. Maybe he thinks I don't want to talk to him after my abrupt hang up this afternoon. I sigh and chew on my fingernail. Then I remember, he works late—that's it. There's no reason to worry.

I plop down on my recliner, and Whiskers jumps on my lap. Suddenly, there's a knock at my door. *Gosh darn it!* I complain. It's probably some solicitor who I'll ignore. I peek out the hole, and there is Ian looking straight ahead. *Oh, crap, and I'm in my PJ's!*

I wrinkle my nose and open the door a crack and peer around the edge. "Ian, this is a surprise." He's in a gray suit, white shirt, black tie, and my legs go weak.

"Can I come in?" He sounds like a little boy asking for a candy bar.

"If you promise not to laugh at my attire, you may enter." I swing open the door and expose myself clad in my black tank top and my flannel bottoms with pink kitty-cats. He bursts out laughing.

"You rascal!" I scold him, grabbing his arm and pulling him inside. God, he looks yummy. He smells divine. He's so pretty. He's fooled around with me. He's everything, and I'm nothing.

"What are you doing here?"

"Had to see you."

I stare at him until my heart jumps in my throat. The next I know, my mouth is on his, and I'm swallowing him whole. Ian doesn't fight it; he relents to my advances. Already my body aches, and I don't want him to be tender. I need him to be rough. How can I tell him? I'm so afraid to expose my desires. Finally, I let go.

"Rachel!" He gulps. "God, woman, you're going to get us into trouble again."

I don't care. Swiftly, I take my hands and lift my tank top off my head and expose my breasts to him. His mouth drops open, and I announce my desires. "I want you."

"Are you sure about this?" His eyes focus on my boobs, where I want them to be.

Take me, don't ask me, my mind screams. I'm the rabid nymphomaniac once again, and it's his fault. For years, I've done nothing but play with myself. Now here he is, in all his glory. He can fondle me all he wants, if I can teach him how.

He stands there gawking at my breasts. Eventfully, his eyes lift to mine. He's hesitating, and I feel naked—really naked—the kind of in-the-garden-of-Eden-naked, and I grab my top from the floor.

"Gosh, I don't know what came over me. Sorry." I pull the top back over my head and cover myself. He looks conflicted as hell, and I don't blame him. Even I'm shocked by my behavior.

"You want to come in and sit down?" I ask, walking over to the couch. I turn and step away, and he grabs my upper arm.

"I've never felt like this with anyone so fast, Rachel. It's crazy." His hand tightens on my arm. "And disconcerting."

His eyes are blazing with desire. I do have an influence on him, and I'm ecstatic. However, his body language tells me he's also hesitant and afraid of where this is going. So am I.

"I know it's crazy. I'm as scared as you, maybe even more so, Ian. There's so much about me that you don't know."

"I don't care."

"I care."

"We'll cross those bridges when we come to them. Okay?"

We gaze at each other with heated longing. He places his hands upon my kitty-cat rear. The next I know, he's pulled me into his hard erection. I close my eyes fighting the love-hate feeling that's flowing through my veins. My head tilts back, and I look at his lips that swoop down upon mine. His tongue thrusts into my mouth, and his hands knead my behind. His erection grows, and I'm at his mercy.

"Ian." I moan. I take his hand and slip it under my tank top and press it against my breast. He fondles me with tenderness, and the disappointment flows through me like ice. Ian lifts my tank top over my head, and I'm bared to him once again. His action sends shivers down my spine. I want him to devour me like an animal.

"This suit has got to go," he says, taking off his jacket. He lays it on a nearby chair. I reach up and undo his tie, because it's enticing. He unbuttons his vest and shirt, and the next I know he's down to a white tee shirt.

My hands start fiddling with his belt, and I pull it through the loops and drop it to the floor. He kicks off his shoes, and the only thing that remains are his pants—all pressed and pretty for work, and they are about to be tossed aside.

"Nice suit," I say, looking at his bare chest. My hands rove over his flesh, and he knows exactly what I mean. "Did you bring a condom?" It's important to check for safety measures before getting too excited.

"Yeah, in my wallet."

He grabs his pants and pulls out the protection, laying it on the nearby table. If this keeps up, I'm going back on the pill so I can get the full feel of this guy, because condoms are a bore.

"Undress me," I beg him. He discards his trousers and the rest of his clothes until he's naked. I see his erection, and I can't look at it. I never can. It brings back memories. *You're pathetic. Yes, I know I'm pathetic*, I acknowledge to my inner tormentor.

Ian pulls down my bottoms, and I step out. Now I'm nude. Where are we going next? Couch sex? Recliner sex? Wall sex? Kitchen tabletop sex? Floor sex? My mind runs rife with exciting possibilities.

"Is your bedroom down the hall?"

It's bedroom sex in the dark? *Boring*, I think to myself as I lead him onward, passing all the fun places he could do me. He doesn't flip on the light, and I'm not surprised. Ian enters his tender, sexual prowess mode. Inside I'm screaming for more—I need more. As he begins a repeat performance of the night before, I begin to wonder if I should fake it for his sake. Maybe I just need to encourage him, and I do.

"Ian, touch me with your fingers, please."

He knows what I mean. His hand slides up my inner thigh and anticipation flows through my veins. *Oh, god yes, please*, I wait in anticipation. He fondles me but doesn't penetrate. Maybe he thinks only his penis belongs there. I don't know, but I want his hand. I want him inside of me and forcefully pushing me to the brink of ecstasy. He doesn't.

Suddenly, he stops, as if he's done his duty. He positions himself on top of me and starts to make love—tender, sweet, suffocating love. Slowly he pushes in and out, and I hear him moan. He wants me to moan, but I can't respond. I can't feel anything. I've never had an orgasm during intercourse—never. This isn't what I want or need.

The only way I can reach that place where the world slips into oblivion is when I'm taken by force and allow myself to submit to a man's domination through his hands. It's all I've known since I was sexually abused as a child. It's the only way my brain thinks. It's the only way my body responds. By force and bondage, not by love and sickening tenderness! I'm screaming in my mind for more, but nothing happens.

Ian keeps trying, and I feel his mounting dismay. Again, I encourage him to release himself. He doesn't. Instead, he pulls out of me, his face is shrouded in shame.

"Don't stop on my account, please," I beg him. I wrap my arms around his neck and pull him back down on top of me. "Go ahead," I whisper in his ear. "Fill me."

He looks at me hesitantly, but I know he's about to explode. He penetrates me again and resumes his gentle pushes. A minute later he grunts and holds me tight as he releases himself into his condom. My arousal sinks into the springs of my mattress, where all unachieved orgasms die a tortuous death. This isn't working for me at all. After years of sexual drought, I'm still fooling around with myself even with a man in my life. I'm so disappointed.

Ian doesn't say anything. He's clearly bent out of shape again. Swiftly, he rolls off me and looks down into my face with an exasperated expression.

"Boy, I'm really striking out in the sex

department, aren't I?"

My lips curl into a pitiful smile. Inside my unsatisfied whore is cursing him. *It's you. You're a bore in bed.* I turn my head away, because I can't stand the scrutiny of his blue eyes.

"It's just me, Ian. I need a lot of stimulation. Some women are like that."

"Explain," he says, pulling my chin back toward him. "I want to understand."

For a few moments, I stare into his insistent gaze. My heart is pounding in my chest as the words leave my mouth. "I like it rough." *There, I said it, you satisfied?* I bitch at my inward demons.

His brow furrows. "Explain rough."

"I can't."

"Tell me, I want to know."

"Gosh, what is this? Defined terms in a contract?" I sit up in bed and scowl.

"I'm frustrated." He huffs. "Because it's obvious I'm not giving to you what you need. Explain rough." His face frowns as if he's trying to figure it out. "You don't want me to hit you or anything, do you?"

"God, no," I quickly say. "I'm not into bruising."

"Then what?"

"Can we talk about this another time? I don't feel comfortable discussing it right now."

He's peeved. I'm peeved. I get out of bed. He gets out of bed. The room turns cold, so I flip on the light and grab the sheet.

"Well, I sure ruined your visit tonight, didn't I?" My voice is curt, as I wrap the linen around my nakedness.

"No problem," he says, in a pissed-off tone.

He stomps toward the living room and picks up his strewn clothes. I watch him get dressed into his white underwear and pressed suit. He remains silent, but I can tell by his hurried movements he wants to get the hell away from me. Finally, the perfect specimen of a man is standing in front of the door ready to leave, just like all the others.

"Maybe we're going too fast. I feel like I'm running blind down a road, and I don't know where I'm going," he rants. He lowers his eyes to Whiskers who has emerged shaken from underneath my bed.

"Whiskers, don't," I say, grabbing him and holding him in my arms. I don't want to see cat hair on Ian's pristine trousers. For some reason, I'd feel guilty if I soiled him in any way.

"I have a tough week at the firm. Big deal going down, and I've got a contract that needs negotiating. How about we take a breather, and I'll call you Friday or something."

I pout. The poor man is wounded, and it's my fault. "Sure, whatever you say, Ian."

"Nite," he says through a clenched jaw. He's gone. For a moment I stand and look at the door flabbergasted that he abandoned me, but why am I surprised?

"Shit!" I bellow in my empty living room.

I set down Whiskers on the floor, and slink back to my bedroom feeling like a whore. I'm devastated, angry, ashamed, and that desire of wishing I didn't exist flows through my veins. Heartbroken, I lie down on my bed and have a good pity-party cry. An hour later, I disappear into the blackness of my mind and fall asleep, exhausted and sore.

Chapter 9

PLAYING A GAME OF HUG

I am inside the two-story, white house down the street from where I live. My hand is being held tight by a teenage boy, and he is leading me upstairs. We walk into a bedroom, and the door closes behind me. He smiles.

"You like candy?"

In his hand is a really big candy bar in a brown wrapper. It's chocolate. I like chocolate.

"Sure, can I have some?" I reach out for it.

"Not until we play a game." He takes it away and sets it on top of his dresser.

"What game?"

"I just want to hug you, is that okay?"

I don't understand why he wants to hug me. He's not my brother.

"Where's my brother?" I feel scared.

"Don't worry. It's okay," he assures me.

I look toward the window and want to go.

"Come here by the bed so I can hug you." I wonder if I should do what he tells me.

"Do you want that candy or not, Rachel?"

My eyes see the candy bar lying on top of the dresser. I really do want it. "Yes, please."

"Then do what I tell you, and you can have it." He holds out his hand toward me. "Come here."

Slowly, I walk over to the bed and stand in front of him.

"I'm going to lift up your dress so I can feel you when we hug. Is that okay?"

"I guess so."

He lifts my dress up, and then gently leans me back.

"I want to hug you on the bed, but we need to take your panties off too."

When he pulls them down, I don't understand why, but I don't say anything because I want the candy. My tummy and bottoms are bare. The boy grins as he looks down at me on the bed. I watch him unzip his pants and pull out something long and big.

It's a part of his body, and it's ugly. I don't like it, so I close my eyes.

"Be still and quiet, Rachel. I'm going to rub myself against you like a hug," he whispers.

I do as he says. He lowers himself on top of me and holds me down on the bed. I can't move. This doesn't feel like a hug. He presses that big, ugly thing on my tummy, and rubs himself against my body. He slides it up and down and it hurts. It's warm and hard. He goes faster and faster, and I whimper.

"Just stay quiet," he tells me. He sounds mad, so I do as he says. "I'm only hugging you, Rachel."

He brings his hand down to my bum. I feel him touch me between my legs with his fingers, and I feel funny inside. I'm tingling in my body.

The boy rubs faster and faster. He closes his eyes and then he groans loudly. When something warm spills on my belly, he stops moving. When it's over, he stands up and looks down at me and smiles. His face is red and sweaty. I watch him push the ugly thing back inside his pants. I'm glad it's gone. I don't like it.

"Don't tell anybody about our little secret up here, okay?" He grabs a tissue from a box and wipes the sticky stuff off me.

I nod my head. "Okay."

He pulls my panties back up and my dress down. I stand up from the bed.

"Can I have the candy now?"

"Sure, here you go."

He hands me the big candy bar, and I smile. I don't know what happened, but I now have candy and something inside of me feels good.

"Thank you."

"Want to come back again? Did you like that?"

"I guess so."

"Good, when you do, I'll have another candy bar for you after we play our little game."

"Okay. Can I go home now?"

"Yes, but don't tell anybody about our secret. Promise? If you do, there will be no more candy."

"Okay. I won't tell anybody."

—·❀·—

I wake up in a start. The red numbers on the clock show two in the morning. My hair is wet from sweat, and my body is aroused. I know why. I've had another dream. It's too hard to dismiss, and I lie quietly in bed waiting for my arousal to subside, but it doesn't. It increases. My heart pounds in my chest, and I ache for release.

My eyes are closed, and the door to the dark room in my mind opens. My tormentors start their usual taunting and tempting to succumb. I'm stimulated because of the boy that touched me and held me down in his bed.

Just think about him hurting you, the voices start. *Go ahead, touch yourself. You know you want to, because it feels good and you need it.*

My self-hatred grows. I've been masturbating since I was six years old. One pedophile stamped my brain with his revolting desires, and I haven't been the same since. I was introduced to the male penis and sexual arousal when I should have been playing with dolls. He rubbed himself against me time and time again, fondled me, and I prostituted myself out for a chocolate candy bar each time he invited me to his bedroom.

I've since learned the sick word for what

he did to me—frotteurism. Why psychiatrists give it a name, I have no idea. Some men get off rubbing themselves against others against their will. Why don't they call it what it is? Sick!

I'm angry, and the torment in my body continues. My hand creeps down, and I fondle myself. I'm wet, aching, sore, and hurting. I just want to make it go away, but it won't go away until I take care of it. I've tried, time and time again, but my flesh is stronger than my spirit, and I can't resist.

In the darkness, I close my eyes and stir my imaginations. I'm bound by some stranger with no face. The abuse begins, and I submit and let the man do to me what he wants. I hate it, but long for it. He violates my body and tells me that I'm worthless. This is my punishment for being a bad little girl.

I imagine the pain, the bondage, the forceful grasping of my flesh, and to my utter shame, I enjoy it immensely. A moment later, my body responds to the captivity, and an overwhelming orgasm rages through me.

My fantasy has conquered me. My abuser has won again by arousing my needs. I hurt myself, because I don't know any other way. At a young age, he taught me how to enjoy sexual arousal through self-gratification, and nothing I do will make it stop. When the dream comes, I'm at his mercy once again.

At last I feel the comfort flow through my stressed body, and the dark desire slips away. My tormentors return to the closet of my mind, taking with them the little girl. I turn over on my side in remorse and disgrace for what I cannot overcome.

It's all I've ever known. It's all I respond to—bondage, hurt, and being forced. How will I ever tell Ian what I want him to do to me, let alone why? He will be appalled, and I will lose him for sure, if I do.

My eyes lift to the clock on the table by my bed. The red numbers stare back at me. It's two-thirty in the morning. I try to go back to sleep, but I can't. After tossing and turning for another hour, I crawl out of bed, start a pot of coffee, and wander over to my computer and turn it on. I wonder if Ian has emailed me. The coffeemaker slurps its last drop into the carafe. I pour myself a cup and add some powdered cream. Afterward, I wander back down the hall to my small desk.

I sit down and know in my heart nothing

awaits me. Sure enough, there is nothing. No notice of Ian's mail, and my heart sinks. This short-lived, tumultuous romance is going nowhere, and he's probably reconsidering suing my ass for running into his spiffy car.

There are no words inside of me to type him a note either, but I click on his page and see his status has changed to "in a relationship." A relieved grin spreads across my face. Maybe there's hope yet, and for the next few minutes I struggle whether to change mine from single to match his. As soon as I do, I'm sure all my nosey friends at work will be asking for specifics.

"Oh, what the hell," I mumble.

Afterward, I pop over to one of many pages and groups created for those who have suffered childhood sexual abuse. One that I frequent now shows over seven thousand thumbs up. I shake my head. My eyes scroll down the wall, reading comments from suffering men and women. It validates to me that I'm not the only mental case around with sexual issues.

There are so many tormented and hurting people that it makes me sad. I wish I could help them, but I can't. What can I offer? Comfort? A hug? Hang in there, it will get better platitudes? *Heal thyself*, my mind reminds me. How, I have no idea where to start.

There are snippets here and there from counselors and quotes from books on how to win the battle. Funny thing is, I'm not sure if I want to beat this rap. That's the sad part. After struggling with myself for so long, I've decided this is who I am and not much can be done about it.

Over the years, I've read about women who have the same tormenting need for bondage. They seek sexual relationships with dominant men. I know there are males in the BDSM community who would do to me everything I crave. However, I'm afraid to go there, even if the thought is pathetically stimulating. There is a word for people like me with bondage and pain propensities—masochist. I can barely admit the dark truth to myself.

Conversely, I want to pollute dear Ian enough to bring me to that edge where he's forceful and hurts me so that I can scream underneath him in utter pleasure. Perhaps I find it more comforting to cross that line with him instead. All he knows is smooth-going sex, tenderness, and respect. I'm horrible. I've been corrupted, and now I want to corrupt another human being with my unusual desires.

I'm so damn conflicted over the entire thing that I stare at my computer screen and zone out for a few minutes. Ticked off at my state of affairs, I walk away and crawl back in bed. For the next hour and a half, I stay in the dark trying to sleep but get nowhere. I decide to stay put, until the alarm goes off, and I need to get ready for work.

Chapter 10

SETTING THE RULES

The next few days crawl by. Ian hasn't called or emailed. I'm filled with worry, but have convinced myself that he's been busy with work.

When Friday morning arrives, I stare at my computer and feel nauseated inside. I don't want our relationship to end so soon, because I know I could easily fall in love with him. He embodies the normalcy that I desire in life, along with an unscathed past and emotional health I lack.

At three-thirty, which seems to be his calling hour, my cell phone vibrates on my desktop. Caller ID shows his firm. I jump up from my chair, run over into the employee lounge and answer.

"Hello?"

"Hey, it's me," Ian announces half-heartedly.

"Hi, me." He's quiet for a few seconds, and I'm petrified.

"Sorry I haven't called, but I've been pulling a few all-nighters at the office."

"That's okay, I figured as much."

"Listen, I need to get away for the weekend to unwind."

My heart drops to the floor. I can hear the thud and see the pool of blood at my feet. He doesn't want to be with me.

"Hey, I understand, Ian. No problem."

"That's not what I mean, Rachel."

I draw in a breath of air and hold it in my lungs. "What do you mean?"

"Come to the coast with me this weekend."

"Are you sure?"

"Yes, I'm sure. We need to start spending some serious time getting to know one another."

I quickly disassociate myself from the threat, and my mind breaks out into that stupid song, "Getting to know you, getting to know all about you . . . ."

"You there?" he asks, since I've wandered off to my safe place for a second or two.

"I'm here."

"Is that okay? You and me, at my place?"

"Yeah, but I'm scared."

"Not of me, are you?" His voice sounds exasperated that I don't trust him yet.

"No, it's that getting to know you part. Well, not you, I mean you knowing me."

"Scared or not, you're coming."

He's telling me what to do and making the decision for me. I nod in agreement, even though he can't see me. I couldn't say no, even if I wanted to.

"Okay." There's that submissive word again from my little girl.

"Can you be packed and ready to leave by seven o'clock this evening? I don't want to leave in the morning. I've got to get away from this damn office and city sooner than later."

"Seven o'clock is fine."

"Good, see you then."

The call ends, and I let out the air I've been holding in my lungs in a huge sigh of relief. He wants to take it to the next step. That's a healthy sign. Well, sort of, or it could be disastrous.

I walk back to my desk with the "King and I" soundtrack blaring in my head. This isn't going to be easy, but at least I'll get to see the ocean again, and that brings a slight sense of peace to my panicked state of mind.

—·✻·—

When seven o'clock arrives, I'm standing salivating at the door. As usual, he's punctual, and I swing it open and smile.

"Hi."

"Can I come in? There's something I want to talk about before we hit the road."

I'm worried, but I surrender to his request. He glances around like he's looking for the cat, but Whiskers is sleeping on my bed, as usual. Then his eyes look at me, and I see a serious expression spread across his face.

"Listen, Rachel. I want to set the rules for the weekend before we leave."

"Rules?"

"Yeah, rules." He shifts his stance as if he's nervous, and then he looks at me straight in the eye. "I've felt pretty crummy these past few days about how fast I allowed our relationship to get sexual. It was disrespectful to you, and I'm thoroughly pissed at myself. We're obviously not ready for such intimacy."

My mouth drops open over his confession. He closes his eyes for a moment, as if he's regrouping, and then looks at me seriously and continues.

"This weekend it is hands off, except for kissing and hugging. You sleep in the loft upstairs, and I'll sleep on the couch downstairs. I don't want us to have any sexual relations whatsoever. The weekend is for us to grow closer together." He lets out a breath of air like he's relieved he got it out of his system. "Do you understand what I'm trying to say?"

For a second, he sounds like my father scolding me. A part of my body is disappointed, but another part of me is relieved. But when I chew on his earlier "getting to know you" comment, I'm afraid I'll be pressured into confessing my past before I'm ready. I think back to my counselor's advice of safe zones. *Boundaries*, I repeat in my head. *Boundaries*. Not that I've ever succeeded in keeping them, mind you, but the thought of trying oddly helps.

"Deal, but I have a requirement too." I can barely speak, as I choke out the words. My voice is trembling.

"Sure, what is it?" He looks intently into

my eyes.

"That when we get into these getting to know you sessions, if I start feeling uncomfortable, I get to say 'time-out.' I can't tell you everything about me in one single weekend."

A worried look spreads across his face. Maybe he wants full disclosure. He probably thinks he can place me on the stand and ask me questions under oath. It's his attorney-brain mentality. *Raise your right hand. Rachel Ann Hayward, do you agree to tell the truth, the whole truth, and nothing but the truth? Hell no!* After thinking far too long about it, he answers.

"All right, if you become uncomfortable over anything I ask, I'll give you the safe exit."

"Whew!" I say, heaving a sigh and wiping my brow. It's going to take every ounce of strength within me to do it, but at least he's left the door open for me to run out.

"Come on. Give me your bag to carry, and let's split this place."

"Gladly." I grab my coat and call back to my cat in the bedroom. "See you later, Whiskers!"

—·�֍·—

Ian has his spiffy roadster back in one piece, and I'm back in the cockpit. It's close quarters, but I don't mind. Our trip is quiet, interspersed with shallow chit-chat. I am curious about this job, because it seems to take a toll on him physically. It's time to poke.

"So, can you tell me what you did this week at work? How come so many hours?"

He pulls his mouth to one side as if he's uncomfortable about the subject. Ian shifts in his seat.

"Can't talk about it much. Client confidentiality and all that stuff."

"Oh, okay." I'm disappointed.

"Just hours of negotiating with the other side over terms and conditions. It's a pain in the ass sometimes, and I'm about ready to think of a career move."

"I don't like seeing you like this," I say sympathetically. "Of course, I'm not the happiest in my position either, but we spend so much of our lives working, I often think we need to find a content-filled job—if there is such a thing."

"You're right, and one of these days I'm going to start looking. I can't right now.

Obligations."

Ian grows quiet, and I sense he doesn't want to discuss the matter any longer. It's only fair that I give him the same out, as I hope he will give me this weekend. I leave the subject and gaze out the window. It's almost dark outside.

We arrive at Cannon Beach at eight forty-five. Ian looks tired when he slips his key into the lock at his beach house, and frankly, I am too. He flips on the lights and expels his thoughts. "God, I'm exhausted."

"You look drained," I agree. "Why don't we just call it a night? I'm kind of spent too."

He lowers his head and climbs up the stairs ahead of me, carrying my bag. "Sounds good to me." After plopping my suitcase down on the bed, he turns and puts his hands on my upper arms.

"I'm sorry. I've only had about eight hours sleep in the past forty-eight hours. My body is shutting down."

"Don't worry about it." I bring my hand up to the side of his face and give him a comforting stroke on his more-than-five-o'clock stubble. "We have the entire weekend ahead of us. Get some sleep."

He forces a tired smile. The light in his

beautiful blue eyes is dim from exhaustion. Sweetly, he lowers his head and gives me a brief kiss.

"I just need to grab a blanket and pillow. Make yourself feel at home, Rach." He walks over to a walk-in closet and swings open the doors. On the top shelf, he grabs a blanket and pillow, some sweat pants, and a clean tee shirt. "See you in the morning," he announces, slowly descending the stairs. I stand and look at him adoringly and feel sorry for the guy.

When he's out of sight, I turn around and look at the vast king-size bed I have all to myself. I feel selfish, and I hear him downstairs flipping the blanket open and tossing the pillow on the couch. My body and mind are exhausted, as well, so I start my own preparations to pass out. It doesn't take long after my usual nighttime bathroom routine to flip back the blankets and crawl into Ian's bed. The light in the great room has already been turned off, so I reach over to the nightstand and dim mine.

My head rests upon his pillow, and I can smell a faint scent of the shampoo he uses. I smile because it makes me feel as if he's here holding me. After closing my eyes, I embrace the cased feathers and imagine his body next to mine, with his strong arm draped over my waist. It doesn't take long before I drift off to sleep in the contentment of Ian's presence passed out on the couch below.

My nose inhales the aroma of coffee and bacon wafting up toward the loft. I hear the faint sizzling of the frying pan and open my eyes to be greeted by a glorious sunny morning. I sit up in bed and look at the view. For the first time in years, I pray. *God, let me die here.* A silly grin crosses my face when I see the white waves rolling into shore. "Just not today," I add out loud, "or anytime soon."

I jump out of bed and grab Ian's robe hoping that he doesn't mind me wrapping myself inside his cocoon. Quickly, I brush my morning breath away, run a comb through my hair, and then slowly sneak downstairs. Ian is standing in front of the stove flipping the bacon over. He's dressed in sweats and a tee, and his hair is a tousled mess. I don't care.

"Morning." I greet him, shuffling across the hardwood floor.

"Hey, sleepy head, you're awake." He flashes me an endearing look.

"Yes. I can't remember the last time I slept all the way through. You've got a comfortable bed." I wonder about his night on the couch and the state of his back. "How about you?"

"Yeah, I passed out until this morning as well."

"Comfortable?"

"Doable," he laughs, rubbing his lower back.

"I'm sorry, you could have slept way on the other side of the bed with me."

He raises one brow at me like I'm naughty for suggesting it. "I wouldn't have slept," he answers with a sly drawl. "Besides, you're off-limits this weekend."

I pout. "Breakfast smells good."

"The coffee is done," he points over to the hot caffeine.

"Where do you keep your cups?" I look at the long line of cupboards over the counter.

"Second one over, on the left."

I open the cabinet and see a perfect line of matching coffee cups on the second shelf and perfect line of clean glasses on the bottom. The sight sends me into a silly giggle.

"What's so damn funny?" he asks, scowling at me.

"You're a neat freak," I say teasingly. Hopefully, he doesn't take it to heart.

"Huh, never been called that before," he says, wiping up the grease from the splattering bacon. "I like order in my life."

"Nothing wrong with that," I quickly agree, pouring myself a cup of coffee. "Most of the time, I feel out of order."

"So what do the insides of your cupboards look like?"

For some reason, I equate the thought to sex. I'm useless around this guy. "Uh, disorganized. Nothing lined up; nothing matches. I'm a mix-and-match girl, myself."

Ian doesn't say much. He looks as if he's digesting the newest tidbit about the girl that crashed into him. I can't help but wonder if his ex-wife was a neat freak, as well.

"How do you enjoy your eggs? Sunny side up, over easy, medium, or hard?"

A laugh escapes my lips, because he already knows I want it hard. I think he sees the devilish twinkle in my eyes, because he starts shaking his head back and forth like

I'm a naughty little girl, and I am.

"Eggs, Rachel. Eggs."

Whatever you do, don't say hard. Go with the flow, I tell my voice. "Uh, over medium?" I seriously hate runny eggs, but if I say hard, I'm going to burst out into red blotches, run back upstairs, and hide beneath the covers.

"Over medium it is," he drawls, making his own sexy comment.

"Eggs, Ian. Eggs." I can't help myself.

He flashes me a wicked grin, but I know there's not a shred of wickedness in him. He's clearly not the bad-boy type, so why do I want to turn him into one for my own selfish pleasure? He's a clean catch, and I'm a dirty trawler.

"So, you don't have problems dining in with me, it's just out?"

The funny thing is I haven't thought about it, because I'm feeling more comfortable around him. "I can do in, not out." Why does everything that comes out of my mouth equate to sexual preferences. Good God, my mind is in the gutter this morning.

"Good to know. I was worried you'd starve this weekend."

He serves me up a hearty breakfast, and

the two of us sit at his dining table. The entire western wall of his house is a window to the ocean, and I'm mesmerized at the view. I can hear the roar of the waves outside and the wind whipping around the building. The sun is shining brightly, and the ocean in the distance sparkles like thousands of diamonds.

"It supposed to be good weather all weekend," he says, while munching on a piece of toast. I'm surprised that he talks with food in his mouth. He does have faults.

"Gosh, it's so beautiful here, Ian. You're spoiling me."

He smiles. "Yeah, I've got it good. I'll admit it. Especially with you to keep me company. It makes the place feel alive again with the presence of a woman."

My mind is back to playing house again, and I stare at him like he's my husband. I merely want to be normal, happy, and at peace, but fear tells me otherwise. There's part of me that wants to live my life in front of him as one gigantic lie. I don't want him to know my past or my thoughts in the dark. It wouldn't be fair to him, and I know it. He has the right to know the full-deal, especially if we take this further between us.

I watch him quietly finish his breakfast. He looks as if his mind has wandered off somewhere. Maybe he's making a mental list of questions for my upcoming interrogation, and they're being neatly penned in his psyche.

"So, what's the plan today?" I say, interrupting whatever he's thinking underneath his morning hair.

"Take a shower, get dressed, go for a walk?"

"Sounds good," I agree excitedly. "Do you have a tide table?" When you're at the coast, you have to have a tide table.

"Uh-huh, but I already know. It will be out in about an hour or so, why?"

"Because, I want to crawl around the tide pool by Haystack Rock." I'm gushing like a tourist again.

"You like doing that?"

"Uh-hum. Love seeing the star fish, anemones, and all the other creatures stuck to the rocks."

"Sure, no problem. We can go dig for clams farther down the coast, too, if you want."

"Uh, just tide pool." I'm not too keen about digging in wet sand.

"No problem. I'll take you up to Ecola Park, if you'd like. Looks rough out there today. The waves should be pounding the rocks pretty hard, just the way you like it."

What is it with all of these comments? Ian smirks, and I know the stinker knows exactly how that sounded coming out of his mouth. The man is definitely dwelling on my last statement to him between the sheets. Maybe he wants to oblige me. I get excited thinking about it.

"I have plans for tonight, but I'm keeping those under wrap," he tells me with a mischievous glint in his eye. I can't help but wonder what he's got up his sleeve.

The attentive, sweet Ian picks up my empty plate and carries it to the sink. My eyes follow his movements, and I'm drawn to everything he represents. He's a remarkable man, kind, generous, attentive, and emotionally healthy. He embodies all that I yearn for, and nothing that I am. I'm falling like a love-starved fool, and it scares me to death.

"Thanks for breakfast, Ian."

"My pleasure, sweets."

I want to attack his body, but it's hands off. *Rats!*

Chapter 11

As promised, Ian drives me up to Ecola State Park. The narrow lane to the point winds like a snake through the Douglas fir and fern-filled forest. When we reach the parking area, I can't wait for him to open the door. Before he turns off the ignition, I jump out of the car and gawk at the scenery. Ian just smiles over my antics and grabs my hand, pulling me down the hill and then back up to the long trek to the end of the cliff. I enjoy our moments of levity.

"I promise not to push you off the edge," I tease him.

"You better not, or I'll come back to haunt you with vengeance." He frowns at me and then playfully tries to tickle my waist.

I scream and run up ahead. By the time we reach the very tip of the outcropping, I'm disappointed to see a crowd of other tourists.

Ian wiggles his way to the edge, claiming a small spot by the railing. He pulls me in ahead of him, and then he pushes his body up behind mine, wrapping his arms around my waist.

The salty wind caresses my face, and I revel in the spectacular sight. Thousands of years of never-ending waves have shaped the rocky spires below. Each time a huge wave meets the obstacle in its pathway to the cliff, upon which we stand, sprays of foamy white water leap high into the air and then sink back into the Pacific Ocean. It's a powerful, roaring thunder that fills my ears and brings delight to my soul.

"Look." Ian points down to a row of flat-topped rocks. "Couple of sea lions."

A pair lazily lie together soaking up the sun. I'm awestruck and at peace standing at my favorite spot in all of the earth. My emotions express my blissful state, and tears trickle down my cheeks.

Ian hears my sniveling. "Hey, what's the matter? Something wrong?"

"No. Everything is right." I sigh in contentment.

"You like it here, don't you?"

He hands me his handkerchief to wipe

my eyes. Why am I surprised over another caring moment on his part? I look at the initials IAR in the corner, and I dab my wet cheeks. He's not getting it back.

"What does the A stand for?"

"Alexander."

"Ian Alexander Richards," I repeat in a dreamy tone.

For a few minutes we stand there, looking out over the blue ocean. Eventually, the others leave, and Ian and I are left together on the wooden platform. I turn around to face him. My back is against the railing, and Ian pushes his frame against mine. His hands grab the railing on either side of my body, and the next I know he has me pinned in a very compromising position. He has no idea what he's doing to me as a woman, or maybe the rascal does.

"You're mine now," he drawls. His dark eyes look into mine, and I see a sexy, mischievous guy making me weak in the knees. Once again, his manhood is rising in his pants, and I'm growing nervous.

"Are you going to pin me against this railing all afternoon?" I stare at his moist lips, wondering how much longer he's going to torture me before I can taste them.

"I might keep you here all afternoon. Feels good."

"Ha! I can feel that it feels good."

"You've noticed?"

"Uh, yes, it's quite obvious," I answer, feeling far too warm.

"Mind if I kiss you?"

"I think you'll probably kiss me whether I mind or not, Mr. Ian Alexander Richards."

Ian lowers his mouth toward mine. By this time, I'm aching for his body. He's such a hunk, and he's got me under his spell. How much more sexy could this moment be? I'm helpless before him. My eyes close, anticipating his warm lips, and sure enough, he leans in even harder against me and clasps his lips to mine. His tongue does this choreographed dance in my mouth that sends shivers through my body. It's more than I can handle.

I put both of my hands on his chest and pull away. "Whoa there!" I exclaim, trying to catch my breath. "If you keep that up, you're going to break your own rules."

He smirks at me. "You're probably right. I shouldn't be testing my limits of self-control, because around you I don't have any."

That's my slut magnetism, I think to myself. *I just pull them in and do them.*

"Well, I don't do well with self-control," I honestly admit. "So it's on your shoulders to keep us on the straight and narrow."

"Fine," he says, giving me a wink and releasing his arms from around my body. I can breathe again without feeling crushed. Our time alone comes to an end, as another group of scenery gawkers arrives at the end of the point.

"We've got company," I announce. Ian turns around and grabs my hand.

"Come on, let's go for a hike." He drags me down the trail, and we spend the next hour trekking through the forest. At least it took our minds off of sex. I smile, because as I watch him walk ahead of me, I'm fixated on his fine rear in his tight jeans. Let's face it, I'm beyond hope.

—·❊·—

When evening rolls around, I'm in a state of ecstasy recalling our enjoyable day together. We have a leisurely dinner, while I watch the sun sink into the ocean. The clouds turn pink and gray, creating a breathtaking sunset that mesmerizes me.

After the dishes are done, and darkness has arrived, Ian is ready for my surprise.

"Go get a warm jacket," he orders. "No questions, just go."

A chill of excitement runs through my body, and I run upstairs. I hear him in the kitchen with what sounds like the rustling of a paper bag. When I'm back down, he's already donned his coat, and slung his backpack over his shoulder.

"Come on, we've got things to do."

I don't complain, but follow him out the sliding glass door. He leads me down to the beach and off to the left a few yards. A smile spreads across my face when I realize we're headed for an outdoor adventure.

"You like campfires?" he asks, as we arrive at the surprise location.

"Yes, I love them," I squeal like a little kid.

He places kindling on the stacked logs, which he must have gathered earlier. With a strike of a match, Ian lights the fire. Soon it cracks and pops, sending smoke up into the air. When the flames are high, embers fly above us and are carried off by a slight breeze. There's a large driftwood log nearby, where Ian places a small blanket on top. We both sit down together, and I'm filled with romantic excitement.

The ocean is dark, the stars are out, and here I am with Ian. Like a fool, I pinch my wrist to make sure it's not a dream. Why I keep doing that, I have no idea. Perhaps I'm afraid one day I'll wake up and this will have been a delusion.

"Oh, gosh, Ian, how beautiful." My heart is bursting with joy.

"I thought you'd like it," he says. "I come down here a lot at night by myself and light a fire. It's peaceful."

It doesn't take long for me to get lost in the surroundings.

"Do you want a beer," he asks, pulling one out of his backpack, "or a Coke?" He brandishes a can.

"Do you always think of everything?" I grab the cold can and pop the aluminum lip open. He twists the bottle cap off of his beer and takes a drink. We both sit quietly and look into the fire as the flames dance before our eyes.

He turns his head and looks at me, as if he's contemplating whether to start a conversation. I've been anticipating this moment all weekend.

"You want to talk?"

"About what?" I ask nonchalantly, but the muscles tighten in my jaw. Already, I'm reacting to the getting-to-know-you session that's about to ensue.

"I'm curious about a few things. Do you mind if I ask some questions?"

Instinctively, I cross my arms across my chest as if I'm protecting my heart. "Uh, sure. You remember our deal, though, right?"

"Yes, of course."

It takes all my strength to look at him and not feel panic. The dancing fire reflects in his blue eyes, and I melt. He must sense my uneasiness, because Ian leans in for a kiss. God, he tastes like beer, but I don't care. His lips make me feel woozy, like I'm the one who drank a six-pack.

When he's through sucking on my bottom lip, he leans back and takes a swig of beer. "Tell me about your family."

The interrogation starts with an easy question. I can handle easy, so I tell him. "Like I said, I grew up in the Midwest. I have one brother, five years older, who I don't see much. My mom died when I was eighteen from cancer, and my dad passed away three years ago."

"That must have been awfully hard, losing both your parents so early, Rachel."

"Yeah, I miss them." And inside my heart hurts thinking about it.

"There's nobody else?"

"I have a few cousins on my mom's side, but they live far away, and we don't talk."

"What about your brother, how come you don't see him?"

"He doesn't want a relationship with me," I say, frowning. "Besides, he lives out of state."

"Too bad," he says, disappointed. "It's sad when family members aren't close."

"Okay, your turn." I lead him away from the subject of my dysfunctional sibling relationship.

"Hmm, family." He muses for a moment. "Mom and dad are still alive. They live down in the Bay area. Dad wants to retire soon."

"What does your dad do?"

"Bank executive."

I shake my inner head, seeing dollar signs. "Brothers or sisters?"

"Yeah, I've got one brother, no sisters. Jack is married and lives in Boston with his wife, no kids yet."

"What does Jack do for a living?" Boy,

I'm into his family career status.

"Doctor," Ian says in a low voice, as if he doesn't want me feeling insignificant over my lack of education again. My simpleton head takes off with the rhyme:

Rich man, poor man,
Beggar man, thief,
Doctor, lawyer,
Indian chief.

I wonder if they sang that little ditty when they were kids to pick out their professions.

"Wow," I respond, feeling like a grain of insignificant sand on the beach. "Do you see your brother very much?"

"No, we're on opposite ends of the country." He narrows his eyes as he's trying to remember when. "Last time we got together was Christmas two years ago, when he came home to see mom and dad."

"Do you talk much on the phone?" Ian chuckles and his eyes twinkle. I'm surprised at his reaction.

"Yeah, I call him a lot to complain. He's got a good ear for listening."

I'm so jealous. The list of positive points in Ian's favor continue to mount. His family sounds wonderful. On the other hand, I feel like I'm sinking deeper into the sand underneath my feet, having come from a pretty dull and highly uneducated family background. What this man sees in me is beyond my comprehension. Maybe he's going for dumb blondes this time, since his intelligent blonde wife filed for divorce. I just don't get it.

Ian suddenly slips away. He takes a large gulp of beer, and I can't help but wonder what emotions he's shoving back down inside of him. Is it his failed marriage or perhaps lack of children? I'm suddenly curious about that point.

"You like kids?"

He turns his head and looks at me with a surprised raised brow. "Sure, I like kids."

"Your wife didn't want any?"

"She wasn't ready. Her career was more important."

Ian pulls his gaze away and picks up a stick and starts poking at the fire. He's as bad as me, with his quick move to disassociate himself when under tough scrutiny. Frankly, I don't want to talk about his ex-wife, so I drop the subject.

"Time for a treat," he announces. He opens up the paper bag, reaches inside and pulls out marshmallows. "Here, hold these," he orders, shoving the white puffs into my hand.

"Ooh, I love roasted marshmallows," I reply, smiling at the thought of the sweet, gooey filling. Next, his hand returns into the bag, and he hauls out a box of Graham crackers and a supersized, dark-wrapped, chocolate candy bar. I take one look at the familiar brand and feel as if someone has punched me in the stomach.

My head spins away in the other direction. I shut my eyes and groan loudly. Revulsion grabs me by the throat, and I can't breathe. As my heart rate increases, I start to gasp for air.

"Rachel, what's the matter?" His voice is filled with alarm.

Slowly, I respond and turn around to look at him. He's still holding that damn candy bar!

"I—I don't like S'mores," I sputter out. "Please, put the candy back in the bag," I scream at him like a mad woman.

Ian doesn't hesitate to shove the candy bar into the paper container. "Shit, Rachel, what's the matter?"

Horrified, I cover my face with my

palms. A moment later, he gathers me in his arms, pulls me toward his chest, and rubs my back in a soothing motion. The candy bar in Ian's hands incited a flashback that I haven't had for years. I saw my pedophile abuser holding out my payment for his latest jack-off on my body. The candy held by Ian, set off an intense negative recall.

As I'm crying on Ian's shoulder, I know he doesn't understand why. I want to tell him, but I'm petrified.

"Damn it!" I blurt out in anger, balling my fists. "I hate it when I do this."

To my surprise, Ian remains silent. He holds me, until my breathing slows, and the blood stops coursing through my veins at a hundred miles an hour. For some reason, I think he can feel my heart pounding against his chest. Slowly, I pull away from him and wipe my nose with the back of my sleeve, because I've forgotten which pocket I shoved his pretty handkerchief into.

"I'm so sorry."

"Something I did triggered a hell of a reaction in you, Rachel. You want to talk about it?"

"Can you just hold me for a while?" I look into his eyes like a helpless little girl.

"Sure, let's put this blanket down on the sand and lie down a minute. Is that okay?"

I nod my head to agree and stand up to watch as he situates the blanket far enough from the fire that we don't roast. He holds out his hand, and I take it, but I can't look into his eyes. Humiliation shrouds my entire body over what happened.

He lies down on his back and stretches out his arms for me to come to him. I don't hesitate, and the next moment my head is on his shoulder, his arm is around me, and he's tenderly stroking me with his hand.

No words come out of my mouth, and he doesn't pry. I let my emotions take an opportunity to regroup, while I count the minutes before I tell him the awful truth. I'm frightened to keep the secret locked inside any longer. He has the right to know why. If he can't accept my past, it's better to break it off before it goes any farther. Already, I'm grieving over the possibility of losing him.

"Feeling better?"

His warm lips touch my forehead, and he plants a sweet, gentle kiss on my cold brow.

"You want to talk about it?"

Some of the past I can, but not all of what it has done to me as a woman. I'm too mortified to show him the totality of the broken child within. I scrunch my lips together, close my eyes, and whisper my painful confession.

"I was sexually abused as a child, Ian. The pedophile used to give me that brand of candy, if I let him do to me what he wanted." I hold my breath waiting for his response.

Ian grasps me tighter in his arms. "Dear God, Rachel, what the hell?"

A moment later, I find the courage to lift my head and look at him in the face. His eyes are dark and intense. He's clearly upset.

"How old were you?"

I bury my head back into his shoulder and hide. "Five, six," my voice trembles.

"Did this go on for long?"

"Long enough," I painfully whisper.

"I'm shocked" His voice is terse.

"I didn't know any better, Ian." Why I need to defend myself every time I tell someone is beyond me. It wasn't my fault! I didn't ask for this to happen to me—it just did. "Please don't judge me and think I'm terrible."

"Good God, Rachel, I don't think you're terrible. That asshole was terrible. I would castrate the bastard, if I knew where he was at this exact moment."

"I don't know where he is. It was a long time ago."

"Did your parents know?"

"I don't think so. He told me not to tell, so like an obedient child I never said a word. I was afraid and filled with shame and confusion. I hid it from them, but I think my brother knew."

"Why didn't he do anything?" Ian asks, his voice raised in anger.

"I don't know. He was young and clueless at ten or eleven years of age."

"Did you ever talk to him about it?"

"No."

Ian sits up and looks down at me. His eyes are burning with anger, but his face is empathetic. "Oh Rachel, what did that monster do to you?"

Tears burn my eyes. "I don't want to talk specifics," I say, turning my head to the side and looking down the beach. I put my hands up in a t-formation.

"Time out. You promised me time out, if I needed it." My face is wet with sorrowful tears rolling down my cheeks.

Ian tenderly touches me with his thumb and wipes them away. "I'm so sorry, Rachel, that you had to endure such a terrible experience."

His heartfelt words make me inhale a shaky breath, and I look at him with profound respect for his compassion and understanding. My bottom lip quivers. "I didn't know any better, Ian. I was a silly, little girl."

He tenderly reaches over and gathers me back into his arms.

"Don't leave me because of it," I beg.

"Rachel, Rachel," he softly assures me. "I have no intention of leaving. It wasn't your fault." He kisses me on my cheeks and forehead.

No, it wasn't my fault, but it changed me forever. My entire life I've envied people like Ian, who are emotionally healthy, loved, and untainted by another's debauchery.

In contrast, I've hated myself, wallowed in shame and guilt, and wrestled with my need for bondage. Every relationship I've had with a man has been unhealthy, until Ian came into my life. The thought of losing him makes me cling tightly. He's my lifeline, and I know it with all of my heart.

Ian remains quiet, and continues to hold me in his arms. The fire begins to burn down, but I don't want to go. Now that my secret is out, my fate is in the balance. I pray to God for mercy.

Chapter 12

THE WEIGHT OF SHAME

The shame I bear is so intense in Ian's presence that I'm having trouble dealing with it. I can barely lift my eyes and look at him without cringing inside. It's horrible. No one can tell me that this man will not look at me any differently. My past has been exposed. My damage is evident. His mind must wonder about every detail of the abuse, and now I fear that he's questioning whether to move forward in our relationship.

When the fire dies, we return to the beach house. His hand is tightly holding mine, until we step inside.

"I'm tired," I announce. I'm not really. My only thought is to hide, so I don't have to look at him in the eyes.

"Yeah, it's been a long day," he agrees. He walks into the kitchen and sets down the unused contents of the paper bag. I see him reach inside, grab the candy bar, open the lid to the waste container and throw it inside. Ian turns and looks at me.

"I'll never buy another one of those again."

I'm having trouble watching how this has affected him emotionally. The man is such a tender creature that I'm convinced he's horrified by my confession. The beauty of our relationship is marred, and I'm deeply saddened.

"What are you thinking?" His face is pensive with narrowed eyes.

"Anger. Confusion," he says, looking down at the floor.

"Toward me?"

"No." He shakes his head. "I'm not angry toward you, but my mind is filled with questions."

"What kind of questions?" I hold my breath and wait for his answer.

"For starters, why you stayed in an abusive relationship with your ex-husband after what happened to you as a child?"

He brings his hand to his hair and rakes his fingers through his wind-tousled locks.

"Second, what you said about how you want sex." He brings his eyes up toward me, and I feel like a whore. "Is that why you want it rough, because you were treated that way as a child?"

How insightful Ian Richards has become. I am amazed over his perceptive psychological conclusion. Emotionally, I shut down. His questions about my behavior have breached my weak defenses, and I can't find the words to answer. As I look at him, I have this sinking feeling he's slipping away from me. He thinks I'm perverted. I am perverted.

"Time . . . time out," I whisper. I turn around and run upstairs to the loft.

"Damn it," he utters in frustration.

I reach the landing and run into the bathroom, close the door, and lock it. I need a safe place.

"Rachel!" he frantically calls after me. I hear his loud footsteps ascend the stairs.

"Time out, Ian," I yell. I back up against the bathroom wall and stare at the door handle.

"Rachel, please, let me in. I won't pressure you, I promise." He knocks on the door. "Rachel, answer me."

I can't talk. My throat and chest are constricted. No air is entering my lungs. He turns the handle again, and I hear him tearfully plead with me.

"Open the door, Rachel. I'm worried about you."

Any moment I'm going to pass out. I can feel it coming. The room is whirling around, and dark blotches dance in my field of vision. I unlock and open the door. As soon as I do, I fall into Ian's arms. He picks me up and carries me to the bed.

"Enough for today," he says in a soft voice. His fingertips gently brush my hair away from my face. I feel a tender kiss touch my cheek. I'm relieved he can still caress me without disgust. It's difficult to look at him, so I keep my eyes shut.

"You need to rest, sweetheart."

He pulls off my shoes and socks and then bends over me. "Open your eyes."

I do and look into his dark blue gaze. "You want me to undress you or do you want to do it?"

There's no strength left in my body or mind. "You," I say, and then close my eyes to hide again. I feel his fingers unbutton my blouse. He lifts me up into his chest, and I slip my arms out. I'm left in my bra as he lowers my body back onto the bed. Ian unzips my blue jeans, tugs them down my legs, and leaves me in my panties. My body shivers in shame as he covers me with the blanket. His kind hand tenderly strokes the side of my head.

"Sleep, sweet princess. Sleep." He kisses my lips lovingly, turns off the light, and heads downstairs. I roll over and cry myself to sleep.

-·❊·-

My eyes shoot open, and I look at the clock. It's three a.m. I can smell the ocean air inside the house and hear the loud sound of the waves outdoors. I sit up in bed and look out the vast windows. The sliding glass door to the patio is open, and I see Ian sitting in the dark. I feel chilled when I crawl out of bed. Quickly, I dress in my blouse and blue jeans and head downstairs.

The inside of the house is cold, and Ian seems oblivious to the temperature sitting outside in his tee shirt. Quietly, I approach the open door and stand there until he realizes I'm nearby.

"Hey, what you doing out of bed?" He glances up at me with sad eyes.

"What are you doing off the couch?"

"Just sitting," he says, in a low voice. "Couldn't sleep."

I stay in the doorway, hesitant to approach. His attention returns to the ocean, and I hear him sigh.

"Do you want me to leave you alone?"

"No, Rachel, come and join me if you want."

I'm relieved by the invitation and walk outside. The deck is cold against my bare feet, but I don't care. Slowly, I make my way to the empty chair next to him and sit down. I lift my head backward and am amazed at the sight. Every star in the heavens twinkles back at me, and surprisingly I feel small and insignificant, in spite of the uncomfortable moment between us.

"God, it's so beautiful."

"Yeah, I know."

Ian reaches over and grabs my hand. He weaves his fingers into mine and locks us together. He has no idea how much I need assurance that I don't disgust him. I hope he still wants me.

"Sorry about earlier and the way I acted." I feel compelled to apologize.

He looks at me with somber eyes. "You have nothing to apologize about. I'm sorry for the way I acted. Frankly, it threw me for a loop. Took me a while to process the shock, I guess."

My face is expressionless as I look at him in the dark. I'm hurting inside, but I don't want him to know.

"Can I ask you one thing?" he earnestly inquires.

I inhale a deep breath. "Yeah, sure."

"Have you sought professional help for this? I mean, seen a therapist or doctor to talk about what happened to you?"

My eyes drop to my lap. I cannot look at him and lie. "I told you before that I saw a therapist for counseling."

"When you left your ex, right?"

"Yeah, and we talked about other stuff," I concede in a half-truth.

My sexual abuse was only fleetingly touched upon between my counselor and myself. She had wanted to teach me how to say no and set boundaries in relationships, but I shrugged it off. I was too spent after years of an abusive marriage to start poking at another sore spot.

Ian squeezes my hand, and I'm reminded that we're intertwined as one. At that moment I realize I need something else besides focusing upon my abuse. I need to learn how to receive love. The deep-seated belief that anyone can love me eludes my comprehension.

No doubt, I'll eventually sabotage our relationship, particularly the closer we become. When you're convinced that nothing good happens in your life, you have a tendency to end a relationship before another beats you to the punch. At least that way, you're not rejected by another human being. Being cast aside is more devastating than walking away on your own terms. I only hope that I get to spend a few more months with him before it all ends.

I turn and look at him. He's still staring out at the dark ocean, and I want to know what he really sees.

"Do you think of me differently now?"

"I'm not sure what you mean," he impassively replies.

I wonder if he's skirting the question so he doesn't have to tell me the truth. "Do you think I'm sick or something?"

A sigh escapes his lungs, while his dark eyes look pensively into mine. "No, I don't think you're sick. My heart goes out to you, because I can see it has seriously affected your life."

I feel like a soiled piece of trash in his presence. My eyes pull away from his, and I turn my gaze toward the dark ocean that mirrors my soul. Tears threaten to fall, as I huff out my frustrated response from between my lips.

"You're right, it has affected me."

Ian squeezes my hand. "Rachel, I don't want it to affect us." He gently touches my chin and encourages me to turn my head. "Look at me, sweetheart."

Like a little girl, I obey his command and submit.

"I want to understand what makes you who you are," he says sweetly, as his thumb gently traces the edge of my jaw. His dark, expressive eyes encourage me to trust. "Because I think I'm falling in love with you, Rachel Hayward."

My heart leaps into my throat. I know there are tears inside of me, but they don't come to my eyes. How can he love me? Men don't love. I'm convinced the male gender is incapable of the emotion, but Ian's eyes beg to differ with me. He looks so sincere, that I cannot deny his confession.

Embarrassed, I glance away from his

intense gaze. I know he's waiting for me to acknowledge his words and express my own. My voice trembles.

"I want to feel the same for you, Ian, but I don't want to be hurt either."

"Listen, Rachel, I won't ever lie to you. If I say I'm falling in love, then I am. Believe me that there is no ruse on my part or dishonesty in my words."

I scrunch my brow as if I'm in pain, and my lips clamp together. It's so hard to expose my feelings when so much is at risk, but I don't want to spurn him.

"Me too." My answer sounds elusive. "I mean I feel the same way about you."

I find the courage to look at him, and my heart is overwhelmed by his loving presence. My mind runs rampant in conversation with the powers above. *God, I do love him. Look at him! He's my Prince Charming—my dream come true. He's normal, and he wants me. Can this really be happening?*

Ian flashes me an endearing smile and gathers me in his warm arms. "Glad we got that settled," he says in a relieved voice. He strokes the side of my head with the palm of his hand. The peculiar feeling of tenderness attempts to melt my heart.

"You're a beautiful and wonderful woman, far deserving of good things," he whispers.

I don't believe him. Ian kisses me, and I relent to his sweet taste at three thirty in the morning.

Chapter 13

THE CONFESSIONAL

I return to bed, and Ian returns to the couch. We both wake up mid-morning. About an hour later, we have a small breakfast. Neither of us possesses an appetite.

Ian appears absorbed in his thoughts, and I don't blame him. He probably wants to know what happened to me as a child, but I'm not sure that I can specifically tell him every detail. The thought of doing so intensifies my fear that he'll leave me. Anxious about the wandering of his mind, I try to pull his thoughts elsewhere.

"Can we go for a walk? Just a short one?"

He turns his head and looks my way. "Sure, sweets, whatever you'd like."

"What is it with this *sweets* thing?" I ask him with a coy smile.

"Because I think you're sweet, sweets."

I have no endearing names for him. One day when I was bored, I did an Internet search for the meaning of Ian. I almost choked when I read that it meant "the graciousness of God." Of course, I wondered if God decided to be merciful to me, even though I'm a masturbating slut. Every now and then, I think the man above toys with us by dangling a carrot of promise and then snatches it away. It feels like that since my relationship with Ian has been tainted. I don't know what to believe any longer.

We grab our jackets and head out the door. The tide is on its way out, but not enough to climb on the rocks looking for starfish. Frankly, I don't feel like it either, since I'm in the dumps.

Ian grabs my hand and holds me tight. The air is a bit chilly as usual when a morning fog lingers offshore. The waves roll in quietly with a soft slurping sound, and it's peaceful.

The farther we walk in silence, I debate the necessity to reveal more of my past. He's too quiet, and it bothers me. Ian deserves answers no matter how frightened I am to give them. It's important that I fill in the blanks before he fills them in with speculation. I squeeze my eyes shut as I open the door for him to peek inside.

"What do you want to ask me, Ian, about my past? You had questions last night."

The grip of his hand tightens. He glances over at me with a sorrowful look upon his face. I think he knows this isn't going to be easy for me. I have my time out word, so for the most part, I feel confident that I can answer some questions before totally disassociating myself from the pain.

"It's a strange question, but it's driving me crazy."

"What is it?"

"What was sex like with your ex-husband? Did he—did he treat you rough, the way you like it?"

I almost want to burst out laughing. "My ex-husband, Ian, pretty much used me as a receptacle. He could have cared less about my pleasure as long as he got what he wanted." I remember how brokenhearted I was when I realized what a mistake I made. Right after we married it was obvious he didn't love me. He wanted a whipping post he could verbally lash.

"Most of the time, he made me feel like crap. When he was done with me, he'd get up and go wash his hands for ten minutes to rid himself of my smell, I guess. He told me that I made him nauseated when he touched me."

Ian halts our steps. He turns and looks at me in disbelief. "You mean he never pleased you?"

I look down at the sand. "What do you think I did? I pleased myself to find release. It was like that for years, until I no longer shared my bed with him."

"What about other men in your life before you got married? How did they treat you?"

I scowl over his question, because my promiscuous tendencies have gathered a long laundry list of past sexual encounters. My mind remembers them all with clarity—Randy, John, Marcus, two Michaels, and Stephen. It's too intrusive to tell him about everyone, and how some of them did give me what I wanted to one degree or another. Of course, after they got what they wanted, they all eventually abandoned me. Even I don't like to think about it.

"Let's not go there," I say, with an annoyed clip. "If you want me to tell you, then I want details about every woman you've done since you lost your virginity."

"Fair enough. Let's not," he replies in an edgy tone.

Poor Ian. I'm corrupting the man with my horrid past. He looks like he's on information overload, and I'm afraid I'm going to short circuit his kind heart.

We walk down the beach a few yards. He's silent, until he halts again and faces me. The palm of his hand touches my cheek, and with a sympathetic gaze he looks into my eyes.

"What happened when you were a child?" He voice trembles. "Can you tell me?"

There's no way I can maintain eye contact and speak the words. I lower my head and grimace.

"Don't look at me when I tell you," I insist. "I can't bear the shame."

"Okay, then. I'll hug you while you tell me. I'll look over your shoulder, you look over mine."

Ian doesn't give me a moment to protest. He grabs me and pulls me against his chest and wraps his arms around me in a bear-hug manner. Instinctively, I know he's holding me up, because probably my knees are going to give way when I'm done. *Okay, you can do this. Suck in a deep breath and just spit it out.*

"He lured me to his bedroom and told me that we were going to play a game and that he wanted to give me a hug." How ironic, Ian is hugging me now. I inhale another breath.

"If I did what he told me, I'd get a candy bar after he was done. Then he pushed me back onto his bed, and stood in front of me and took out his penis. I remember how I thought it was ugly, and frankly, today I still cannot look at one with any great pleasure." I cringe over my words. "No offense to you, sweets."

"None taken," he whispers.

My tears start, and Ian holds me closer. He's stroking my back.

"After he lifted my dress and pulled down my panties, he laid on top of me and masturbated by rubbing himself against my body."

The suffocating feeling that overcomes me starts to squeeze my chest. "He ejaculated on my belly. When he finished, I earned my candy bar."

"Did he ever penetrate you, Rachel?"

"I don't know," I say, shaking my head. "If he did, I've blocked out the memory. I think he must have fondled me often, because I can remember being aroused as a child and wanting release."

By now, I think Ian is going to crush me in his embrace. I pull away from him to catch my breath, and when I look at his face, he has tears in his eyes.

"Oh, Ian, don't cry for me," I tell him. "Please, you'll make me feel worse."

He's upset. I'm drenched in shame. His eyes have more questions, and instinctively I know what they are.

"You're wondering why I want it rough after what happened to me as a child, don't you?"

He nods his head.

"I don't know, frankly. I think it's because he held me underneath him, and I couldn't move. Something happened inside of me, because he aroused me by what he did." I'm feeling frustrated. "You know, I'm not a psychiatrist. All I know is that I respond to bondage, and I'm sure it's because of the sexual abuse." I start to tremble as I stand before him. My veins feel as if ice is flowing through my body.

"Okay, okay, that's enough, Rachel. Time out." It's obvious that I'm about to lose it.

I nod my head in agreement. It's time out.

Our conversations for the rest of our day together avoid my past. I take the little girl within and hide her back into the closet of my mind, where there is only darkness. I replace her by roleplaying a carefree and happy young woman again. There are times I think I deserve an Oscar for my performances, and this is definitely one of them.

— ·❄· —

We are back in the car, driving toward Portland. I feel a distinct sadness leaving the beach house. Not only is it my dream home, but my dream location to live out my life.

"It's too bad you can't live here all the time, Ian."

"Yeah, but the commute would kill me. Two hours a day back and forth with my hours, doesn't make sense."

"Ever thought of going into practice in a small town like Cannon Beach or Seaside?" Ian turns his head and gives me a smile over my suggestion.

"No, because there probably isn't much

need for a corporate attorney in such small communities."

"Can't you practice any other kind of law? You know, handsome criminal lawyer or something like that for the county?"

Ian bellows a husky laugh. "God, Rachel, you are watching too many television series about attorneys."

"Well gosh," I boisterously respond, "I thought it was a brilliant idea."

"If I ever went into criminal law, I surely wouldn't defend the bastards. I'd be a prosecuting attorney and put them in jail."

His voice sounds stern, and I wonder if he's thinking of a certain person that tainted a little girl's life. After all these years, I have no idea if that asshole is dead, alive, or in jail for hurting someone else. All I remember is that eventually his family sold the house, and they moved away.

"Yeah, you're the good-guy type," I agree. "Frankly, I'm glad, or I'd probably have a court date by now for having rear-ended your prissy sports car." I smirk at Ian, and he flashes me a wicked look that surprises me.

"Missy, you owe me for not suing your ass," he snarls. "I'll admit that I was pissed when you initially hit me." He pauses for a moment and then narrows his eyes looking like a bad-boy. "One of these days, you're going to have to pay up."

Suddenly, my body is on fire at the thought. Does he mean what I hope he means? It doesn't take long for my mind to picture him making me *pay up* in all sorts of cruel ways. I start to squirm in the seat next to him feeling aroused. My neck bursts out into red blotches, and I quickly roll down the window halfway and thrust my face into the wind. I hear him chuckle as if he knows exactly what's happening to me.

"Did that turn you on *that* easily?" he asks curiously, with his sweet voice again. "The making you *pay up* threat?"

My lips are sealed, but I'm aching with the thought of it. I wonder if he even has it in him to follow through with his threat. He's too sweet to be mean, and in my heart I know it. If he continues to taunt me though, we're going to be in trouble.

Suddenly, he hits the button and rolls down the window all the way. "Apparently, so. You better cool off, because this car is way too small to get screwed in."

I burst out laughing, and so does he. The

sexual tension between us fills his roadster, and I turn and look at him.

"That was definitely a getting to know you moment," he slurs.

"Stinker!" I glare at him. I shove my face back into the wind, close my eyes and imagine him attacking my body while I'm helpless beneath him. I'm so damn pathetic.

The following morning I drag myself into work in a fit of depression. I have missed a few of my purple pills over the weekend, and now I'm all screwed up on my dosage. My melancholy mood makes it difficult to get motivated, and my mind drifts back to the weekend with Ian.

He brought me home, walked me to the door, and to my chagrin gave me a short goodnight kiss. It's obvious that he's serious about the no sex interval between us. I'm saddened and horny, but for once I leave myself alone when I crawl in bed.

It's obvious that I've moved into my next mode in the relationship—it's my usual religious guilt tactic. It's time to bargain with the higher power. "I'll be faithful God and not fool around with myself, if you give him to me."

For some reason, my former religious education tells me that I must obey, before God can give me anything good. If I sin, he's going to slap me down, bring me troubles, or make me sick; and masturbating is sin, or so the church tells me. I should be going blind one of these days or my hand will fall off with leprosy. My theology is as screwed up as the little girl I still have shoved in the closet in the back of my mind. The poor slut wants out, but I'm keeping her captive for the moment.

Immediately, I start my morning routine of checking my social page to see if Ian has popped by to say hello. Instead, of an email, I find a picture posted on my wall of a dozen red roses. My face bursts into a cheek-hurting grin when I read his note.

"Thanks for the weekend. How about next—same time, same place?"

It's useless, and I bring my hand up to my mouth and stifle a giggle. Is he serious about another weekend at his beach house? Maybe he is asking me to be his permanent weekend live-in? "I can do that," I say out loud.

"Do what?" Julie comes up and plops on

the chair next to my desk. I quickly close out my page, turn my head, and give her a quirky grin.

"Nothing."

She squints her eyes at me like she knows I'm lying through my teeth. "What did you do this weekend? See your victim again?"

"Sort of."

"You guys hitting it off?"

"Sort of."

"A woman of words this morning, aren't you?"

It's impossible to look her in the eye, so I look at my computer instead and open my email. "I'm feeling a bit private about the whole thing. Don't want to jinx it."

"You've hardly dated anyone since your divorce, Rachel. I'm dying to know."

"I can't tell you. Okay?"

Julie's face falls into a disappointed frown. "Thought we were friends," she mumbles, moving to her feet.

"Listen, Julie, I don't want to hurt your feelings. This one is important to me, and I'm kind of protecting it. Does that make sense?"

"No. You afraid I'll get all hot and

bothered for him, too, or something?"

"It's nothing like that."

"Whatever."

Julie mopes back to her cubicle and sits down. I've offended her, no doubt, but I don't want to spill my private life around the office like everybody else does about theirs. It bugs me. *I have a right to boundaries,* I remind myself, sitting up straight in my chair with a bit of an air. That's a first.

Suddenly, I remember that I haven't answered Ian's question. I quickly look around to make sure no one is watching and then I reopen the page.

My humor is raw this morning. I type in the comment line. "As your cook or your housekeeper?"

He must be staring at his page, because he comes back within a few seconds and answers. "I prefer lover, but if you want to cook and clean, go for it."

"Oh, brother," I mumble. He's something else. I'm so happy that he's being sweet to me and hasn't run the other way in spite of my awful confession.

I hear Mr. Stewart's voice coming up behind me, and my heart leaps in my throat. Quickly, I get out and greet the boss. "Good morning." As usual, he grunts, walks by, and goes into his office. Reality has returned, and so has the long work week.

Chapter 14

HUMP DAY VISITOR

Hump day rolls around, and I haven't heard from Ian. I try to attribute it to his crazy job, rather than to the fears I entertain like old friends in my wounded heart. I miss him and can't help but wonder if he's pondering my confession and what to do with me.

Frankly, I wouldn't blame him if he started to have second thoughts. Nor would I be surprised if he hasn't been on the Internet entering search terms trying to figure out what's wrong with me. If he lands on the BDSM pages and discovers there's a term for my tendencies, I'm probably never going to hear from him again. I try not to worry, but with my brain, it's difficult.

If that wasn't enough of my problems, at two o'clock all hell breaks loose. Mr. Stewart announces that one of the attorneys from the firm that represents our company will be coming within the hour to peruse some files in regards to a nasty litigation we've been dragged into. A disgruntled client is suing, and one of the attorneys on the defense team needs to review some of the background files on the case.

"Book the conference room and make sure it's cleared out for the rest of the day," he barks. He shoves a list in my face with file numbers. "Pull these files and have them ready for the attorney. I expect you to be available to help in any other requests that come up for information."

"Yes, Mr. Stewart," I reply congenially, cursing him inside like I always do. The man is an ungrateful sod.

I book the conference room, and then start my trek to the file area to look for the matters on the list. As usual, most of them are missing. They are probably sitting on a desk somewhere in another office and now I'll be off on a scavenger hunt trying to find them.

When three o'clock rolls around, I get a call from Melanie at the reception desk that our legal guest has arrived. I smile, wishing it was really Ian, but alas his firm doesn't represent the company.

I round the corner to the reception and see a tall, slender, blonde woman in a gray skirt and jacket. She's strikingly elegant, even if she is a lawyer. Melanie gives me a nod: she's the one.

"Ma'am, I'm Mr. Stewart's assistant." I smile at her, feeling terribly insecure. She whips out a business card and shoves it at me, displaying her manicured French nails. I take it in my hand and read the name.

Susan J. Richards, Attorney at Law.

The blood drains from my face. Slowly, I lift my eyes and look at her. *Damn! Is this Ian's ex-wife?* I have no idea if she kept her married name after the divorce, but for some reason, standing here near this woman, something tells me I'm not wrong in my conclusion. What are the odds of meeting Susan Richards? My inward preconceived ideas are confirmed—she's a freaking knockout. I hate her already.

"Well, are you going to let me stand here all day?" Her haughty and demeaning tone slaps me in the face as she eyes me with disrespect. I'm the scum at the bottom of her world, and the woman is putting me in my place. Oh, I see where this is going. I chew on my lower lip for a second so I don't blurt out some rude comment.

"No, of course, not, Ms. Richards." I make sure to enunciate the *Ms.* in her face. *Bitch.* "If you'll follow me, I'll show you to the conference room we have set up."

I turn around and lead the way. My jaw is clenched, my eyes are wide with contempt, and I'm spitting angry. She wants to intimidate me, and I want to wrestle her to the floor. Well, actually, I'll like to turn around and tell her that I've been doing her ex and see how she reacts. *Uh, ma'am, I'd just like to tell you that I've been screwing an Ian Richards—any relation?* I grin over what I know and she doesn't.

We arrive at the conference room, and I inform her of the state of affairs. "Mr. Stewart has arranged for you to work here. I've already pulled some of the relevant files." I try not to let her presence intimidate me, but it's not easy. "You'll find them there on the corner." I point to the stack.

"Fine. Are there others?" she asks, flipping her brief case down on the conference tabletop with an attitude.

"Yes, but I've not been able to locate them as of yet."

"Well, locate them," she snidely replies,

looking at me in the eye. "I don't wish to return again. It's my preference to finish this up this afternoon."

"Of course, Ms. Richards, I'll do my best." I can think of so many words I'd like to tell her. What a freaking attitude! The woman is horrible. If this is how she treated Ian, then I'm glad she walked out. I'm really pissed now.

I turn to leave the room, and she calls after me.

"I'd like a cup of coffee, if you please. Light cream, no sugar."

My steps halt, I scrunch my lips together, and spin around to glare at her. She's already got her face in one of the files, flipping through the sheets of paper. I really don't want to wait on this witch. She's expecting that I will with a snap of her fingers. Go fetch. If I don't, Mr. Stewart will probably give me the riot act for not taking care of her needs.

"Sure thing," I say, gritting my teeth, and walking out the door. I fantasize coming back into the conference room, tripping, and spilling the hot cup of coffee on her dainty little lap. *Control yourself, Hayward.* I try, but it's not easy.

After doing her bidding, I stroll back to my desk. It's now three thirty, and I can't help but think of Ian this time of the day. I'm half tempted to pick up my telephone and call him. My cell phone is sitting on my desk top, and I stare at it contemplating what to do next. Apparently, he's sensing vibes from my end, because suddenly my phone starts to vibrate across my desk. It's him. Swiftly, I grab it and run over to the employee lounge.

"Hello?"

"Hi, sweets."

"Hi, Ian." My voice is melting at the sound of his and a smile spreads across my face. "How are you?"

"Just had a minute and you popped into my mind. Thought I'd call."

"I'm glad you did, frankly. I have something strange to ask you," I say, lowering my voice.

"Strange?"

"Uh-hum." I glance around the corner, looking at the snob sitting in the conference room going over the files. "Although, you'll probably think I'm loony."

"So ask me, and I'll let you know if you're loony," he chuckles.

"Okay, here it comes. Did your ex-wife

keep your last name when you divorced?"

Ian is silent. I'm surprised he's not responding right away to my question. Finally, he reluctantly answers. "Uh, yeah, she did. Why do you ask?"

"Oh, because one of the lawyers from the firm that represents our company arrived at the reception, and I had the pleasure of greeting her." *Pleasure my ass.* It takes me a few seconds to continue. "She handed me her card with the name of Susan J. Richards on it."

"Shit, you're kidding me!" He definitely is mortified by the sound of the "shit" comment.

"Uh, shit I'm not." Ian is quiet. "So what does the J stand for?" I might as well pry.

"Jolene," he answers. His voice is strained.

"Well, what a small world, isn't it?" I glare over at her with my evil eye.

"Rachel, I'm sorry about this. I knew her firm represented Kennedy Advertising, but I had no idea that the two of you would ever cross paths because of it."

"I don't like her." There I've said it. "She's condescending."

"That's Susan." Ian sighs.

"If she treated you that way, then I really don't like her." I'm feeling angry just thinking that she did. He's not answering, and I'm gathering he doesn't want to either.

"You haven't said anything to her about us, have you?"

There's a definite panic to his voice. I narrow my eyes, wondering why he'd care about her knowing about us. I'm a bit peeved at his question.

"God, no, Ian. Not to say the thought didn't cross my mind, but I wouldn't do that to you."

"Thanks, Rachel."

"Why? Does it matter?"

"I . . . I'm just not too keen on Susan knowing my private affairs, that's all."

This conversation is now bothering me big time. Why don't I believe what he's telling me? I can feel it in my gut that Ian's still attached to her in some way. If he didn't care what she thought about his actions, it shouldn't bother him.

Maybe he's embarrassed. That's it. He's ashamed of me, because I'm not a gorgeous, intelligent woman. I'm the plain Jane administrative assistant making an hourly wage. He's lowered his standards, and he doesn't want Susan to know. I'm really getting grouchy now.

"Well, I better go." I don't want to talk about it anymore.

"Hey, you." He stops me from hanging up.

"What."

"You're not mad at me or anything are you?"

"I'm not quite sure how to articulate what I'm feeling right now, frankly."

"How about dinner at my place tonight?"

"Huh?"

"I'd like to cook you dinner tonight."

"Are you serious?"

"Yeah, I think after being exposed to the ex-wife, I need to give you some extra comfort."

"Think so, huh?"

"I know so. Pick you up at your place at six o'clock?"

"You're really going to show me your Portland digs?"

"Sure, why not? It's about time."

I can't resist the thought of snooping around his other residence. First order of business is to find lingering pictures of his ex-wife.

"I'm in," I answer with a big smile on my face.

"Great. See you tonight."

"Bye, Ian."

Our call ends, and I walk back to my desk. I look up at her in the conference room, and she's waving at me to come in and wait on her. *Oh, brother, why don't you just finger snap?*

"Yes?"

"Did you find those other files?"

"No, but I'm working on it." I don't give her the chance to say anything in return. My back is turned, and I leave her disgruntled face behind me. *Wouldn't you like to know who I'm having dinner with tonight?* It's rare, but I'm feeling a tad smug.

Chapter 15

THE WINDOW WITH A VIEW

Like with other surreal moments, I reach over and pinch my wrist to make sure I'm not dreaming. Yes, he has a small place, somewhat the size of mine, but what a view! I'm blown away by the modern décor and tall windows that look over the city lights. It's really nice. The fact that he has money is quite obvious.

"You're into views," I say, walking over and gawking.

"Yeah, I guess you could say that."

Ian comes up behind me as I stand and look out his living room window. I feel his warm arms wrap around my waist. He pulls me back into him, and I'm putty. Tenderly, he leans over and kisses me on the cheek.

"Glad you're here, sweets."

I'm not surprised to feel his growing adoration in his pants, but with this no-sex gig between us, it could mean trouble.

"That's a dangerous position," I whisper.

"I know," he says, turning me around. "Sorry. It's hard to control myself when I'm around you."

"I'm glad, Ian. I was frightened that I would disgust you after this past weekend, now that you know about my childhood. I still feel bad I was such an emotional wreck." I search his eyes looking for a hint of aversion, but all I see is acceptance.

"Never," he says, lowering his lips and kissing me.

Why does he always taste so damn good? As soon as his tongue enters my mouth, I'm wishing for more. He has such an effect upon me, and immediately my mind ends up in bed with him. His body is rock hard, toned, and smooth to the touch—except for his six o'clock stubble that is now poking me in my chin. It's becoming uncomfortable, so I pull away.

"Stubble, babe," I tease. "You're prickly."

"Oh, sorry about that." He rubs his face with the palm of his hand. "Yeah, about this time of the day, I'm getting the old shadow."

"You say that word too much," I complain.

"What word?"

"Sorry."

"Oh, yeah, well, bad habit."

I wonder if that was because Susan was always right, and Ian constantly apologized.

"So, you don't like my whiskers?" he teases, trying to rub his chin on my neck to give me a stubble burn.

"Stop it, you rascal!" I laugh and push him away. "I only like whiskers on my cat."

Ian relents. "I'll try and remember to work on that stubble business," he says, "but I make no apologies for my morning face, babe. They grow overnight, and I'm not getting up to shave at three a.m."

He's right, they do grow overnight. His face is a dark mass of spiked facial hair in the morning. "Then I won't apologize for my morning breath," I tease.

"Deal."

His hand tenderly strokes the side of my face, and he gives me his adoring look. "I'll be right back. Need to change before I start dinner."

"Okay." *Good, I want to snoop around*, I secretly muse.

Ian takes off down the hall to his bedroom, and I hear him close the door. I quickly turn around and start taking in more than the view. It's time to find out who this guy really is in his Portland home. I'm thinking it's a bit different than the weekend-beach Ian I've come to know.

As usual, the house is in order the way he likes it. Nothing is out of place. I'm thinking that it's really weird, finding a man who is actually neat and clean. I suppose if we ever marry, I'll never have to worry about dirty clothes strewn around or towels on the bathroom floor. I can handle that.

The atmosphere of the room is quite different than his earth-tone décor at the beach house. The walls are off-white, with a tint of gray. A large corner black leather couch takes up most of the living area, with black ebony end tables. The floors are light hardwood, and an area rug with a gray, white, and black modern design covers the center of the room. It's stunning, and I wonder if he decorated it himself.

A wall entertainment center sits on the other side, with a big screen TV, and bookcases on either end. I'm curious as to what he reads, so I walk over and check it out. All of the books are hardback, rather than paper, and the shelves are filled with titles from famous authors who write intriguing mysteries or spy thrillers. *Very interesting*, I muse.

To my disappointment, I don't see any pictures anywhere. No family, no ex-wife, no nothing. It's sort of sterile in an odd way and void of emotional attachment. I find that very puzzling.

"Want a drink?"

Ian has returned, dressed in jeans and a tee shirt. I want to attack, but I control myself.

"Coke?"

"Uh, probably not," he says, scratching his head. "Didn't think to buy any. I usually don't stock soft drinks at home. How about a beer?"

"Uh, no beer. Ice water would be fine."

"You sure?"

"Yep." Of course, he's got a huge, stainless steel refrigerator with an icemaker and water in the door. I quickly glance at his kitchen. Everything is in its place. *Neat freak*.

He hands me the water.

"So, what's for dinner?" I ask, feeling my stomach growl.

"How about I order a pizza?"

"Pizza? You've got to be kidding me?" I protest. "Where's my candlelight dinner, with steak and a baked potato?" He's conned me into coming over for delivered bread and cheese? A sheepish look spreads across his face.

"I guess I wasn't totally honest about making you dinner," he says, scrunching his nose. "There's not much in the fridge, and I didn't have time to shop."

"Well, Ian Richards, I'm surprised you've actually duped me into thinking you'd cook dinner."

"Forgive me?"

"I suppose."

"Good, I already called and ordered a pizza while in my bedroom."

"You sneak," I say, looking at him wide-eyed. "Then why did you invite me here?"

"To console you for today, I guess."

"Yeah, that wasn't my most pleasant experience, meeting your ex-wife. Like I said, I didn't like her."

Ian doesn't say anything. He goes to the refrigerator, grabs a beer, and then pops the top. He takes a big swig as if he's looking for fortitude. Now I wish I had more than water.

When he's finished, he stares at me with

his dreamy eyes. I wonder what he's thinking, and when the smoldering look starts to creep in, I know. Sex. I'm in his territory right now, and I bet he has duct tape somewhere stashed in one of his kitchen drawers. I wish he'd tie me up.

"Come here," he says.

He's looking very playful. His free hand grabs me around my waist, and he pulls me into him. Here comes the beer breath, but I don't care.

"Hope you like pepperoni," he says, taking his tongue and licking my bottom lip.

What is he doing to me? "You smell like beer," I complain.

"First the stubble, now the beer. Deal with it," he says, kissing me and shoving his tongue in my mouth.

When he's done devouring me, I look at him with a sly grin. "Pizza, Ian, pizza."

He gives me a wicked laugh, and I can't help but wonder what has gotten into him.

"All right, I'll behave." He walks toward the living room and invites me along. "Come and sit with me for a while. Food should be here soon."

He flops on the couch, drapes an arm along the top, and puts one foot on the coffee table. It's definitely not safe to be near him, so I take the other end of the couch with my ice water in hand.

"I'm sorry, Rachel, if Susan treated you with any disrespect. She can get a bit snooty when she's in her element at work."

"I guess. Although, I'm not surprised. Assistants are scum, let's face it."

"Well, not to me."

"Yeah, you're a rare breed, Ian, and a respectful man."

He shakes his head in embarrassment. "I don't think that way. People are people no matter what job they perform."

"She's quite attractive." I'm curious whether I can get a reaction out of him. He takes another swig of beer, and then makes an odd facial expression.

"Outside perhaps. She's average on the inside."

"Do you think I'm beautiful?" I'm comparing myself, I know it. Susan Richards is ten times more gorgeous than I am. She's perfection and grace, dressed in expensive clothes, manicured, primped and primed with the best hair and top-of-the-line makeup. No doubt, she pays a hundred dollars for a bottle of perfume.

Ian gazes at me. His arm drops from the back of the couch, and he scoots toward me at the other end.

"Yes, I think you're beautiful, Rachel."

I know that's what he sees on the outside, but inwardly, I'm ugly and tainted. The two don't mix, and it's that part that I can't accept.

I lower my eyes from him. "I'm glad that you think I'm beautiful. I wish I felt the same way about myself."

"I do too," he says with clear remorse in his voice.

He's going to get tired of my low self-esteem. It's not exactly a very attractive quality to showcase to the male race. Thankfully, there is a knock at the door.

"Must be the delivery."

Ian answers it, and sure enough the pizza has arrived. He pulls out his wallet, pays the tab, and comes back with a large pizza that smells mouthwateringly good.

"Time for my dinner."

"Smells great."

"Let's eat and then make out on the couch." He gives me a wink.

"Make out? What are we, teenagers?" I look at him dumbfounded over his silly statement.

"I need some dessert after dinner," he boasts, opening the pizza box and handing me a plate.

He's really in his element, being home with me here. It's nice to see this side of him—makes me adore him even more.

"Okay, if you shave your stubble, get rid of your beer breath, and promise not to go to third base."

"Well, forget it then." He sneers at me. His eyes twinkle mischievously.

As we chew our pizza, I doubt he'll forget anything. I can see in his eyes that he's going to tease the hell out of me tonight. He's dead serious about a necking session on the couch. It's obvious I'm feeling like a giggling juvenile over the thought.

It doesn't take long after we finish eating, before we end up there. We both smell like pizza sauce and pepperoni. Of course, he's laced with the smell of beer on top of it, but as his lips start nibbling on mine, I don't care. He's such a sweet kisser. After drawing the air out of my lungs, he lets me take a breath.

"You going to make it to second base, law man?" I have to tease him, because he's being far too good. "Third base, still off-limits," I remind him. "That is if you want it to be off-limits."

"Don't tempt me. It's off-limits," he drawls, "but this isn't." His warm hands slip underneath my blouse, and I feel him unhook my bra. Wow, he's being aggressive tonight. As soon as my boobs slip out, he's got both hands on them, having a good feel.

"God, isn't this torturing you?" I heave, ready to burst into a nymphomaniac at any moment. It sure is torturing me.

"What do you think?" he says, grabbing my hand and placing it on his hard erection in his pants.

I flinch feeling him. "Ian, what's got into you?" I pull my hand away, feeling embarrassed over touching him. I'm not very good in that department, and he should know that by now.

"Nothing has gotten into me," he says. His voice is sexy and low. "I want you to know how sincere I am about you, Rachel. You mean a lot to me."

"I do?" It's obvious by now I'm totally drugged over his smooth talking and caressing hands.

"You're a wonderful woman that I

deeply admire."

"Oh, I'm glad" I moan. I close my eyes as he comes for my mouth again and fills it with his tongue. I'm thinking he's on a mission to make me forget about Susan or maybe not. Perhaps he wants to make me feel better about all that he's learned about my past and my childish breakdown in front of him.

Whatever the reason, it's working. He makes me feel safe and secure, and a part of me really wants to open up my heart and trust him completely. Maybe one of these days I will.

Chapter 16

CONFLICTING HEARTS

When Friday evening arrives, I'm proud that we actually made it through our pizza party without having sex. Instead, we had a great make-out session, which ended in more conversation and close sharing.

Later that night, Ian drove me home. By that time, I had completely forgotten about Susan. Since we had both confessed that we were falling in love with one another, I pushed away any threat she might possess.

I'm sad, though, when we arrive at the coast Friday night, that the forecast is rain for most of the weekend. It is Oregon, after all, but I'm disappointed we can't enjoy the outdoors. Nevertheless, the view from Ian's great room is worth the show. I dream of the winter storms, which should be spectacular to watch at Haystack Rock.

By the time Saturday night rolls around,

we both have cabin fever after being cloistered together watching television and talking. Since we arrived, the sexual tension in the air has been palpable, and both of us have been teasing one another like teenagers. We're at a breaking point.

Ian's resolve not to touch me is crumbling like a sand castle battered by the Pacific Ocean. I'm definitely tuned to my easy-lay channel. His defenses are weakening by the look in his eyes, and mine are non-existent.

After dinner we make it to the couch again, and I'm ready for another make-out session. Only third base is wide open for the taking, as far as I'm concerned.

I'm cuddled next to him, with his arm wrapped around my shoulder. We've both been quiet for a while, looking at the fire and listening to the pelting rain outside. As usual, the distant sound of the roaring waves puts me in a romantic mood, to say the least. I'm aching just sitting next to him.

I turn and look at him. His face is aglow from the golden flames in the hearth. He looks deep in thought, and I wonder if he is dealing with the same torturous feelings that run rampant through my body. I almost want to peek and see if he has an erection. The slut in me is hopeless.

"Kiss me," I invite him in a sultry voice. Ian's head turns toward me. He looks at me with a questioning gaze, and I look back with the invitation of an available woman. He puts his warm lips upon mine, and I feel his tongue find its way between my lips. I part my mouth to grant him entrance and enjoy the wonderful taste.

A moment later, it feels as if the fire before us leaps into our hearts. Ian comes alive with a brash longing that I've never seen him display. His hands aggressively roam over my body.

"Are you sure you want to go down this road?" I gasp, searching for breath. He says nothing for a moment, and just clasps my breast with his hand, pinching my nipple with his fingertips.

"I've gone long enough being good," he says in a heated tone.

He unhooks my bra from underneath my tee shirt. My naked breasts loosen in his hands, and his warmth clasps them tightly. This isn't the Ian that's fondled me before. My only conclusion is that the man is really horny.

"Are you going to close the drapes?" I ask worriedly. "Or are we giving Cannon Beach a show tonight?"

"Forget Cannon Beach," he says, pulling my tee shirt over my head and stripping my bra from my body.

"You and me. Now. Upstairs."

He rises from the couch, pulls me to my feet, and leads me up the stairs in my topless condition. When we reach the landing, Ian takes off his shirt and throws it on the floor. Enough light from the fire below filters up to his loft, and I melt at the sight of his six-pack abs and taut chest.

The next I know, he throws me onto the bed and attacks my neck and lips like a devouring animal. Sweet Ian is on fire, and his actions engorge my body with longing.

"God, what's got into you?" I cling to him like a desperate woman.

"It's time to pay up, babe." His voice is dark and threatening.

My eyes bulge out of my head. *Did he say "pay up"?* Just the thought and I'm wet and ready.

He pulls away and unzips my jeans and tugs them off my body. A moment later, his fingers claw at my panties. After pulling them down, he tosses them over his shoulder. I can't help but giggle at his antics.

Afterward, he stands by the bed looking at me with dark eyes as if he's deciding what to do next. Suddenly, he retreats to the bathroom. I'm confused, until he comes back with the tie to his robe between his fingers. My heart jumps into my throat as he heads toward me.

"Give me your hands," he commands.

I do. He wraps the tie around my wrists, draws a knot, and then binds the other end to the bedpost bringing my arms over my head.

"Ian, what are you doing?" My voice quivers.

"You told me you wanted to be bound, so that's what I'm doing." His voice is empty of emotion.

I can't believe he's tethered me like this, but I'm excited as hell feeling helpless before him. He pulls his eyes away from me as if he can't acknowledge, even to himself, what he's done.

Ian unzips his pants and disrobes in front of me. My eyes see his hardened erection waiting to take me, and as usual, I glance away at the sight. I close my eyes for a moment, until I hear him pull open the nightstand. I turn and look, and he has grabbed a condom from the drawer. A moment later, he's rolled it on, and he's ready.

"Tell me what you want," he demands, looking down at me with narrowed eyes. "You said you want it rough. How rough? What do you want me to do to you?"

His words send a chill down my spine. The sheer thought of him giving me my desires nearly bring me to an orgasm. I pull on the restraints that send a coursing surge of fire through my veins. The throbbing in my body is overpowering.

"Tell me," he demands. "I want to know. You're not leaving this bed until I hear you scream in satisfaction."

Dear God, I melt into a puddle in the middle of the bed. "Touch me," I whisper, barely able to speak. My eyes are staring at him in disbelief, and then I quickly close them to hide in my dark room.

"Open your legs," he orders. I part them a little, and Ian pushes his knee against my inner thigh and spreads me open so I can't close them again. "Look at me," he orders.

I'm hesitant, but obey. I open my eyes and see a changed man leaning over me.

Suddenly, I'm not sure if I like this Ian or not. A rush of fear captivates me. With a drugged look of pleasure, he parts my cleft, and quickly slips a finger deep within my vagina pushing it in and out.

"You're so wet, Rachel," he drawls. He lowers his head and watches his fingers fondle me as if he's finding pleasure at the sight. His other hand squeezes my breast tightly. After a few moments, I beg.

"More," I gasp.

"More what?"

"Another."

"Another what? Another finger?" he teases, slipping his index finger alongside his middle one.

The entrance into my body is intense. "Oh, my god." I moan, pulling on the restraints and pushing my breasts into the air. Ian shoves his fingers in and out, but it isn't enough. He still is too tender, too careful, too detached from the hurt I need.

"Do it harder. Hold me down, Ian. Take it from me. Hurt me."

I know it's a horrible thing to ask of him. A part of me is sorry. As soon as the words leave my lips, he removes his hand from between my legs. My eyes shoot open, and I see his troubled gaze. I've scared him. He looks at my hands tied above my head, and a moment of remorse flashes in his blue orbs. This isn't him. He's acting this way because I want him to. Ian looks at me with hesitation mingled with desire.

"Please, Ian," I plead. "I need it as rough as you can give me, if you want me to come."

My words ignite something in his soul and darkness fills his eyes. The kind countenance I know disappears, and Ian looks as if he's possessed. He's angry. I don't care, because I want him to do me like I've imagined in my mind every night.

A moment later, my dreams turn to reality. He leans his massive, muscular body against mine and pins me helplessly against the mattress. His knee shoves my thighs apart as far as he can. I can't look at his face any longer. When I close my eyes, I feel his long fingers bury themselves into my craving body.

I scream at the onslaught of pain, but Ian has disappeared into his character of the sadist I crave. He partakes in my carnal lust and takes me beyond the point of my endurance. My fantasy turns to reality as his hand relentlessly pushes deeper into my body. I love and hate him, all at the same time.

"You want me to fuck you with my hand, is that it?" he grunts, doing it faster and harder.

He inserts another finger. I think he will tear me at any moment.

"This is what you want, now take it! Come on my hand!"

His forceful command of domination pushes me over the edge. An orgasm bursts within me, and I let out a bloodcurdling scream from the surge of discomfort and pleasure that racks my body simultaneously. My heart feels as if it has stopped beating for a few moments as I slip into the ecstasy of dark pleasure.

Slowly as the peak subsides, I open my eyes and behold his face. I'm shocked at what I see. He's bitter, undone, and wild. Swiftly, he unties my hands and roughly flips me over on my stomach. Ian grabs me by my hips, lifts my ass up, and shoves his penis into me hard and deep. I gasp as he fills me, astonished over what he's done.

"Now it's my turn. I'm not finished with you yet." His voice startles me.

"Ian!" I grab the pillow with my fists.

My body trembles at the onslaught. Again and again he bangs me in anger. Then with one throaty roar, he comes within me, digging his nails into my hips. When he's finished, he stops and pushes himself deeper into me as if he's punishing me for taking him to this place of wantonness. Then slowly he pulls out, and lets me drop to the bed.

Tears stream down my face. I'm satisfied but troubled. Relieved but embarrassed. A myriad of emotions drown my soul. It was what I always wanted, but now I feel ashamed, violated, and yet—I immensely enjoyed every depraved moment.

I'm so fucked up, I cry inside. I bring my hands to my face and hide behind them in disgrace. My body curls into a fetal position.

"Satisfied are we?"

His tone is demeaning and filled with disgust. I feel stripped before him.

"Answer me!"

I dare to roll over and look into his face. He has changed, and my heart breaks.

His angry eyes narrow. "Why the hell are you crying? I thought that's what you wanted," he snaps. "I finally performed to your liking, didn't I?"

I can't bear it any longer. I've ruined

him. "Ian, I'm so sorry."

"For what?" After taking his condom off and throwing it into the waste basket near the bed, he grabs his tee shirt from the floor and pulls it over his head. Next, he takes his jeans, and one leg and a time, steps into them. He zips them up and looks at me curled naked upon the bed.

"I decided the next time we made it to the sack, I was going to give you rough." He looks at me in contempt. "Don't ever fucking ask me to do that again," he says clenching his jaw. "Do you hear me?" His voice cracks as if he's on the verge of tears.

I shake my head in obedience and watch him turn around and run down the stairs.

"Fuck this sick crap," he growls.

Ian's anger bursts into a tirade. His wrath fills the house. I hear him stomp back and forth across the carpet for a few moments like a crazed man, and then he stops. His voice bellows at me from below.

"Rachel, don't you *ever* ask me to do that to you again. Do you understand? Ever! I'm not some goddamn abuser like your pedophile neighbor for you to get off on!"

Then I hear his voice break. Ian gasps into a sob. "Christ," he cries. "I'm sorry."

I bury myself underneath the pillow and cover my ears, hiding from the sound of his voice, but it doesn't stop the anguish that I feel. I have sullied the kind and tender heart of the man I love. My hunger for pain dragged him to my level, and I forced him to succumb to my depravity.

The sound of the ocean fills my ears when I hear the sliding glass door open. Ian pulls it shut behind him with a bang. The house grows deadly quiet. I sit up in bed and see him disappear into the dark toward the water. My whole body trembles. The only thought I have is to run, and I do.

I rise from the bed. My body hurts from the assault. Quickly, I dress, grab my sweatshirt, purse, and leave the rest of my things in the upstairs bedroom. I descend the stairs. Ian is nowhere in sight. The rain sounds as if it has subsided enough so I won't get soaked. As soon as my shoes are on, I pull my hood over my hair, open the front door, and disappear into the dark.

At that moment, my world crashes down around me like shattering glass. I can never look into the sweet, tender face of Ian again, after turning him into an abusive monster. My heart is heavy and sorrowful as I walk up

Hemlock Street and head into town in the middle of the night. It's a mile walk, but I don't care. I creep along in the shadows, crying the entire way.

When I arrive downtown, Cannon Beach is a ghost town. All of the shops are closed and the road deserted. I find a bench near the courtyard of a variety of stores and sit down. The rain has subsided, but I'm chilled to the bone. I wonder if Ian has discovered me gone or if he even cares about me any longer. My phone in my purse rings, and I open it and look at the caller ID. It's Ian. I ignore it.

Numb, I sit there for ten minutes wondering what to do next. I can't walk to Seaside; it's too far. I'm too scared to hitchhike. There are no car rentals in the resort town. I'm screwed. Maybe I can find an empty room in some hotel somewhere, but I know it will cost me more than I can afford. I see headlights coming up south from Hemlock, and I wonder if it's him. When the car gets closer it slows down, and I see the emergency lights on the roof. It's a cop.

The police officer takes one look at me, stops the car, and gets out. Instantly, he's in an authoritative stance as he hovers over me.

"Problem, miss?"

I don't say anything.

"Shops are closed. We don't like loitering. Can I see some identification?"

I nod my head, open my purse, and search for my wallet. My hands are shaking like a leaf. A minute later, I find my driver's license and give it over. He takes it, runs his flashlight over the information, and then looks at me.

"What are you doing out here, Miss Hayward? It's late."

I raise my eyes to him, and my lower lip quivers. "Fight . . . I had a fight with my boyfriend."

"Did your boyfriend assault you?" he asks in concern. He shines the flashlight into my face, no doubt looking for bruises. I squint and turn my head away.

"No. Nothing like that. He doesn't have a mean bone in his body."

"Well, you can't sit out here all night. I suggest you go back to your hotel or wherever you're staying."

"I can't officer. Please, can't I just stay here?"

An exasperated look crosses his face. Another set of headlights approach from the south, and I immediately recognize Ian's car.

"Oh, God, it's him," I moan. Quickly, I pull my hood over my head as far as it will go and lower my face to my knees and hide. "I can't talk to him right now. Please, officer, make him go away."

The policeman doesn't say anything. I hear Ian's roadster pull up and stop. The officer walks away, and Ian's window rolls down. They are talking, but their voices are low and I can't decipher the exchange of conversation. A minute later, the cop is back in front of me again.

"Mr. Richards would like you to return home with him. I think it would be in your best interest to do so, Miss Hayward."

"I don't want to," I protest, keeping my face buried and out of sight.

"Look lady, I'm not playing the role of some shrink here. You either go with him and work out your lover's spat, or you're going to spend the night in a jail cell for vagrancy. What's your choice?"

"You wouldn't," I say, lifting my head and looking into the policeman's disgruntled face.

"I would. Ian Richards is a decent guy. He's well known in the community, and I have no qualms turning you back into his care. You can't stay here, and yes, I'll haul you off to jail."

Figures. Kind Ian has a stellar reputation even in Cannon Beach. I hear Ian's car door open, and his footsteps approach.

"She's all yours," the cop says, walking away. He climbs into his car and drives off, leaving me alone with my victim.

Ian knells down on one knee in front of me.

"Rachel, I'm so sorry for losing it."

He touches my knee with his hand, and I push it off. "Go away," I whisper.

I hear an exasperated sigh expel from his lungs. "Come home with me, sweets. You can't stay out here all night in the cold and dark."

Why not? I think to myself. It's how my soul feels at this moment. I pull the hood even tighter down over my face. There is no way in hell I can look into his blue eyes and not die at his feet.

"Take me home . . . to Portland. I want to go home," I plead like a little girl.

"Rachel, it's almost midnight."

"I won't get in the car with you unless you take me home." I pout. He remains silent for a few moments, and then relents in an exasperated tone of voice.

"If that's what you want."

He rises to his feet, and I see him offer me his hand. I don't take it. How can I touch him? I so ashamed that I want to slink down the sewer grate alongside the road.

Ian withdraws his offer of help and walks toward his car. He holds the door open for me, and I crawl inside. Once he closes it, I scrunch up in the seat and hug the door, still hiding my face underneath my hooded sweatshirt. A minute later, we're heading north on Interstate 101. I feel like crap.

"Rachel. We got to talk about this," he says in a sweet, loving voice. "I'm so sorry for the way I treated you. Please, forgive me."

"I don't want to talk about it. Not now," I whisper. "Time out."

He heaves a heavy sigh and accelerates the car. I can tell he's upset with me.

"If that's how you want it," he replies, annoyed. "Have it your way then."

"That's how I want it." My voice is emphatic but trembling.

The entire one and a half hour trip back to Portland transpires in complete silence. I think of the horrible thing I've done to him, and I wish to God I would have never been born. I'm such a whore, and I dragged him down to my level. He was right. I turned him into my abuser, and there is no forgiveness for what I've done. Now God is going to make me pay for sure.

As soon as he pulls into my apartment complex and stops the car, I jump out and run up the stairs toward my door without saying goodbye. When I reach the third floor and insert my key into the lock, I glance below. His car drives off into the night, and the man I love is lost to me forever. I'm a wreck and want to die.

Chapter 17

INTENSE PERSONAL INJURY

The morning arrives, and I drag myself into my bathroom. My eyes are nearly swollen shut from constant crying since Ian dropped me off early Sunday morning. I can't show up at work today—I just can't. I pick up the telephone and dial the number for my boss. It goes to voice mail.

"Mr. Stewart, this is Rachel. I won't be in today," I declare as my voice cracks. "I'm ill."

I hang up and walk over to the couch and sit down. Whiskers jumps into my lap and purrs. He always senses when I'm upset. I pet him and silently cry. My mind can't stop thinking of Ian and how I've ruined our relationship.

My cell phone pings for the hundredth time, announcing the arrival of another text message. I'm afraid to look, but I can't help myself. It's Ian again.

"Rachel, I need to know you're okay. Please, text or call."

I finally answer his multiple pesky messages. "I can't talk. I need time out. Find someone else. I'm not worth the trouble."

He doesn't give up. Another ping announces the arrival of a return text. "I'm not letting you break up with me."

I text him back. "Too bad, I already have."

The phone rings. It's Ian. I answer it, angry as hell. "Why can't you leave me alone?" I bark into the receiver.

"I won't let you break up with me. We're going to fix this."

"You can't fix it. I'm broken, don't you get it? Nobody can fix me. Not you, not God, not anyone. Just go away." I hang up.

A moment later another text arrives. "I won't give up on you . . . ever." I want to find a hammer and smash my goddamn telephone. Instead, I turn it off and then throw it in the kitchen drawer.

The rest of the day, I can't function. For hours, I lie in my bed in a fetal position. I'm tired of living. Thoughts of killing myself run through my mind—from overdosing to slitting my wrists—but I've always been afraid to act out. At least when I think about it, I feel better. I hate emotional pain, and I want it to stop. If I die it will stop, but then my theological thinking kicks in and the risk of hell compels me to suffer through it instead.

I relive in my mind how Ian sexually gave me what I craved. The thought turns me on thinking about being bound, and I start to ache for a repeat performance. I can't do this to myself. I can't reach down and recreate it in my mind, for I know I'll be feeding my vile desires.

Slowly, I crawl out of bed and wander over to my desk and scour the center drawer. Somewhere, there is the card to my former counselor, and I have to find it. I'm going to end up in an insane asylum, if I don't get help.

After a few minutes, her card resurrects to the top of my messy drawer. I dial the number, and her answering service kicks in.

"This is Dr. Grayson. Your call is important to me, please leave a message, and I will contact you as soon as possible. If you are in a crisis and need immediate help, call the Suicide Prevention line at . . ." Blah,

blah, blah. I wish she'd stop talking so I can leave a message. At last the beep comes.

"Dr. Grayson, this is Rachel Hayward. I don't know if you remember me or not, but you helped me through my divorce five years ago. I need help again. Please call." I leave my number and hang up like a sniveling little girl. An hour later she telephones back.

"Rachel, it's Dr. Grayson. What can I do for you?"

"I need somebody to talk to," I cry. "I just broke up with my boyfriend, and I'm a mess. When can I see you?"

"Well, I actually have a cancellation today, and I'm free at three o'clock. Would that be convenient?"

"I'll be there."

"Looking forward to talking with you, Rachel. Hang in there."

Our call ends, and a sense of relief flows through my veins. At least I have someone to spill my guts to, even if it will cost me $120 an hour. I have to fix this somehow.

—·❋·—

The location hasn't changed, and I feel relieved when I enter the door. She has the usual "in session" tag on the outside of her office, so I know the routine remains the same. I pick up a magazine and flip through the pages waiting my turn. Nothing registers and I don't even know what I'm looking at. Finally, the door opens, another woman departs.

"See you next week," Dr. Grayson says to her departing patient. She looks over at me and smiles. "Rachel, come on in."

The familiarity of her office returns. Nothing seems to have altered—from her chair to the two-seater couch near the wall. The familiar brown pillows are on either side, and I notice her plants that need watering. It's not the most inviting atmosphere, and I wonder if I should bring up the suggestion it's time to redecorate. She sits down in her chair, and picks up a pen and pad.

"So, what brings you here today, Rachel?"

I'm amazed at how psychologists can jump from one troubled mind to another with ease. That's all it takes. The floodgates open, and I'm bawling like a little girl. She hands over the box of tissues.

"Take your time. When you feel like you can tell me, go ahead."

After blowing my nose, I glance up at the clock on the wall keenly aware I've wasted ten minutes of my $120 fifty-minute session.

"I don't know where to start."

"You said in your phone call that you broke up with your boyfriend. Is this your first relationship since your divorce?"

"Yes, first serious one. I've hardly dated anyone in five years."

"How long have you been seeing him?"

"Not very long." I don't give specifics, because I'm embarrassed to tell her I jumped in the sack with him on the third date.

"How did you meet?"

The absurdity of it breaks out a relieved smile upon my face. "I rear-ended him on the Sunset Highway on the way to work."

Dr. Grayson raises her eyebrows. "Well, that's the first time I've heard of a couple meeting that way." She looks at me. "That memory seems to make you smile, at least."

"Yes, from the moment I met him, he's been the kindest person I've ever known. He's Mr. Perfect, and I'm Miss Screwed up. We've been colliding hearts ever since."

"Do you mean your personalities?"

The sadness returns. I look at Dr.

Grayson, but then pull my eyes away from her before I utter the words.

"My abuse issues." I gulp. "My sexual abuse issues, to be honest."

Dr. Grayson flips through my file. "Yes, I remember we touched upon your past briefly in our sessions before, but you indicated at that time you didn't want to delve into that area."

"I guess it's time to delve," I sheepishly reply.

"And what's changed your mind?"

"Because my relationship with Ian Richards is the closest to normalcy I've ever been. I feel as if I've dragged him down to my sexual perversion." I start to cry again. "I want to change. I don't want him to change for me. It's wrong."

"What type of perceived sexual perversion are you talking about, Rachel?"

"The fact that I need to be hurt to feel wanted and have an orgasm."

"All right," she says, making a comment on her pad. "We can talk about that behavior."

I look at her, wondering if this is really going to help or not.

"Where are you currently in your

relationship with Mr. Richards?"

"We're not. I told him that I didn't want to see him again."

"And what prompted that?"

My lower lip quivers. With each damn minute that ticks by it becomes harder to express my thoughts.

"We had sex the other night, and I asked him to hurt me."

"And did he hurt you?"

"Not really bad. I don't want you to think he beat me or anything."

"All right, thank you for clarification. What did he do?"

"I asked him to be rough. It's the only way I can come."

"And he was rough, I take it."

"Yes."

"Did you like it?"

"Yes."

"Did he like it?"

"Obviously, no." I glare at her like she needs to get the point. "He was angry afterward. I think he was angry at me for making him do it."

"Hmm," she says, as if she's digesting my statement. "Did you make him or did he have a choice?"

I think for a moment. "No, I guess I didn't *make him*, per se."

"Then he had a choice."

"I guess so, but he did it for me."

"And what happened afterward?"

"He yelled at me and asked me never to ask him to do it again, then started crying."

"I see. Why do you think he acted that way?"

"Because I forced him to be someone he's not. He said he felt like my pedophile abuser."

"You're saying you forced him, again. There's that lack of choice."

"Okay, I guess I didn't."

"All right."

"You have to understand that there's not a mean bone in the man's body. I selfishly didn't care if he could handle it or not." When the words come out of my mouth, I suddenly get what Ian must have felt.

"Do you think that maybe he was angry at himself for going down that road, rather than at you?"

"Maybe."

"Have you talked to him since?"

"Only to tell him to leave me alone."

She jots a few notes down on her pad,

and then leans back further in her chair looking relaxed and in control. It's irritating.

"So, what do you want, Rachel? Why are you here today?"

It takes me a moment to think about her question. I know what I want, and it's Ian. I don't want to hurt him with my issues.

"Understanding," I say with a quivering voice. "Understanding as to why I want to hurt myself or be hurt, and the courage to turn away from it."

"Is that all?"

"I want to believe I'm worth loving, and also that I can give love in return."

"That's an admirable goal. Have you told Mr. Richards you are here?"

"No, I can't talk to him."

"Do you think that's fair to him, shutting him out of your life with no explanation because it's uncomfortable for you to talk to him?"

"Boy, you're filled with questions, today." I frown at her. She smirks. I know I'm hurting him by pushing him away. Now I feel even guiltier since she shined the spotlight on my insensitive behavior.

"No, it's not fair."

"I'm glad you see it that way. Will you

call him and let him know how you feel?"

"Yes," I relent.

"Will you give him the chance to do the same?"

"Yes, but I need a break from our relationship. If I'm going to go back into therapy with you, I can't deal with being with him. I won't be able to focus."

"Then tell him how you feel. If he truly has your best interest at heart, then he should allow you the time that you need." She pauses for a moment and continues in a serious tone. "And no texting or emails to get it out, either. I want you to pick up the phone and hear his voice or see him face-to-face to discuss it. "

Busted again, I groan inside. Texting and emails are so much easier. Doesn't she realize that kind of communication was made for me?

I sit there and process all that we've talked about, and a sense of relief flows into my heart. I know this isn't going to be easy, but I love Ian too much not to find out why I want to keep my broken child locked in that room.

We spend the rest of my few minutes talking about how we'll approach our sessions, and I set up a payment plan. After making an appointment for the next session, I drive home feeling like a zombie.

It's been almost an hour since I arrived home. I've procrastinated carrying out my promise to communicate. Finally, I sit down and write my thoughts down on a piece of paper to read during our conversation. I might as well run over that deer staring into the headlights ahead of time.

When I'm done, I check the time. It's five-thirty, so I call his cell. He's probably still at his office, but maybe he can talk in private. His phone doesn't ring but once, and I hear his desperate voice at the other end.

"Rachel . . . sweetheart." His tone is edgy, and I can sense his sorrow at the other end of the line.

"Hello, Ian." I look down at my written dialogue and start reading it aloud. "I wanted to let you know that I've gone back to counseling."

"Can I see you?" he interrupts.

"No, Ian, not now. I need time to figure things out."

"Rachel, I love you. I'm so sorry for last

night. I don't know what came over me."

"Ian, don't apologize. You made the decision and gave me what I told you that I wanted." My lower lip quivers. "It broke my heart afterward, because I know that's not you. It can never be you. I'm ashamed over what happened."

"God, Rachel. Afterward, I felt like your abuser. I don't want to feel that way ever again. I want to love you, not abuse you."

"I know . . . I know . . ." I tell him, with silent tears rolling down my cheeks.

"I need to see you," he begs.

"I think we should stop seeing each other, so that my mind isn't muddled in the months ahead while I am in counseling. I need a three-month break."

"Three months?" He sounds mortified.

"Yes, three months. I've got to figure this stuff out in my life, Ian." He's silent at the end of the line. "It's not fair to you."

"All right," he relents. "If that's what you need, I understand."

I imagine the pain and disappointment flitting across his face, and my heart breaks over pushing him away.

"I want our relationship to work," his voice pleads. "Do what you need to do, and

I'll be here waiting."

"Maybe you need to take this time, too, in order to figure out why you love me. I'm screwed up, Ian. You can't rescue me." I really don't think he is, but I still feel so unworthy of his love. "You can do so much better. You're a wonderful man, and you shouldn't love a wounded girl like me."

"I never thought that I was rescuing you." His voice is defensive. "Besides, you're a wonderful woman, but you just don't see your value. I don't want anyone else."

"Okay, I get it, Ian, but in my heart I don't understand it." I hesitate for a moment feeling it shatter in my chest. "I'm sorry, but I have to go."

"Rach, keep in touch. Don't drop off the face of the earth," he begs.

"Bye Ian." I start to cry and end the call. "I love you too," I say, looking at the phone. I wish I would have told him.

After a few minutes of struggling whether to call him back, I lay down my cell phone. Most of what I had written on my cue paper never got out of my mouth, but a least the important parts did. Frankly, I don't know how I'll handle three months without him.

Suddenly, I feel stupid, like I shot myself in the foot or something. Second thoughts flood my mind as to the wisdom in this counseling thing, but my heart tells me that I have to do this.

I go to my computer and click on his page so I can look at his pictures and blubber. As soon as I do, I see a new comment on my wall.

"I'll be watching for you in my rearview mirror. Love you always, sweets, Ian."

That's it. I'm back on another crying jag.

Chapter 18

CONFRONTING DEMONS

It's been two months since I started therapy, and I feel like chopped liver. Each time I walk into Dr. Grayson's office, I see chain saws and shovels. It's a damn torture chamber. As soon as I sit down, I wonder what pain she'll put me through during the session. It irritates me even further that I have to pay for this torment!

The process usually starts with the chain saw. Dr. Grayson pulls that damn cord, and then I hear the roar of the engine and the smell of gasoline and smoke. She starts with slicing into my mind and bombarding me with stupid-ass questions.

"Tell me about that."

"How did that make you feel?

"Why do you think you reacted that way?"

"Have you forgiven your abuser?"

Blah, blah, blah. She stands and knocks

on the door where I have my inner child locked up and demands a conversation with my five-year-old self. She's trespassing where I've never let another soul, and frankly it just plain hurts.

When the interrogation ends, she turns to my heart and attempts to shovel out the shit I've buried there. At times, I want to leap to my feet and say, "fuck this crap" and slam the door on my way out. To my chagrin, something keeps me tied as if I'm bound in invisible duct tape. I blame Ian. As soon as that thought is articulated, Dr. Grayson reminds me I should be doing this for my sake, not his. I hate the woman.

To top it off, it's been too long since I've spoken to Ian, and I'm dying inside. The out of sight, out of mind torment is keeping me up at night. I have visions of him slipping away.

Every day I check cars in front of me on the Sunset Highway looking for his spiffy car. I want to talk to him, but I'm afraid and vulnerable. He hasn't posted anything on my page, or his, for that matter, since the day we parted.

On top of that, I'd really like to get laid, even if I don't have an orgasm. Just feeling him being part of who I am would be comforting. After our last tryst, though, I don't think he's going to be too keen on banging me again for pleasure anytime soon.

To feed my frenzy, I've printed out one of his photographs with his bare chest from his online photo album. I had no guilt whatsoever using the color printer at the office to do so. I cut it to size and hid it underneath my mouse pad on my desk. When I'm feeling lonely, I lift the corner up and drool over him, get lost in his dark eyes, and wonder if I'll ever seen him again in the flesh.

Then it happens. I get caught one day gawking at him with tears in my eyes, and everything turns upside down. Julie catches me in the act.

"What's this?" She grabs the picture right from under the pad. "Ooh, nice picture. Great body."

Swiftly, I try to snatch the photo back. "Yeah, great body." *I miss it,* I think to myself.

"I thought that you broke up with him, right?"

"Well," I say, looking at the image and crying inside. "We're taking a break."

"Let me see that again," she says, snatching it back.

"Do you mind?" My voice is terse, but she's staring at the picture and poking her finger at it.

"I could swear I saw this guy last weekend."

"Where?" I blurt out. Suddenly, I'm a captive audience.

"At that Italian Restaurant a couple of blocks down on Fourth. I was there with my boyfriend having dinner."

She looks at me with a smug look like she's one up on me having a date. "Oh, that's nice." My scatterbrained answer makes me feel insecure when I see Julie's face.

"I don't know if I should tell you or not."

"Tell me what?"

"Are you sure you want to hear this?"

"Yes, tell me." I grab her arm and give it a little squeeze.

"He was having dinner with a really pretty blonde."

My heart flies out of my chest and plops upon my desk bleeding. Instantly, I close my eyes and see him with another woman. I'm shocked.

"Were . . . were they friendly?" My eyes

plead for the right answer.

"Oh, yeah, friendly, all right. I noticed them right away, because she giggled really loud over something he must have said. I turned and looked over at their table, and he was holding her hand and smiling."

My mouth drops open, and I'm devastated. I can't breathe. "Excuse me," I rashly say, rising to my feet.

"I'm sorry, Rachel. Maybe I shouldn't have said anything."

My mouth is wired shut. I take the picture away from her and run off to the ladies' room. My eyes are stinging with tears. "You fool," I berate myself under my breath. "You damn fool." I knew it would end this way. It always does. Hurt and rejection.

My hand pushes the restroom door open with a bang, and I run for the nearest stall and lock myself inside. I head bang against the door as I lose control over my emotions.

When I hear someone else enter and get into the stall next to me. I back up to the toilet, lower my pants, and have a seat. I might as well sit down and get it out of my system. I stay there for a few minutes, numb and remorseful that I pushed him away. The flushing of the water next to me reminds me of my life. I'm back in the commode again. After a few minutes, when the coworker leaves, I've made my mind up.

"Screw this," I mumble. I pull my pants up and open the door. I look down at my hand and realize my fist has crunched Ian's picture up into a little ball. The wastepaper basket beckons, so I throw it in and walk out the door. There is no way I can continue to look at that picture.

I pass Julie's desk, and she glances at me, seriously concerned. As soon as I sit down, she's back over beside me.

"Listen, Rachel, I'm so sorry. I feel terrible. Maybe you should call him. It could have been his sister or something and not some new girlfriend."

I swallow the lump in my throat. I'm wondering if that blonde was his ex-wife. "He doesn't have a sister," I mutter.

"Oh, well sorry, Rachel."

Julie returns to her cube, and I sit and stare at my computer screen. I have a terrible urge to call Ian. The clock ticks closer to that three-thirty hour when we've talked before. My cell phone flies out of my purse, and I go over to the employee lounge and hit the speed dial for his number. It rings four times, and I'm trying to decide whether to leave a message or not. At last he picks up.

"Rachel."

His caller ID alerted my arrival, no doubt. There is no excitement in his voice, but rather an awkward tone speaking a name from his past.

"Ian."

Silence.

"Is this a bad time?" My voice quivers.

"Um, no. Hold on, while I close my office door."

I grip the chair in front of me for support. In the background, I hear a door close. His breathing sounds heavy, and finally he speaks again.

"Hey, how have you been?"

His half-hearted question stabs me in my heart. My throat closes, but I try my best to squeak out an answer.

"Fine," I answer in a high-pitched tone. "Been thinking about you a lot. How have you been?"

"Uh, busy, as usual. Work, you know."

Not too busy to go out to dinner with some blonde broad, I rail inside. "Sorry," I reply with no emotion. I'm lost for words.

"How are you? You still in counseling?" His tone sounds a tad more interested in my welfare.

"Yes."

"Is it helping any with your issues?"

Oh, crap. Now I have issues? I bite my tongue wanting to say something snarky, but I don't. "Yes, seems to be helping."

"Good, I'm glad to hear that."

"Can I see you?" I blurt out. The ice beneath my feet is thin, and I hold my breath waiting to fall into the cold waters.

"Uh, yeah, maybe. I've got a pretty busy schedule this week." His lackadaisical answer sucks.

"You don't sound very keen on getting together." Even I surprise myself as the words come out of my mouth. I hear a deadly silence at the other end of the line. "I guess that answers my question." I'm about to end the call when he speaks.

"No, it's not that. It's just things going on in my life right now. Kind of bad timing."

"Well, I don't want to pressure you, Ian. Maybe all this time apart has cooled us both off. I understand. I should leave you alone."

"How about Thursday night? I could have a quick drink with you after work. We probably should talk."

Now I don't know what to say. It's obvious what the talk will be about. Nice knowing you. You're too screwed up to be bothered with. I've found a normal, beautiful woman, and I'm moving on. I can hardly bring myself to agree to meet him, because I already feel the pain of rejection inside my heart.

"Having second thoughts?" he asks. My silence must have gotten to him, because I hear a pang of sadness in his voice.

"No, just afraid to see you." I might as well admit what I'm feeling.

"If you're not ready . . . "

"No, Ian. After work Thursday is fine. Meet you in the lobby of my building?"

"Sure. Like old times when we first met."

"Yes, like old times. See you then."

I don't wait for him to say anything else. The call ends, and I look down at my hand. My poor fingernails are bent from grabbing the back of the chair. Instead of going back to my desk, I pull the chair out and sit down. My head buries itself in my palms as I contemplate our meeting. It's too much to handle alone, so I call Dr. Grayson.

"You've reached . . ." Blah, blah, blah, the message plays. "It's Rachel. I need to talk to you ASAP. I'm losing it."

My voice cracks. I end the call, and lower my head upon the table and try to control the feeling of being out of control. *Being a woman sucks. I wish that I had been born a man,* I complain to myself. Men always have the upper hand in every situation. Whatever he says, I'll be at his mercy, whether I like it or not.

Dr. Grayson hands me the box of tissues and patiently waits for me to blow my nose. "I feel so stupid," I growl.

"Why?"

"I should have known this would happen!"

"I don't think you know anything at this point, Rachel, except that you're having a drink with him Thursday night."

"Yeah, he's so nice he's going to dump me face-to-face. He's not the telephone, text, or email type. Always treating me with kindness."

A sly smile curls her lips, she looks down, and jots something on that damn notepad of hers. She is probably penning, *"Patient doesn't have the ability to receive courteous treatment."* She lifts her eyes and looks at me after my snide remark.

"Is that another conjecture on your part, or something you've realized on your own?"

"He's a man. Men leave me. Men hurt me. Men use me."

"You must not think very highly of Ian then, if you think he's another one in a long line of abusers."

Now, I feel like a fool. I inhale a deep breath. "I think very highly of him."

"Why?"

"Because he is the only man who has ever treated me with respect, except for that one night when I asked him to be someone he wasn't."

"Don't you think you should give him the benefit of the doubt that he intends to continue that kind treatment, no matter what he has to talk to you about?"

My lips pull off to the side while I feel self-conscious over my overreacting. "You're right. I'm sure if he's found someone else, he will tell me kindly, and probably apologize profusely while doing it."

"Have you thought about how you'll

handle that, if he does have someone else?"

"Oh, probably crawl under the table, grab his legs, and beg for him not to go."

"You don't really mean that, do you, Rachel?"

She narrows her eyes at me and scowls. It reminds me of my mother scolding me as a child. I sit and think about how pathetic I would look if I did act out. It will justify his need to leave the crazy lady behind, and I don't want him to see me being unstable.

"No. I want to be mature about it. Wish him the best of luck, and leave like a gracious woman. Then I'll go home and cry in private."

"You know what the right thing to do is, and I have faith in you that you'll be strong, no matter what the outcome."

"I am not confident right now, Dr. Grayson. I'm beginning to think I should give up this counseling gig and forget about it. I was happier with my cat. Now that I realize how much I love Ian, I'm miserable."

"I don't think you really want to give it up, Rachel. Frankly, I think your love for this man inspired you to return and get help. You've come to a point of wanting a healthy relationship with a healthy man. In the end, it may not be him that you end up with. If it isn't, by the time you meet Mr. Right, you'll be ready to be loved and love in return."

She's a freaking romantic pie-in-the-sky person, and I know it. "You're just saying that so I'll come back next week."

"Well, I hope you do. I'll be interested in finding out what happened when you have your drink with Ian."

"My Coke, you mean."

"I hope so. Alcohol and—"

"Anti-depressants don't mix. Yeah, I know."

She smiles, and so do I.

Chapter 19

PAINFUL REUNION

The week flies by and Thursday arrives. Before work, I decide to forgo a pantsuit and dress in a skirt with a matching blazer. I choose a white blouse, a few pieces of cheap jewelry, and spend more time on my hair than I usually do. It's obvious I'm trying to impress someone. By the time five o'clock rolls around, my makeup will probably have faded, so I stick a few extra items in my bag for a quick touch-up in the ladies' room before meeting Ian.

My nerves are on edge, and I try to remember points in my conversation with Dr. Grayson. I need to keep my emotions in check and part of me teeters on disassociating myself from the entire experience. I know if I go that far, my eyes will glaze over, and I won't hear a thing he says. Instead, I'll be busy constructing the brick wall so I won't get hurt.

After blowing a breath of air from my lungs, I glance at the clock. It's time to revive my makeup before I take the elevator of doom down to the lobby. As I glance at myself in the mirror, I appear outwardly confident, but I can see the fear in my eyes. *Jesus, please help me get through this.* I haven't uttered a prayer like that in ten years.

"Okay, let's rock," I mutter aloud, giving myself a team rah-rah. I get into the elevator, press L, and count the stops to let on more homeward-bound workers. A few minutes later, I emerge and round the corner.

Instantly, my eyes pick him out of the crowd. I stop dead and stare for a moment. It's been so long, and he is so handsome. Ian is dressed in a dark, pin-striped suit, with a powder blue shirt and dark-blue tie. I want to jump him, but at the same time my knees are knocking together. He turns and sees me standing there like a scare crow. Thankfully, his face brightens into a smile. I melt.

My feet propel me forward like I'm on a conveyor belt, and the next I know I'm standing in front of him. The cheeks on my face puff out, and I smile from ear to ear. "God, you look good," I say, eyeing him up and down like a crazy woman. He gives me his classic smirk, and then leans over and kisses me on the cheek. I'm surprised.

"God, you look good too" he says.

My heart bursts forth like a stream in the desert. "So, where are we off to, law man?"

He chuckles and gives me his arm. There's isn't an ounce of hesitation, as I wrap myself into Ian and yank him to my side.

"How about where we had our first drink?" He looks at me with hopeful eyes.

"Sounds good." I am slightly miffed. It seems he takes all his women to that little Italian restaurant.

We take a short walk of a few blocks. Both of us are quiet. I'm scared, but thrilled to be in his presence. I have no idea why I let this man go, and the fears that I have lost him start to haunt me as we enter the bar. It takes me a moment to adjust my eyes to the dim lighting. Ian leads me over to a secluded table, helps me into my chair, and sits down across from me.

"Boy this sure is familiar," I say, looking at him. He's avoiding eye contact with me. My stomach tightens.

A waitress approaches. "Coke," I say.

"Bud," he says. Afterward, he guardedly looks at me and parts his lips with a small smile. His eyes have that familiar glimmer in them that I love.

"You really look fabulous, Rachel."

"Thank you for the compliment. I accept." He raises his eyebrow at me.

"Well good," he replies. "I'm glad to hear it."

I want to tell him that I'm feeling better about everything, but I don't want to go down that road yet. How can I tell him the things that I've told my counselor?

My pop and his Bud arrive, and we both take a sip. My mouth feels like a ball of cotton, so I quickly suck the liquid through the straw. Ian remains aloof, and I try to draw him out.

"So how have you been, Ian, really?"

He lowers his eyes into his beer and clears his throat. "Uh, okay, I guess. Just busy." He lifts his head and looks at me like he wants to say something, but the cat has his tongue.

"You have something to tell me, don't you?" I'm afraid of what he'll say, but I might as well open the door. "Go ahead."

Ian quickly pulls his eyes away and hides

in his frothy beer. "Ah, Rach," he says, heaving a puff of air from his lungs and shaking his head. "I'm kind of confused, I guess."

"About what?"

He brings the beer to his mouth and takes a sip. After he swallows, he bites his upper lip nervously, and then sheepishly raises his eyes to mine.

"My ex wants to get back together again."

At first, I wonder if I'm hearing him correctly. His answer reverberates in my brain, and the light in my eyes disappears. My soul crawls into a fetal position, and I know what's coming. Now, I avoid looking at him and jump into the bottom of my glass. I was right, it was Susan having dinner with him. My heart rate increases in both fear and anger.

Take charge of things, Rachel. Buck up, I tell myself. I know I have to get through this.

"Wow," I answer, trying to keep a cheerful look on my face. "That's a surprise."

He tilts his head to the side. "Yeah, it was to me too. She broke up with her former boyfriend, and said she was having second thoughts about having divorced me."

"I thought you said you were over her," I remind him of his statement clearly announced the day we went to Multnomah Falls. I remember the look in his eyes, and I believed him.

"Well, she didn't want me then." He quickly replies with a lame-ass explanation.

"And now she does, so now you're *not* over her?" I'm sounding miffed. "Sorry, I just don't get it." My mouth pulls to one side of my face, showing my disapproval.

He shifts in his seat uncomfortably, and then takes another drink of beer. "Like I said, I'm confused."

"Have you been dating her again?" I already know the answer, but I want to see if he fesses up.

He nods his head. "Yeah, we've had a couple of dinners out and have done other stuff together."

Other stuff. What the hell is that supposed to mean? Has he done her? My nails dig into my palms of my clenched fists. I want to slap some sense into his confused pretty little head.

"Define *other stuff*," I press, sounding annoyed.

"Not here," he says, lowering his voice like he's ashamed to mention it in public. He avoids looking at me.

I shake my head in disbelief. "You don't need to articulate the *other stuff*, Ian. I get the picture."

He doesn't affirm or deny. His silence really irks me now.

"Well, I guess then if you're confused, I'll call it a night. No use sticking around where I'm not wanted."

As soon as the words leave my lips, he reaches over and grabs my hand. His actions surprise me. I look into his eyes, and I see the Ian I know. He wants me, too, but he's conflicted.

"No, don't go, Rachel. Tell me about you. I have missed you, really I have." He looks pitifully at me, like he's a little boy again. "How are things with counseling?"

I look down at his hand that clings tightly to mine. His flesh is so warm and inviting, that I feel my eyes water. *Shit. I can't start crying now*, I tell myself. I blink a few times to avert the flow.

"Uh, it's going good. Learning a lot about myself and why I do the things I do. I'm trying to learn how to be loved." I look him directly in the eyes. "And to love."

"What about the other stuff?"

Oh, now he wants to know about the *other stuff* with my sexual issues. I feel a coldness flow through my veins. Anger rises in my heart, because I feel threatened. I lean forward and whisper.

"You mean my propensity for wanting rough sex and bondage when you fuck me?" He scowls at me, and his hand slips off mine. "Well, that's what you mean, isn't, Ian? You've met a masochist, and you want to know if I still want you to be a sadist with me in the sack."

I'm shocked at my own words and admission to another human being. It's like AA, only for sex addicts. *Hello, my name is Rachel Ann Hayward, and I have masochist tendencies.*

He doesn't say anything. I sound perturbed, but I'm being defensive. It's far too difficult to dwell on the thought that I disgust him at this moment. I try to soften my voice.

"Let's just say that I'm working on it, but I won't know if I've conquered that desire until I get fucked again by another man."

I'm saying the F-word far too much, but I'm irritated at myself for being so screwed up. If I was a normal woman, I wouldn't be having this god-awful embarrassing moment in front of the man I love. I'm convinced now that he doesn't love me, and all he sees is an emotional, unbalanced train wreck. It's better that he goes back to his prissy and arrogant Susan.

Suddenly, I'm floating off somewhere in my head to where I want to be hurt and bound, because I don't deserve him. I look into his eyes and realize that I am being hurt—by him, the man I love—only it's an emotional thrashing and not a physical one, which is by far more painful.

Ian lowers his head, and he's staring at the tabletop. His fingers play with the corner of his white napkin, turning the edge down and folding it. He's hiding, and I can't take it any longer.

"Listen, Ian, I'll make it easy for you. You figure out what you want. If it's me, I'd like to rekindle our relationship and see where it goes. If you want to go back to your wife, and hope she doesn't get *bored* with you again, then I wish you all the happiness in the world. Let me know, and if you need a good counselor, I can recommend one."

I rise to my feet slowly, flash him a gracious smile. Ian lifts his pathetic gaze and looks at me dejectedly. His lips remain closed in a hard line.

"I'll be watching for you through the windshield of my car."

My body turns to leave, and then I stop. I have to say it, or my soul will burst. "By the way, Ian, believe it or not, I really love you. You're the best thing that ever happened to me."

Quickly, I run out the door and sprint to the parking garage. Tears stream down my cheeks. I pray with every footstep I take in my high-heel shoes, which are clicking across the concrete sidewalk, that at any moment he'll come up from behind me and grab me by the arm. I want him here with me, telling me he loves and wants me, not with his haughty ex-wife; but he doesn't, and I'm crushed.

I've done my duty. Kept my cool. Now I'm going to go home, cry, and probably masturbate with thoughts of some man hurting me to punish myself. It's all I deserve in life. It's all I've ever known. When someone hurts me; I hurt myself, validating my lack of worth.

"To hell with counseling," I scream, as I push my key into my car door lock. "Why put myself through this torture? For what? Nothing ever changes."

I crawl inside my car, slam the door shut, lay my head on the steering wheel, and lose it.

-·✻·-

My drive home is scary. After sitting in my car and crying for twenty minutes, I can't process where I am or where I'm going. It's that feeling you get when you drive through a light and get on the other side trying to remember if it was red or green. The road is a blur through my tearing eyes, and I'm afraid I'm going to crash into the concrete barrier on the Sunset Highway.

Finally, I take my exit and make my way down the street to my apartment. I'm numb and angry at myself, at him, and at his stupid wife for playing with his feelings. Inside I'm damning her left and right.

My firm grip on the steering wheel lessens as I turn into the driveway of my complex. I pull into my assigned parking space under the covered portion, turn off my car, and look in my rearview mirror. My heart stops when I see the back of Ian's trunk. He's standing there waiting for me. I don't know whether to shoot him or kiss him.

For a few moments, I hesitate getting out. It's obvious I'm avoiding him, because he walks over to the driver's side of my car door and opens it for me.

"What are you doing here?" I look at him with my swollen eyes and tear-streaked face.

His face is distraught. "I couldn't let you go."

"You're not making this any easier for me," I complain, stepping out of the car and facing him.

"It's not easy for me either," he admits, closing the door with a bang.

He's upset; I'm upset. It's a standoff. We're staring at each other eye-to-eye. I have no idea what he's thinking or feeling. The urge to throw myself at him tempts me, but the thought to be gracious and mature brings sense back into my head.

"Let's go upstairs," I say, scooting by him and heading for my apartment. He follows me up the stairs, and the next moment my brain registers is when we're standing in the living room ogling each other. My cat wanders out to greet me, and immediately the traitor runs to Ian and starts doing his dance around his legs.

"Whiskers!" I lift him into my arms, horrified at the thought of cat hairs on his suit.

"Hi Whiskers." Ian's voice is kind, and he reaches out and rubs my cat behind his ears. Instantly, the animal's eyes glaze over, but I don't blame him. If Ian rubbed me behind the ears, I'd probably do the same.

"Let me stick him in the bedroom so he doesn't bug us." Quickly, I walk down the hall, lay Whiskers on the bed, and then lock him inside. I can already hear him scratching at the door, but I'm going to tune him out.

I get back into the living room, and Ian is sitting on the couch. He looks relaxed. One arm is draped over the back, one leg is extended, the other in, and he's placed his other arm on the rest.

"Would you like anything to drink? Coffee, tea, pop? Sorry, no booze here."

"No, nothing." His dark eyes have clamped upon me, and I feel uncomfortable under his piercing gaze.

"What are you looking at?" He's annoying me.

"You."

"Well, that's obvious." I plop myself at the other end of the couch and gape at him in return. "So what are you doing here Ian Alexander Richards?"

He's silent for a moment, and I wonder what he's thinking. All the while he continues to stare at me with his piercing blue eyes, and it's making me anxious.

"Our conversation ended too soon, and I felt like more needed to be said between us."

I can't handle his intense look any longer, so I pull my eyes away and fiddle with the hem of my skirt.

"Besides," he continues. "You said you loved me."

I find the courage to look at him again, and I see his smart-ass smile. "Oh, you caught those words, did you?"

I feel anxious wondering where he's going with this. A part of me hopes it's the couch, floor, or wherever. I'm aroused looking at him, but then I think about the *other stuff* he's been doing with his ex-wife, which douses me with a bucket of cold water. I'm angry he didn't keep his pants zipped, or maybe she seduced him and that was her plan all along. My anger shifts toward her underhanded tactics.

His face turns deadly serious. "Did you mean it, Rachel?"

All right, now I'm really frustrated with him. Does that suddenly make a difference in his confused brain? *Men*, I bitch inwardly.

"What do you think?" I'm learning the tricks of my counselor—skirt the issue and ask questions instead.

"Don't know."

"Well, I guess you can either ignore it or figure it out for yourself."

I'm sounding really bitchy, as I pull my eyes away from him and glance out of my sliding glass door. It's really dirty, and I wander off thinking about how I need to grab some paper towels and squirt it with cleaner. My thoughts wander back where they should be.

His presence on the couch reminds me how much I love him, but I'm afraid to let my guard down. I don't want to lose him to another woman, who never learned to appreciate him in the first place. It takes restraint, but I keep my face impassive and voice calm.

"Tell me what you feel about your ex-wife. I want to understand."

My question breaks his stare and all of a sudden the relaxed Ian turns into pensive Ian. He drops his arm from the back of the couch, pulls in his leg, and inhales a deep breath. His body language screams volumes of agitation, but I'm not going to let him off the hook.

The seconds tick by, like he's hoping I will relent, but I keep a constant, patient gaze in his direction. *Oh, this is good. Rachel Hayward has the upper hand for a brief moment.* At last, one word slips between his lips.

"Failure."

His answer stuns me. I narrow my eyes. "Failure?" He bobs his head "yes." Boy this guy needs a counselor too. "Explain."

"I genuinely loved Susan when we wed. Having a lasting, happy marriage with her was an important goal in my life. When she left me, I knew I had blown it. I wasn't the husband she needed." His voice is trembling. "Now she's back, I'm thinking it's a second chance to make it right."

Rachel the counselor kicks in. "Why do you take all the responsibility for the failure of your marriage? Don't you think she had a responsibility to strive for a happy marriage too?"

"Well, sure," he sighs. "However, it's the man's responsibility foremost." He gives me a stupid look.

I can't believe the words coming out of his mouth. Clearly, the woman is manipulating Ian. Mr. Goodie-Two-Shoes, without a mean bone in his body, is as screwed up as I am—only in a different sort of way. I'm finding a strange sense of comfort in this dilemma, and a release of guilt for dealing with my problems.

"Don't let her take advantage of your kind heart, Ian. Be wise and make sure she's sincere, if you want to continue down that path of reconciliation."

He's back to staring at me again. I want to know what is going through his muddled mind. Where's the chain saw when you need one?

"What are you thinking?" I pry.

"I'm thinking that I'm still attached to you, but I'm dealing with our conflicting sexual desires."

We're back to that subject. It's clear the man isn't going to give up his poking.

"Point taken," I say, a bit annoyed. "Does it bother you that much?"

"I don't want to hurt you Rachel. It's not in me. There's nothing sexy to me about causing you pain. It's disrespectful to you as a woman." He pulls his eyes from me and lowers his head. "In fact, it sickened me after what I did to you that night at the beach house. I felt like shit for days. After you left, I almost lost it."

"Yes, and I felt satisfied but filled with shame afterward for leading you down that road." I inhale a deep breath and scoot a bit closer to him. It's time to get this out of my soul once and for all.

"Look, Ian. I didn't ask to be this way. At five years of age, a monster pinned me to a bed, fondled me, masturbated upon me, and brought me to sexual arousal repeatedly. I've been abusing myself because of it for twenty-five years. In fact, I started masturbating alone as a child, because I didn't know any better. All I knew is that if I put something hard between my legs, I'd feel good, and then relieved. I can remember hiding under the covers of my bed to keep that secret away from my parents."

My cheeks feel as if they are on fire. I'm so embarrassed to be telling him these secrets, but I feel like I need to get every detail out on the table so he can make a decision about me one way or the other.

"Every time I think about being bound and hurt, I get turned on—really turned on. It's revolting to you, I get that. But for me, I don't know anything else, because I was molded that way as a child." I'm sounding like a psychiatrist now. "I'm trying my best to understand why I react as I do and find a way to overcome the part of me that I despise. Somewhere in my soul is a little girl that needs to be set free and healed."

After that long, ranting confession, tears well in my eyes. Ian looks shocked, but not repulsed. I see a hint of sympathy in his gaze.

"Even if you never hurt me in bed again, Ian, and you make the most beautiful and tender love to me in the world, I'll probably fantasize in my mind that you're doing to me what I honestly want—being rough and forceful. That alone will bring me to an orgasm, but I don't think you'd want me to even imagine such degeneracy on your part. You're too respectful of a person to be painted in that light."

I'm emotionally spent and naked in front of the man I love. It's clear that he's trying to process all that I'm saying. He looks down at my hand and then reaches out and takes it into his own. His fingers are ice cold, and my hand is burning hot.

"You went to counseling because you loved me, didn't you?"

"At first I did. After I got into it, I realized that I was also doing it for myself. I came to a place where I wanted to change." I inhale a deep breath and squeeze his hand in return. "Now, I'm not sure if it's worth it, if I don't have you."

My heart stops a beat as I look at him for a reaction. He's rubbing my hand with his thumb and thinking. Then he leans forward heading for my lips. I see him coming, so I close my eyes. When he touches me tenderly, I can't believe it, but he tastes like honey— sweet, warm, and loving. It's wonderful to open my heart and accept the tenderness he gives.

Ian pulls away and lifts his hand to the side of my head. He affectionately strokes my hair for a few seconds and then brings his index finger across my lips.

"I've missed you," he dotingly whispers.

A smile curls my lips, because he didn't totally wipe me from his mind while we were apart. Yet, I feel like he's committing adultery, because in the back of my mind, I see his ex-wife looking over his shoulder. He may miss me, but I still don't think he's decided which road to take.

"Come with me to the beach house this weekend."

My mouth drops open at his invitation. I wasn't expecting that move. The first reaction I have is to call Dr. Grayson for advice, but there is no time to talk it out.

"Why?"

"It's important to me, that's why. I can't say any more than that."

There's longing and urgency in his eyes. I really do want to spend time with him, so I agree with a smile. "All right, I'll come."

"Pick you up at seven after work tomorrow?"

"Sure, but what about . . ."

"Susan is out of town."

"So you're cheating on her?"

"No, I'm not cheating on her." He gulps. "There's no agreement between us right now. I'm free to do as I will."

I don't want to let it go. "Does she know about me and what we had?"

"She doesn't know it's you specifically.

Susan only knows that I had been in a relationship."

I'm irked. The prospects are compelling, because I want to weasel my way back into his life and get my claws in him and be sure that she doesn't. My lips release a puff of air, thinking that he's made love to her. Trust issues come to the forefront, as I feel like he's cheated on me or something! *God, this is screwed up*, I think to myself. He was probably horny, and I'm reading too much into this. Men get horny and unzip their pants without thinking.

"Okay, then, seven p.m. I'll be ready."

"I've got reservations at a nice restaurant for dinner Saturday night. I'd like to take you out, so would you bring a nice dress for the occasion?"

I look at him cockeyed at his unusual request but comply. "All right." If he's suggesting a romantic evening together, I'll do the dinner thing.

Ian smiles. I see in his eyes a glow of relief. He wants me with him, that's all that matters.

"I need to go," he says, rising from the couch. He walks toward the door, and I follow.

"Thanks for coming over, Ian. I wanted you to follow after me." My eyes are filled with gratitude.

"Yeah, I knew you did. Just took me a minute to act upon it. Sorry." He lowers his eyes to the floor as if he's been reprimanded.

The moment is overwhelming, and I can't help myself. Guardedly, I draw near to him, wrap my arms around his waist, and lay my head on his chest. The beating of his kind heart fills my ears. It's peaceful.

He wraps his arms around me in return and rests his chin on the top of my head. Ian releases a sigh. For a few moments, we hold one another. In our embrace I sense a healing flow between us.

"Forgive me," I whisper, tightening my hug.

"For what, sweetheart?"

"For hurting you."

"Ah, Rachel, you know I forgive you."

He pulls away from me and puts both of his hands tenderly on the side of my face. Ian's eyes look deep into my soul. "Have you forgiven me for hurting you?"

In my heart, there is nothing to forgive, except for my resentment over his weakness with Susan. It's obvious, though, by the look on his penitent face, that he needs a release of guilt for what transpired between us that awful night at Cannon Beach.

Tears threaten to undo my resolve, and I give him a warm smile. "You know I do." He gives me a sweet kiss again, which fills my heart with hope that I may still have a future with him. The next I know he's out the door and gone.

I hear Whiskers scratching at my bedroom door, and then one white paw reaches out from underneath clawing to get out.

"All right, all right." I open it, and he runs past me looking for Ian. "Well, nice to see you too, traitor!" Frankly, who can blame him? All I want to do is run after Ian too.

Chapter 20

KEEPING SECRETS

Ian seems happy when he picks me up Friday night, but I can tell he is exhausted after another long work week. Our conversation remains superficial for the entire one and half hour drive. I feel tired and slightly apprehensive myself, anticipating the weekend.

When we arrive at his beach house, I can't help but wonder if he spent a night here with Susan. The thought of crawling in his bed gives me the creeps. I don't think I'd be too happy to smell a different scent of perfume on his pillowcase. In fact, I know I wouldn't. After entering his living room, I look at the couch and offer up a sacrifice.

"How about I take the couch this time and you the bed?"

"Are you sure?" The poor guy has dark circles underneath his eyes.

"Yeah, that's fine. There's a bath

downstairs, and I have everything that I need. Besides, I would like to sit outside for a while on the deck. I don't want to disturb you, if I do."

I wonder if he suspects why I asked for the couch, but he doesn't argue the point. He looks too tired to care.

"All right, then. Let me run upstairs and get you a blanket and pillow."

Ian heads up to the loft, and I walk over to the sliding glass door and unlock it. My hand pulls it open a bit and immediately the invigorating ocean air kisses my face. The sounds of the waves soothe my soul. I feel as if I have arrived home where I belong.

"Here you go."

A pillow hits the floor, and I swing around to look up at Ian about ready to toss the blanket down to me as well. He's definitely not getting off that easy.

"That's it? Blanket and pillow toss and no kiss?" I cross my arms and glare at him. A look of guilt flashes across his face, and immediately I'm sorry for the tease. He reminds me of a sensitive Golden Retriever that always wants to please you.

"Sure sweets," he says, trotting down the staircase. "Give me a smooch."

He's acting like a dork, and it makes me giggle. He's carefree for the moment, and that means he's relaxed, or I think it does. I wrap my arms around his neck and tilt my head back. "Ready," I whisper, closing my eyes. A moment later his lips mold around mine, but he doesn't invade me with his tongue. I take what I can get, albeit a tad disappointed over his presentation. In my head, I hold up the score card. He only gets a six, and I smirk over my thoughts.

"Thanks. Now go to bed."

"Night, Rach," he says, turning around and slowly dragging himself upstairs. He stops at the top of the landing. "Come get me if you need anything."

"Go," I wave him off, "I'm fine. Get some sleep." He nods his head and disappears into the back of the loft.

After picking up the pillow and blanket, I arrange it on the couch so I can look out the window. I'm not going to pull the curtains shut and block out the atmosphere. Suddenly, I think about the dress packed in my suitcase. I don't want it wrinkled, so I take it out and hang it up behind the bathroom door. After my nighttime routine, I crawl under the cover and get comfy.

For a few minutes I lay staring into the dark toward the ocean. My ears hear the soft, soothing rush of water rolling up and down on the sandy beach. The sound embraces me, and it doesn't take long before I'm off to the land where dreams are made.

-·❄·-

Morning arrives and I hear Ian clinking around in the kitchen. My nose picks up the aroma of freshly brewed coffee. I slightly panic over how I look, because I'm not exactly a beauty queen when I wake up. My hair always looks like a bird's nest.

Quickly, I sneak off to the bathroom without him seeing me and do quick repairs by brushing my teeth and combing my hair. I decide to remain in my PJ's—might as well feel comfortable.

I wander out and follow the smell of hot caffeine.

"Hey, you're up," he says, turning around and eyeing me up and down. A smirk spreads across his face. "Cute, but where's your kitty PJ's?"

I roll my eyes cringing that this handsome man actually saw me dressed in child's apparel. Then I'm reminded, I am a little girl inside my mind—if he only knew.

"At home where they belong," I say, heading for the cupboard where he keeps his cups. I'm smiling because I know where they are. The coffee maker makes its last steamy slurp into the carafe.

"What cup do you want?"

"Nothing special. Here take this," he says, shoving an empty cup with his law firm's name on it.

I stare at it then say, "Cute." And pour him a cup, along with mine. "So, what's on the agenda today?" I climb on top of one of the stools by the kitchen island.

"Nothing specific, except for dinner tonight." Suddenly, a look of panic flashes across his face. "You will do dinner with me, right?"

He's really anxious about this night out. Maybe he thinks I'm going to back out, but I'm not afraid to dine out with him anymore. *I can handle this*, I remind myself. Besides, I could use a decent meal.

"Yes, of course. Where are we going?"

He smiles, and a sparkle flashes in his blue eyes. "Stephanie Inn."

My mouth drops open. "Oh, wow, I've never been there." It's too pricy for my wallet, but Ian can afford it. Nevertheless, the look on his face bothers me. I can't help but wonder what the reason is behind the date. Perhaps, he's romancing me. The thought gives me hope.

Suddenly, his cell phone on the kitchen counter rings. He looks at it and instantly snatches it up.

"Excuse me," he says, while running up the stairs to the loft. I scowl, wondering if it's Susan.

I strain to hear Ian's conversation from the kitchen, but I can only catch a few words spoken here and there.

"Good . . . trip okay?"

Damn, he's talking to Susan, I seethe. Cautiously, I sneak a little closer to the bottom of the stairs, but stay out of sight.

"Yeah, sure, that's fine. How's mom?"

Mom? Now I'm thoroughly confused. Maybe it's not Susan. Ian breaks out in laughter. "You got to be kidding me?"

This conversation is driving me bonkers.

"Uh-huh, yeah . . . sure . . . okay."

His voice drops really low, but I still hear him talk. It's obvious he doesn't want me to know what is going on. I skedaddle back to the kitchen and start sipping the brew, acting innocent. A few moments later, Ian walks in and plays dumb.

"Everything okay?" I pry looking up at him.

"Yeah, sure."

He avoids eye contact with me. Apparently, that's becoming a habit, and I find it irksome because I can't read what he's thinking. Okay, he doesn't want to talk or tell me who was on the telephone. He's hiding something, but I can tell from his body language he's nervous as hell. I don't want to push it, so I let it drop.

"So, you *are* okay about dinner with me tonight?"

He looks at me checking my response one more time. This dinner thing is important. "Yeah, I think I can handle it now that I know you better." He flashes a relieved smile.

"Great," he replies.

"I think I'll go shower and get dressed," I announce, emptying my coffee cup and heading off to the bathroom.

"You want to go for a walk on the beach later?" he calls out after me.

I glance outside. A slight morning fog is lying off shore, but later on it should burn off. It's supposed to be sunny this weekend.

"Yes, I'd like that."

"Good, I'll go get cleaned up. We can have a bite to eat before we head out."

"Okay," I say, walking into the bathroom. I close the door and wonder what's going on with him. He's acting secretive, and I'm dying to know who was on the telephone.

Chapter 21

HANG IN THERE DOLL

One last glance in the mirror and I'm pleased. God, I look hot. I have to admit that since I started back in counseling my self-esteem has moved up one notch. I'm feeling more confident about myself, in spite of some of my screwy sexual desires.

I'm dressed in my black dress that hugs my curves. My legs are covered in sheer black panty hose, and my shiny patent leather four-inch heels are making me feel tall. Thank goodness Ian is taller still. Wearing them makes my ass look good, and my boobs thrust temptingly forward.

My hair is upswept on the sides, but I've let my long blonde locks cascade down the back. I brought a few pieces of my nice, gold costume jewelry to wear. A few dabs of my favorite perfume, the last touch of mauve lipstick, and I'm ready. *Watch out Ian, you're in for it*, I smugly think while looking at myself.

Slowly, I emerge from the bathroom and walk out into the great room. Ian is pacing back and forth. I'm shocked over his behavior, because he's usually the cool cucumber. He turns around and takes one look at me, and his eyes grow wide. The man is speechless. I can't help but feel powerful and provocative. I've got the upper hand on the law man.

"Good Lord, Rachel, you're a knockout."

"Why thank you, Mr. Richards," I say in a soft drawl. "I'm glad you like it." I turn around and give him the complete view.

Afterward, I stop and assess him. Ian is dressed in a black suit, ivory-colored shirt, and dark gray tie. He's smoking hot. I like it when he wears dark colors, because it accents his hair and dreamy eyes. "Not bad yourself. You look extremely handsome in that suit, sir."

He approaches me like he's going to give me a kiss. I raise my hand in protest. "No messing up the makeup. Hands off." He shoves out his lower lip in a pout.

"All right," he sighs, lowering his eyes

to my cleavage. "You ready?"

"Let me get my wrap." I take the black silk shawl that came with the dress and drape it over my shoulders and arms. Now I truly feel like a million dollars. Ian looks mesmerized, and I feel as if I'm gaining ground in my favor.

We climb into the car and drive south about a mile to the beautiful inn that sits right on the ocean. I've never been there, and I'm frankly excited for a romantic dinner for two.

After we pull into the parking lot and park, Ian's face looks as if he just ate a sour grape. He sits motionless for a moment and then turns his head and looks at me.

"You okay?" I reach over and touch his hand. It's hard not to question his odd behavior.

"Yeah, sure. I've got something to tell you when we get inside."

"All right." The whole situation is becoming confusing, and I don't understand what all the mystery is about.

We walk inside the lobby of the hotel. The resort is beautiful with wood and stone decor. A sense of excitement flows through my veins, because I know it's one of the most expensive places to stay and dine in Cannon Beach. Ian walks me around the huge stone fireplace that faces the front door to an elevator on the other side.

He pushes the button and the door opens. Once in, he pushes two, and then turns and looks at me with a worried look in his eyes.

"Hang in there doll."

Hang in there, doll? What the hell is that supposed to mean?

The elevator door opens, and we step out into the reception area of the restaurant. Ian stops, and I assume we're waiting for the hostess to greet and take us to a table. Instead, I see a strange man heading in our direction. He's extremely good looking, brown hair, and I guess that he's a few years older than we are. He's dressed in a fantastic, well-tailored, three-piece, gray suit, which makes him look intriguing and important. I'm aghast that he has come to greet us. He heads directly to Ian and gives him a manly bear hug.

"God, Ian, it's been far too long! Good to see you." He pats him a few times on his back. Afterward, he squeezes Ian's upper arm and looks at him up and down. "Shit, you look good." He nods his head with a broad smile on his face.

Ian flashes a grin from ear to ear. "Shit, you look good too, Jack."

Jack? Jack? Where have I heard that name before? Suddenly, it dawns on me that Jack is his freaking brother! My head spins to Ian like I'm possessed or something, and I give him the Rachel evil eye. Ian ignores me, keeping his focus on Jack, who suddenly turns his attention to me. He flashes the typical male once-over from my boobs to my toes and up again, then looks me in the eye with obvious curiosity.

"And who is this beautiful, young lady?" he asks. His voice is enticingly warm.

"Jack, this is Rachel Hayward."

"Nice to meet you, Rachel," he says enthusiastically, extending his hand out toward me.

I look at it for a moment and glance at Ian. He's got a stupid look on his face like he's pulled one over on me. All I think about is how I'm not going to be able to eat anything, and I'm starving. Hesitantly, I take his brother's hand.

"Nice to meet you also," I say, trying to be the mature, graceful, young woman. All the while inside, I'm a raving lunatic. "This is a surprise." Jack doesn't say anything and turns his attention back to Ian.

"Mom and Dad are waiting for you in the dining room. We've got a large table by the window."

"Great," Ian says. "We'll be right in."

Mom and dad? What trick has he played on me? Jack seems to understand that this is all news to me. He turns and heads toward the dining room leaving us, for a moment, alone in the lobby.

"What is going on?" I say, giving Ian an angry glare.

"It's my family, Rachel. My mom and dad are celebrating their fortieth wedding anniversary. They drove up from California for the weekend. Jack and his wife flew in from Boston for the occasion. They're staying here at the inn."

I can't believe what he just told me. My stomach balls into a hard knot. I'm livid and scared to death.

"Then why did you bring me here this weekend, when you should be spending it with family?"

"Because, I realized that I wanted you to meet them, and I wanted them to meet you." His sincere eyes are pleading with me.

"I don't know if I can do this, Ian," I say, shaking my head. My body trembles. "I told you how I am eating in front of strangers. You, I can handle, but your brother and parents?" I shake my head again. "This is too much."

Ian reaches out and grabs my hand. He brings it to his lips and kisses it softly. "You can do this, Rachel," he encourages me. "I have faith in you. *Please*, it's extremely important to me that you meet my family."

Now he's beseeching me to relent. I guess that I should be glad he's decided to introduce me. Does this mean I'm up for approval? Maybe he wants to see their reaction to his crazy girlfriend before he makes a decision as to who gets him for the rest of their life. If this gives me an upper hand on Susan, I should suck it up and go with the flow. I swallow the lump in my throat and draw in a deep breath.

"Okay, for you, but I hope you don't have any other surprises up your sleeve."

"Thank you, sweetheart." He kisses my hand once more and then flashes a smart-ass smile before escorting me to their table.

I'm sure the restaurant's interior is gorgeous, but I can't focus on my surroundings. Ian directs me to a large table, and before I can completely collect my wits about me, I'm up for scrutiny before the whole lot of them. I'm trembling in my heels. Thank God, Ian slips his arm around my waist and holds onto me for support.

"Mom, Dad, I'd like you to meet Rachel Hayward." Ian looks at me and gives me the scoop nodding toward his parents. "Rachel, this is my mother Grace, and my father, Bill."

I smile and my eyes look at his parents. I'm in a daze. I see them, but I don't see them. I'm on the verge of zoning out. His father stands from the table like a gentleman and gives me a warm, welcoming smile.

"Nice to meet you, Rachel," he says enthusiastically. "It's good of you to join us for our anniversary celebration." He places his hand on his wife's shoulder and smiles down at his cherished companion. "This is my wife, Grace."

"Rachel, how nice it is for you to join us this evening." Her tone is welcoming, and I see in her eyes, what I hope is pleasure, that Ian has brought a date. "Please, I insist that you sit down next to me."

Grace invites me to the empty chair to

her right. His mother's voice is warm and friendly, and it's quite obvious where Ian learned his manners. The man grew up in a loving, caring family. I'm in a fantasyland and definitely out of my element amongst these people.

"Rachel," Jack interjects. "This is my wife, Karen.

I look across the table and see his wife flashing me a warm smile. "Nice to meet you, Karen." I nod in her direction. She's very pretty, too, with short brunette hair and a swan-like neck. Karen is dressed in a classy red dress. It's obvious, by their attire, that they have money. Since Jack is a doctor, I'm not surprised.

"Hello, Rachel, glad you could join us." She smiles, but I see a curious look in her eye that catches me off guard.

Swiftly, I turn and look at Ian, pleading for his help. He slips his hand underneath the table and grabs mine, rubbing his thumb along the top of my knuckles. I glance at his brother, who is intently watching me. His face is serious, and I'm wondering what has gotten into him. Maybe he doesn't like Ian's choice in women.

"So, you have a nice drive up the coast,

Dad?"

Ian starts a conversation with his father. A waiter comes up and gives us our menus. The dinner has started, and I'm a basket case.

"Yes, not bad, actually. We took our time and stayed at a few towns on the way. It's a nice drive this time of year."

"Have you lived in Oregon long, Rachel?" Grace turns and looks at me, sweetly starting up a conversation.

"Uh, yes. I was born in the Midwest and came out here about twelve years ago."

"I love Oregon, frankly. I keep telling Bill when he retires we need to move up here."

There are no airs about his mother and father at all. Even though both of their sons have successful careers, I can't see a hint of snobbery in the family whatsoever.

Ian's mother is wearing a modest blue dress, adorned with a gold necklace. She's sparkling in personality, lovely to look at, and has a beautiful complexion for a woman who is probably in her late fifties. Grace's hair is light brown, but looks as if she's had it tinted to cover any gray.

Bill is unpretentious, attentive toward his wife, dressed in a brown suit. His hair is graying at the temples and a little thin on the top, but he's quite a decent-looking man for his age, and slender. I see the resemblance in Ian and Jack immediately. They both appear to take after their father, more so than their mother.

My eyes scan about the table at everyone as they peruse their menus. I can't see the words in front of me. I know I have to order something, but I also know I'm going to be picking at my plate for the next hour, dreading each bite. My anxiety is growing, and I catch Jack's eyes again watching me. Quickly, I look back down at the menu. I wish he'd knock it off. What is it with him?

The waiter returns to the table to take our orders. I still haven't decided what to do. I read my options—filet mignon, duck breast, sea bass, and crab. God, I'm out of my league. Where are the burgers? The waiter makes it around to me, and I order fish. It's the lightest thing on the menu, and something that I think I can manage after six months of eating frozen dinners and carry out.

Ian's father orders two bottles of wine— one white, the other red. I have no idea what they are, but when they start filling up glasses I'm mortified. I choose the white, and ask for a small portion. The waiter pours half a glass. My purple pill is going to be complaining.

I try and smile while the table turns into family chatter. Quietly, I listen and take in all the conversation. Ian asks his brother about work.

"Jack, how's the practice going?"

"Fine. Busy as hell."

Karen adds, "He's never home." She flashes a tender smile. "But I love him anyway."

I stare at them both, and then my curiosity gets the better of me. "Jack, what is your medical specialty?"

He looks at me square in the eye with a straight face. "Psychiatry. I'm a psychiatrist, Rachel."

Jack picks up his glass of wine and takes a sip, keeping his eyes on me. *Shit! A psychiatrist?* Now I know why he's been looking at me like a hawk. Ian has told him about my past, I'm sure of it. He's checking me out big time, doing a little psychoanalyzing of my behavior at the dinner table, no doubt. I try not to feel threatened, but it's hard. I reply calmly, but I'm perturbed.

"Oh, Ian, didn't tell me that you were a *psychiatrist*," I say, turning my head and looking at him with one of those "when were you going to tell me" looks. Ian smirks.

"It just never came up in our conversations."

I feel his hand back under the table again searching for mine, which is now balled into a fist. He finds it and then holds it tight underneath his palm. It's obvious that I'm having a slight hissy fit in private. I glance back over at Jack. He's saying something to Karen, but I can't hear the words. Maybe my brain wants to tune him out. I wish Dr. Grayson were here to protect me.

Ian leans into my ear and whispers. "You okay?"

I don't want to make a scene, so I nod and give him a forced smile. "Yeah, I'm fine." Jack suddenly pipes up and picks up his wine glass.

"I'd like to propose a toast to Mom and Dad on their fortieth wedding anniversary."

Ian looks lovingly at his parents and all eyes are upon them. Bill puts his arm around Grace and gives her a quick peck on the cheek.

"Mom and Dad, I think I speak for all of

us at this table that we are happy to be here to share in the joy of celebrating your anniversary. You have been an inspiration in our lives. The adoration and respect that you show one another have taught your sons the meaning of unconditional love. Dad, you especially have been a wonderful example on how to respect, love, and honor the women in our lives, and for that, sir, I thank you."

"I thank you too," Karen announces. Everybody laughs.

I feel so foreign to the world in which they live that a deep sadness flows over me. Jack continues.

"We wish you many more happy years together. God bless you both."

Everyone raises their glass. I hear Ian, "Bless you, Mom and Dad." His voice is trembling, and I wonder if he's revisiting the failure of his marriage in comparison to the success of his parents' life together.

Unexpectedly, I feel truly sorry for him and understand the pain in his heart, let alone what I encouraged him to do in bed with me. I feel ashamed, and for some odd reason, I comprehend why he's struggling about making it right with Susan. A moment later, I join in the toast and smile at them both.

"Happy anniversary."

I add my congratulatory remark and take a small sip of white wine. When I'm through, I set my glass down on the table and look at Ian. I feel my eyes tearing, but I suppress my emotions.

"I hope you know how lucky you are," I whisper.

He looks at me affectionately and squeezes my hand underneath the table. "I do, Rachel."

I'm so jealous that he has it all. Dear God, I want it too—a kind, loving family and unconditional love.

It's all I can do not to cry. Warily, I look over at Jack. He's watching my obvious struggle over the unfamiliar territory I'm exploring. Jack nods his head in my direction and gives me a sympathetic glance and a kind grin.

My eyes break away, and I lower my head to stare into my glass of white wine. It's obvious by the look on his face that he knows the secrets of my heart.

Chapter 22

THE AFTERMATH OF SURPRISE

For the next hour and a half, I feel as if I'm having an out-of-body experience. I'm there at the dinner table participating in the festivities, poking at my food, chitchatting, but my mind is elsewhere. It's difficult to process normal, when most of my life has been abnormal.

As the event draws to a close, I fear that I will never fit in. I've come to the awful conclusion that I'm not right for Ian. On the other hand, I still want him more than I want Susan to reclaim him. I'm feeling terribly confused.

Everyone rises from the table. Grace turns toward me and gives me a little hug.

"It was wonderful getting to know you, Rachel."

"You too," I manage to say. Ian's father approaches me.

"Rachel, I hope we get to meet again

someday. Thanks for joining the family affair tonight. I hope we didn't bore you."

"Oh, heavens, no, Mr. Richards. It was an enjoyable evening, and I'm thankful for the opportunity to have met you both."

"I'm glad, too, dear," Grace replies with sincerity.

I'm overwhelmed at the reception I'm receiving from Ian's parents. There is so much more that I wish I could articulate, but I can't get the words out of my mouth.

I notice that Ian is over by Jack and Karen talking. When he's through, he turns his attention to his mother and father to say goodbye. From the conversation, I gather his parents are leaving in the morning to drive further north up the coast into Washington State to continue their vacation on the San Juan Islands. I'm not sure about Ian's brother, and then I see Jack and Karen head over toward me.

"Very nice to meet you," Karen starts. She leans into my ear and whispers. "Make sure that rascal treats you good."

I'm surprised at her comment, but I presume she's trying to make light of my uneasiness. "Oh, I will," I reply, forcing a grin.

Jack looks at me sympathetically. "I hope I didn't intimidate you, Rachel, with the psychiatrist business. People often feel uncomfortable in an informal setting when they first meet me."

"No, not at all." He knows I'm lying through my teeth. "Just surprised Ian left that little tidbit out." I turn and look at him, and he's playing innocent.

"You still coming over tomorrow afternoon to watch the game?" Ian asks.

"Yeah," Jack replies. "What time?"

"I think it starts at Noon. I'll check and give you a call."

Apparently, my exposure to the mind bender isn't over yet. Karen smiles.

We say our goodnights, and Ian escorts me to the car. I'm emotionally exhausted. As soon as we climb in and sit down, we both stare out of the windshield. Apparently, this wasn't easy for him either. After a minute, which feels like an hour, he turns and looks at me. Even in the dark interior of the car, I see his eyes sparkle with approval. He reaches over and takes my hand.

"You did fantastic, Rachel. I was proud to introduce you to my family. Felt good."

Why do I want to tell him that I don't

feel the same? Yes, his family is wonderful, but I'm out of my comfort zone. My self-esteem issues are reminding me that I'm a messed-up female with a long road of healing in front of me. One thing I'm sure, though, this evening I learned more about the man sitting next to me.

"I'm glad you pulled this fast one on me, Ian. It's given me a deeper insight into who you are as a person and how your parents have formed your character. You're the kindest and gentlest human being I've ever met. Your entire family is gracious."

He gives me a vulnerable look as if he's uncomfortable with what I've said. Apparently, he has trouble receiving honest accolades as well.

"Is that a bad thing or a good thing?"

"For you it's a good thing, but for me . . . it's not bad, per se, just strange and uncomfortable. I feel like the square peg trying to be shoved into the round hole." Disappointment spreads across Ian's face.

"Oh, Rachel," he affectionately expresses, "I honestly hope that one day you see your worth. You are a beautiful woman that warms my heart. You deserve happiness."

My brain doesn't process worth. My ex-husband's belittling voice screams into my gray cells, *Look at you! Who would want someone like you? I wish you were dead.* I'm not sure if I'll ever believe anything else. I want to silence that bastard's voice, but I can't find the erase button.

Ian inserts the key into the ignition and pulls out of the parking lot. We are both quiet during the short drive back to his beach house. As soon as we enter, I want to flop on the couch and pass out.

"I'm really tired," I announce, taking off my silk shawl.

"Me too," Ian replies softly, coming toward me. He stands a few inches away from my body and looks at me fondly. "Why don't you join me on the other side of the bed tonight? I promise not to incite anything."

I suck in my lips and think about his offer. His couch isn't that comfortable. "Okay, but no sex."

"No sex."

"Take me to your boudoir," I tease.

He raises his eyebrows at me. "Well, my boudoir will be a tad boring tonight," he says, grabbing my hand and leading me upstairs.

After we're ready for bed, I climb in with my panties and bra and he with PJ bottoms, but no top. We're between the sheets. I look at him; he looks at me. It's awkward. I have an overwhelming need to be held in his safe and loving arms.

"Hug?" I sound like a little child.

Ian reaches out his arm and draws me into his warm body. I find that comfortable place in the crook of his shoulder and lay down my head. My arm wraps around his waist. The sense of security and peace cover me like a warm blanket. He kisses my head and strokes me gently with his hand. I want to tell him that I love him, but I'm afraid to utter the words. Ian is quiet, but I don't care. A few moments later, I fall into peaceful sleep in his strong arms.

—·❈·—

The morning light wakes me up. I'm still wrapped in Ian's arms and it feels wonderful. He stirs when I do.

"Good morning," he says, with a grin and sleepy eyes. "It's nice to wake up next to you."

"Morning," I whisper, afraid to breathe

into his face lest I have a bad breath.

"Sleep good?"

"Yes, you're very comfy and make a good pillow."

"You think so, do you?" He reaches over to my waist and starts tickling me.

"Ian!" I squirm and try to wiggle away, laughing at him, but he won't let up. Suddenly, he's on top of me looking into my eyes, and I feel his morning erection. *God, this is not good.*

He looks as if he's examining every inch of my morning face and wild hair. I'm losing it physically. Ian lowers his mouth and kisses me with his prickly face and bad breath. His tongue slips in between my lips, and he still tastes sweet to me. God, I love this man.

When he's finished, he rolls off me. "Boy, I better get out of bed, or I'm going to break my promise."

I watch him throw back the covers, stand up, and disappear into the bathroom. My body is on fire, and I have this urge to be loved—not hurt. My psyche is surprised over that emotion.

Okay, I say to myself, getting out of bed. I hear him turn on the shower, so I trot downstairs to the bathroom and take a cold shower myself.

-·❈·-

An hour later, I'm sitting at the kitchen counter munching on cereal and toast. Ian and I are both off somewhere in our thoughts. The anticipation of his brother's arrival is driving me insane. I have to know.

"I need to ask you something," I say, looking at him, somewhat afraid of the answer.

"Sure, what?" he replies, talking with his mouth full again. I have the urge to scold him, but I enjoy his rare foibles.

"What have you told Jack about me? Does he . . . does he know about my sexual issues?"

There, I've said it. A tremendous relief rolls off my shoulders, but now my stomach is in a knot waiting for Ian to answer. I can see by the look on his face, he's already spilled the beans. It didn't take me long to figure it out last night, after Jack's relentless notes he was taking in his mind about my behavior at dinner.

"Okay, I'll fess up," he sighs.

"Please do."

"Yes, I have."

"Okay, I can deal with that. Why and when?" I sound pushy.

Ian drops his eyes into the cereal bowl. He looks embarrassed. I'm surprised he's having trouble maintaining eye contact with me.

"Well, the first time was after you told me about your abuse initially. I was concerned."

"Okay, that makes sense. If I were in your shoes, I probably would have done the same."

"Then after we separated, I really needed to talk to Jack. I nearly lost it when you left." His eyes look into mine, and he flashes a timid grin. "It's convenient having a shrink in the family—saves money."

"Funny," I reply with a chuckle. I try to keep the conversation on the light side. "Did it help?"

"Yeah, sort of."

"What did he say about my past?"

Ian draws in a deep breath. "He asked me some questions, and I told him what I knew, but didn't understand."

I pull my gaze away from him, because now it's my turn to feel embarrassed. The shrink is going to be back at noon, and I'm wondering if he has a poking session planned. For a few moments, I ponder my predicament. More than anything, I want to put Ian's mind at ease.

"Would you feel better about my issues if I sat down with your brother and talked to him?"

Ian sits up in his chair and intently looks at me. He seems shocked and intrigued over my suggestion.

"You don't have to do that, Rachel. Besides, whatever you tell him is confidential, so he can't discuss it with me anyway."

"True," I remind myself. "But I suppose he can counsel you one way or the other and help you make a decision."

"What decision?"

He looks confused, and I wonder if he's hiding what I know is going on inside of his soul. He's at a crossroads; it's obvious.

"Whether you want to be with me or Susan."

I swirl the smidgen of milk left in my cereal bowl with my spoon in order to find a safe place to escape. It's too hard to look at him, and I'm afraid of what he might say. It's apparent, he's not going to say anything either by his silence.

I slide off the stool. "Mind if I take a walk on the beach alone?"

"No," he answers without looking at me. Apparently, I've put him on the spot.

"I'll see you in a bit." I grab my jacket and head out the sliding door to the path that leads to the ocean. The cool morning air touches my face, and I draw in a deep breath. I walk toward Haystack Rock and try to calm my fears of rejection.

He's not the only one at a fork in the road. I know how hard it must be for him to think about me in a long-term sense. It will take commitment on both of our parts—me to continue counseling and seek healing; and him for the patience to endure the long process. I don't want to think of him as my abuser when we're in bed. My desires have begun to yearn for something else.

As I near the rock, I stop and watch the waves crash against the hard monument. Seagulls and other ocean birds are circling above my head squawking. Amidst the beauty, I wonder what Susan's motives are in getting back together with Ian. Is she on the rebound from her last relationship or using him for something else? The whole matter unsettles me, because I don't know. Conjecture is useless.

I do know, though, that this weekend with Ian has brought me closer to him in many ways, and for that, I'm thankful. Hopefully, when it's all over, he'll choose me, instead of her, regardless if I think I'm right for him or not. There is a deep longing in my soul for goodness and a loving relationship, and it's that smidgen of hope I decide to cling to instead of fear and doubt.

Chapter 23

The noon hour arrives, and Karen and Jack are at the door with a six-pack of beer, chips, and pretzels. I can see where this is going, but I'm not a football fan. Karen acts enthusiastic over the forthcoming game, so I assume she shares her husband's interest in sports. I'm feeling out of my element again.

As we sit down with drinks in hand—me with a cola and everyone else with a beer, I look at Karen and ask her if she actually likes the sport.

"So you're a football fan, I gather, like your husband?"

"Oh, God, no," she says. "I try and show an interest in what he likes." She leans into me and whispers. "I find more entertainment watching my emotionally stable husband lose it screaming over a pigskin ball. It gives me an odd sort of comfort that he has tendencies of lunacy once in a while."

She sits back, takes a swig from her bottle. Jack turns his head and glowers at her. "Yeah, yeah, very funny."

Ian laughs.

"You want to go out on the deck and talk?" Karen asks.

I've never been much of a talker with other women, but Karen comes across as someone who could be a real friend. It's compelling. "Sure, I'd like that."

"See you boys," Karen says, as we head for the door.

"Hey, don't go talking about me," Ian calls after us.

I flash him a mischievous, toothy grin. He looks nervous. Good.

We plop on the two patio chairs, and I look out at the ocean. "I really love the ocean. It's my favorite spot in the entire world," I sigh, letting her into that small part of my likes versus dislikes.

"So, Ian tells me how you ran into each other." She's grinning at me.

"Yeah, wasn't that a hoot? I rear-end an attorney."

"I will admit that when I heard the story, I laughed. Hope you don't mind."

"You kidding? When I look back on it, I laugh too. I thought he was going to scream and yell, but he was compassionate and concerned over my welfare right from the beginning."

"Yep, that's Ian," she muses.

"What about you? How did you and Jack meet?"

"Well, not quite as colliding as you two. I was working at a hospital in Boston where Jack did his internship. I was a clerk in the residency office. We sort of took care of the incoming residents and interns during their tenure."

"Really?" I'm surprised as hell.

"Yeah. We just hit it off right away, and he asked me out on a date. The rest is history. We got married in his third year of residency. Best thing that ever happened to me."

I'm flabbergasted. Suddenly, I don't feel so out of league with Ian. The two of them seem genuinely happy together.

Karen and I spend the next hour talking about anything and everything. I like her. She's down to earth, easy to talk to, and I don't feel intimidated by her at all. She is the first woman that I've ever met who I think that I could have a lasting friendship with. It's sad that she lives clear on the other side of the country.

The sliding door moves back, and Jack pops his head out. "What are you two up to?"

Karen rises from the chair. "Just talking about you," she says, patting him on the side of the face. She looks over at me. "Excuse me while I find the ladies' room."

A moment later, Karen disappears, and Jack keeps his gaze on me. It's obvious he's waiting for my invitation. "Come on over, shrink. I know what you want."

It doesn't take him long to close the door and sit down next to me. "What do you think I want?" he asks with a smirk.

"You are curious about the crazy lady that's dating your brother." I look at him square in the eye. "Ian told me that he mentioned to you my childhood sexual abuse." I inhale a deep breath. "So, you want me to tell you where I'm at with that?"

"If you want to," he says, leaning back in the chair and folding his arms. "I don't want to cross lines, though. It wouldn't be ethical of me to take your therapist's place."

"Yeah, I get that, but I want to tell you, because I think as Ian's brother you have the right to know what he's getting into, if anything."

Jack's eyes convey compassion. I don't feel ashamed, for some odd reason, because I know what comes out of my mouth on this deck will remain between the two of us and go no further. It's a free session that I don't have to pay for. Regardless, I am a bit nervous.

"Okay, I'll get this much out of the way so you don't have to fret over these points." I count on my fingers. "Number one, I don't cut myself. I've never had the urge to either. I hate the idea of blood."

I glance up at him, and he's intently looking at me. "Number two, I don't throw up my food, nor do I starve myself. I've never had those problems either."

"That's encouraging," he says to me. "What do you do?"

"Ah, the questions begin," I tease him.

"You started it."

He's a snarky guy, and I like it. "For most of my life, my self-esteem has been in the toilet. I've been back in therapy for almost two months. I know it's not much, but I can say I think my self-esteem has made it to the toilet seat."

He laughs. "Well, that's a powerful analogy."

"Hey, works for me. One of these days, I hope to get off, wipe myself, and get on with life."

Jack's face turns serious. "Are you on meds?"

"Yes, I've been on anti-depressants for a few years."

"Have you ever thought or attempted suicide, Rachel?"

I give him the eye-to-eye contact I know he's going to want when I answer this question.

"I've never attempted suicide, but there have been times in the past I've wished that I didn't have to live, so the emotional pain would end. Frankly, my religious background threatens hell, and I'm more afraid of burning for eternity. Therefore, doing myself in, isn't an option." For a moment, I stop and think of my answer, then clarify further. "Those thoughts of not wanting to live are few now."

"What have you dealt with as a result of the sexual abuse?"

Okay, now the questions are getting tough. "The usual, like poor choices in relationships. My ex-husband was verbally abusive, and it took some doing to get me out of that situation. The other laundry list of symptoms, which you know already—self-esteem issues, depression, flashbacks, nightmares, self-loathing, eschewed ideas about sex, promiscuous behavior, inability to receive love, irrational fears—stuff like that."

I inhale a deep breath and painfully admit my other shame. "I've had trouble with self-gratifying sexual behavior." I can't say the "M" word, but I'm sure he knows what act I'm referring to.

"Is the counseling helping you?"

"Yes. I have a good counselor, who I trust. But I'm still worried about one aspect."

"And what's that?"

I flash him a worried squint. "You won't talk to Ian about this, will you?"

He shakes his head. "No, I'm not going to cross ethical boundaries here, Rachel. You're right that I care about Ian. When he told me of your past, naturally, I was concerned. I've worked with quite a few women who have deep emotional scars from sexual abuse. It's not easy to overcome the effects."

"You're right, it's not easy, but I'm trying for Ian's sake, and my own, of course."

"Why?"

Confession time. I bite my trembling lower lip to suppress the urge to cry. A few seconds later, I tell him what's in my heart.

"Because I love him, and I want to be loved. I've got to stop abusing myself and reliving that part of my life over and over again if I'm ever going to beat this. I know that."

My eyes start to well with tears as my little girl comes out of the back room and tries to talk about the hurt.

"It's my hunger for bondage and pain during sex that bothers me. I fantasize about it often, and I don't know if I can win that battle. I certainly don't want Ian to stoop to my level. It's not fair to him. Besides, he's not wired that way. He's the opposite of sadistic behavior. He gives respect, not pain."

Jack sighs deeply and keeps his eyes on me, giving me a concerned, but kind glance.

"I'll tell you what I think, Rachel," he pauses for a moment, as if he's collecting his own thoughts before he continues. "I have patients who have never been sexually abused who still fantasize those thoughts and ask their partners to act on them. Some women like the bondage gig—it turns them on. I think it's in the female DNA from the cavemen days to want a strong man to dominate, although I'm sure some liberal women will vehemently disagree with my take on the matter."

He flashes a knowing grin, and I'm shocked over his opinion.

"If consenting adults enjoy it and nobody gets physically hurt, I'm not that opposed to the practice. However, that being said, I don't agree when the need interferes with a person's ability to function normally and indicates a deeper mental problem under the surface that turns into criminal activity and torture of a non-consenting adult." He's sounding quite serious in his clarification of the line he's drawn.

"I'm surprised you think that for some it's okay," I burst out nervously. "I constantly struggle with the guilt that my bondage fantasies are morally wrong."

"You struggle with it because that behavior was forced upon you as a child. In your developmental years, a male implanted that idea into your brain, and it took root and grew. You don't know anything else, Rachel. Bondage and pain during sex is wired into your personality, because you were taught to relate to your sexuality that way by another man."

He pauses for a moment and then bombards me with a shockingly intimate question.

"Do you get aroused when you just think about it?"

I pull my eyes away, and stare out at the ocean. The shame covers me. "Yes. My body betrays me. Just the thought of it, and I'm aroused. It really bugs me, because I can't control it, even if I try."

"That's because you're tuned to that frequency."

"Yeah, I get that," I admit in a frustrated voice. "But I don't want to have these masochist tendencies, because I keep reliving what my abuser did to me. That's why I think of them as deviant behavior and perversion and not kinky sex to enjoy like other women."

"That's quite understandable. Actually, the psychiatric community doesn't categorize masochist tendencies in consensual relationships as a mental illness like it used to be, unless it adversely affects your life to a place where you can't function or you put yourself in physical danger."

"My counselor told me that, too, but I don't think it brought me much comfort, frankly. I feel terrible having these urges, and I carry a lot of guilt over it, as if something is terribly wrong with me as a human being."

"Rachel, in your case, if you keep abusing yourself privately, it only reinforces those beliefs, because you keep reliving the instance of abuse over and over in your mind. You'll never think any differently. You need your hard drive erased and a new program installed."

I chuckle at his comment. Yeah, I'm a broken computer, that's for sure. "I don't get tenderness and love," I admit. "It's hard for me to comprehend or understand it. All I get is the does not compute error."

Jack takes a deep breath, and then reaches over and takes my hand. I'm shocked that he's actually touching me. It's clearly not the psychiatrist coming out of him now; it's the brother of the man I love.

"Rachel, being in a loving relationship

with someone like Ian can help rewire your desires. If you stick with counseling and open your heart to learn to receive love, eventually you'll want to experience it rather than the abuse. The desire to be hurt and bound will give way to the desire to be loved and freed. Believe me. It may be there even now under the surface waiting to be released at the right time when you decide to open that door."

That's it. I lose it. The waterworks spill over my lower lids and run down my cheeks. "You two are unreal," I say, looking at him and chuckling through my tears. "I didn't know kindness still existed in the male species until I met the Richards family."

"Hey, we're not perfect," he quickly corrects me. "If you stick around long enough, I'm sure you'll see our little quirks."

"I hope so. I know that Ian is trying to decide what to do about Susan."

"Susan?" Jack heaves a puff of air from his lungs and his face surprisingly turns dark. "Confidentially, between you and me, I've never liked the woman."

I'm astonished at his raised voice and intently look at him as he continues.

"She was all wrong for Ian from the get-go. Susan is an arrogant, controlling, selfish bitch, and I'd wish she'd leave him the hell alone. She's only screwing with his head and emotions, and that pisses me off," he says angrily.

"Wow, you do have faults," I tease him.

"Hey, I tell it like it is when it comes to family."

The door slides open, and Ian pokes his head out. "What's going on out here?"

"Wouldn't you like to know," Jack says, shifting to his feet. He gives me a wink and I smile. "What's the score?" he asks, walking back into the great room.

Karen returns with a bowl of pretzels in hand and another pop for me. She gives me a knowing glance, and I feel relieved.

"You've got a nice husband," I say, taking a pretzel and shoving it into my mouth.

"Yeah, he's a keeper," she says, taking one herself. We both sit there munching the snacks and looking out over the ocean. I feel relieved the quiz is over and hope that I didn't flunk the test.

The game ends and Karen and Jack are

standing at the door saying their goodbyes. I feel like I've known them both for years and am sorry to see them go. Jack is remarkable, and so is Karen.

"You guys leaving in the morning?" Ian asks.

"Yeah, driving to PDX. We have an eleven o'clock flight back to Boston.

"It was good seeing you both with mom and dad," Ian says, reaching over and slipping his arm around my waist and pulling me to his side. I think he's giving some kind of signal to Jack, but I'm not sure.

"It was nice meeting you both," I say, smiling. "I hope I get to see you again." There, I've made my own statement of sorts.

"Well, that's possible." Jack looks at Karen with a mischievous grin upon his face.

"Might as well tell him now," she chides him.

"Tell me what?" Ian asks.

"I got offered a position as assistant head of psychiatry at the university medical center up on the hill."

"No kidding, bro! Did you take it?" Ian's voice is ecstatic.

"I'm thinking about it."

"Take it, damn it!"

"I don't know," he says, shaking his head. "It rains too much in Portland."

"Yeah, and when the Nor'easter blizzard hits you this winter in Boston, don't go calling me up and complaining," Ian ribs him. "I hear it's El Nino this year, so you're in for it."

Karen pokes Jack in the side. "Stop teasing your brother and tell him."

"I accepted," Jack confesses with a big grin.

"Great! Do mom and dad know?"

"Yeah, I told them not to say anything until I had a chance to tell you. Mom's delighted to have both of her boys back on the west coast."

"God, that's great, Jack."

"I'll be calling you to help me with housing."

"Hey, I'm on it. When you moving?"

"The hospital is giving me a couple months to relocate."

I can sense Ian's joy, and I'm happy for him. After we all exchange hugs, Jack and Karen drive back to the inn. The house feels empty. The day is coming to a close. I look at Ian feeling sad that it will soon end.

"It's late, are we heading back to

Portland?"

Ian closes the door. "I don't feel like driving back, Rachel. Would you mind staying the night, and I'll drive you back early in the morning in time for work?"

I smile at the thought. "Sure, I'd love to." Ian looks at me adoringly. "So, what did Jack have to say about me?" I'm dying for him to spill the beans.

"He said that you're on the right track, and that I should keep you around." Ian brings me into his arms and gives me a passionate kiss. I passed the exam and melt with relief.

Chapter 24

A HEALING MOMENT

Ian and I share the same bed and fall asleep hugging each other. A few hours later, a bright light suddenly awakens me. My eyes open, and to my horror, Susan Richards is standing at the foot of the bed. The vile look on her face gives me the shivers. She is dressed to the hilt and looks like a Vogue cover model. I can't believe that she is here.

"Ian." I nudge him gently in the side.

"What?"

"We have company."

He stirs, and for a brief moment confusion flashes across his face as he wakes up.

"Ian," she hisses through her clenched jaw. "What the hell are you doing?" She thrusts both her hands on her hips and postures herself boldly.

Casually, Ian sits up in bed, while I grab

the sheet and cover my bra.

"Sleeping" he answers. "What does it look like?"

I can't believe he's so calm while the three of us are in his bedroom.

"More like sleeping after fucking a whore, you bastard."

Suddenly her attention turns to me. She eyes me for a moment, and then the light goes on in her pretty little head. "I know you." She scowls. "You're that inept assistant at Kennedy Advertising."

Inept. What kind of shit remark is that? Now I'm pissed.

"Boy, Ian, you must have been desperate for a lay to stoop to her level," she spits. Susan glowers at me as if I'm a prostitute.

"Shut your condescending mouth," Ian angrily jabs back.

He turns and looks at me and heaves a frustrated sigh. His eyes are ablaze, and I can see he's mad as hell. "Stay here sweets, I'll be right back."

I nod in an agreement, because I'm certainly staying out of this argument. He swings his legs out of bed, and gets to his feet. Quickly, he takes Susan by the upper arm and escorts her down the stairs.

"Why are you in bed with that trash?" she snaps at him.

I sit straight up in bed and scoot to the end so I can see them at the other end of the great room. They're standing by the sliding glass door. She's postured in his face. Ian is raking both his hands through his unruly hair, but holding it together.

"Would you stop yelling at me?" he calmly asks.

"Why are you with her?" she yells again.

"It's none of your business."

"Like hell it isn't."

"What are you doing here anyway?" His face turns into an angry scowl.

"I ended my trip early and thought I would surprise you, and it is my business! She's in our bed in our house, you bastard!"

Ian raises his palm in the air like he's halting oncoming traffic. "Now wait a minute. Last I knew this was *my* house and *my* bed. We are still divorced, and you don't fit into the equation of property ownership."

Susan's face seethes. I can see her turning multiple shades of red from where I'm sitting. This is not good.

"You bastard, see if I'll ever take you back now." She snarls at him.

"You act like taking me back is doing me some kind a favor. That's a bunch of horseshit, Susan," Ian spits back at her. "You just lost the last man you failed to control, now you want to weasel yourself back in my life and start controlling me again. Well, it isn't happening."

Way to go, Ian! I think to myself.

To my utter horror, she hauls off and slaps him in the face really hard. I want to jump up and run downstairs to strangle the woman. It's all I can do to contain myself. Ian doesn't react. He merely holds out his hand palm up.

"I want the key back that I gave you. Then, get the hell out of *my* house."

"Fine," she says, taking it off her key ring. She throws it against the wall and glares at him like a witch. "I hope you rot in hell with your whore."

Susan turns around, stomps toward the door, and slams it on her way out. Ian disappears, and I hear him lock it behind her. I scoot back toward the headboard and wait for his return. He looks frazzled when he reaches the landing.

"I'm really sorry about that, Rachel," he says, crawling back in bed. "Come here."

I quickly scoot to his side and let his arms encircle me. *Does this mean I won?* A flood of relief flows through my veins that she's gone, but I have to hear it from his lips.

"Are you done with her, Ian?" My voice is trembling.

"Done."

He turns my face up toward him and kisses me. Ian's tongue enters my mouth, and I'm putty in his hands. A moment later, he looks into my eyes. "I love you Rachel, and I'm not letting you go . . . ever."

Oh, my God, I can't believe the sincere adoration in his eyes. It's impossible to contain myself, and I hug him tightly. "I love you too, Ian."

We hold each other, and I revel in the moment of being in his arms. The embrace between us is warm and inviting.

"I need you, Rachel—need you bad."

I know what he means, and I want him too. The no-sex gig is off.

"Then I'm yours," I tell him sweetly, touching his reddened cheek where Susan slapped him. "Why don't you take my bra and panties off and let me comfort you." Wow, I can't believe that came out of my mouth.

"You sure?" He's hesitating, but I don't want him to wait.

"I love you Ian, and I want you to make love to me."

He tenderly strokes the side of my face and smiles sweetly. "I love you too, Rachel, and that's exactly what I'm going to do to you—make love."

Oh, God, I can't believe this is happening to me. Jack was right. I want Ian to love me, and he does. My whole body feels as if warm honey has been poured upon me. He kisses me with sweet passion, and my tongue swirls around his. I'm aching for him.

My body begins to tremble as his warm hands embrace me. He slips his smooth palm across my breasts, down my waist, and over my thighs and legs. My panties and bra disappear somewhere between kisses. His mouth finds my nipple, and he sucks on it making it erect in his mouth.

The whole experience is dreamlike. I can sense his love through his fingertips, and I arch as his fingers slide up my inner thigh and enter me. The door in the back of my mind is closed, and a new awareness of self-worth keeps it shut. I trust him and have no doubt of his sincerity as his love begins to consume me with his skillful hands.

Ian takes his time to make sure I'm enjoying every movement of his long fingers, while he kisses me and keeps my legs parted.

"You like it like this?" he asks in a dreamy voice, as he stimulates me with one hand and fondles my breast with another.

I look at him like a drugged woman and nod.

After a few moments of deep penetration, I feel him take my wetness and spread the lubrication. His actions surprise me.

"What about this," he asks, with a devious looks upon his face. He takes his finger out and inserts his thumb instead, and then slides his middle finger gently backward and brings pressure against his penetration into my vagina. I can't believe what he's done!

"Oh, my God, Ian, you're driving me crazy. What are you doing?" I'm literally having spasms of pleasure over his little trick. My eyes widen with astonishment that he even knows how to do that or wants to, for that matter. I see him hovering over me with a self-assured smile, and I wonder if he's been reading dirty magazines to find ways to do me.

"What do you think I'm doing to you, Rachel Ann Hayward?" He pushes his thumb into me deeper. "I'm making you wet and ready for me."

I moan in the pleasure. It's almost unbearable, and I never thought I would ever think those thoughts.

"Ian," I beg, gasping for breath. "Please, stop."

"You don't like?" he says, pulling his thumb and finger out and looking a tad disappointed.

"I love it, but I need you now. Fill me," I beg. I sound desperate.

Ian licks his lips and stares into my eyes. There's a wicked glint in his gaze as he stands up, takes off his pajama bottoms, and exposes himself to me. He reaches for the nightstand drawer and grabs a condom.

"Oh, so you want my cock, is that it?"

God, he's talking dirty and driving me berserk. When he's through with the protection, I wish he didn't have to wear, he climbs on top of me. I open my legs to receive him. Slowly, he slips inside of me and thrusts deep. My eyes roll back in my head, and then he starts his movements. He's more aggressive, but still laced with tenderness. The fullness feels incredible, and I lose myself to the sensations.

His hands slip underneath my buttocks, and he pulls me up into him and angles my body to bring more pressure. Back and forth he glides deeply into me. He's pressed hard against my clitoris, and it's sending shivers through my body. The feeling is glorious and intense. My legs are wrapped around his waist, so that his penetration is deep and unhindered.

"Rachel," he whispers with a heavy breath. "Open your eyes and look at me."

I do. His blue-eyed gaze is piercingly intense.

"You're the most delicious woman, I've ever known," he says. "You have no idea how tight and wonderful you feel inside, sweetheart."

His breathing gets heavier, and he doesn't take his eyes off me. The sexual tension in my body is rising to a place of explosion. I start to close my eyes again to go to that dark place, but he gives me a command.

"No, Rachel. Don't go there. Keep looking at *me.*"

My eyes shoot open, and I look into his face. I'm mesmerized by his call to remain.

"Look at me and think about what *I'm* doing to you right now. Feel it," he exhales, with a deep voice.

Oh, my God, I can barely handle it. It's almost there—at that place where you peak and know at any moment that ecstasy will throw you over the side into pleasurable oblivion. Our eyes are fixed upon one another, and I'm lost in his love.

"Keep looking at me, Rachel. Don't leave me." He lowers his head and fervently kisses me, pushing his tongue deep into my mouth.

Ian will not let me go into that dark room. He's purposely keeping me there with him, as if he owns me and rules me now instead of my past. It's insane to think I'm so close to actually experiencing it with a man who is drowning me in passionate love. I don't want bondage. I want Ian's lovemaking, and that's all my mind feels— his pressing fullness making me one with him.

He releases my mouth and looks at me again. "Come on, Rachel, give it to me. I want to feel it."

His thrusting intensifies, and then it happens—I burst with pleasure. "Oh, my God," I scream like a wild woman. My hands grab his back and a rush of sweet release fills my abdomen. Ian is right there with me, and with one hard thrust, he groans loudly over his own climax.

This is insane, I scream in my mind. The orgasm is deep, lingering and pleasurable as it flows through my body. I'm overwhelmed that he's captivated me in love. It's too much, and the tears start rolling down the side of my face and into the pillow.

"Oh, sweetheart, what's wrong?" he asks tenderly, stroking my face with the palm of his hand. Ian looks sadly at me, but stays inside of me. I don't want him to pull out. I want to be part of him forever.

"Nothing," I blubber. "I'm just so thankful for you because you love me . . . really love me."

A small smile parts his lips as he looks adoringly at me underneath him. "I'm thankful for you too, Rachel. You're the best accident I've ever had."

I glory in the release that flows through my head to my toes. Ian is indeed one gracious gift from heaven above.

Chapter 25

THEY DO EXIST

I am back at work Monday morning and feeling wonderful. My appointment with Dr. Grayson is after work, and I'm anxious to tell her about the weekend. You wouldn't think that having an orgasm, without the thought of bondage and pain, would be front page news, but for me it was a milestone.

I know that I can't quit now, and I don't intend to either. Ian means the world to me, and I want to totally recover. There are still lingering fears and doubts, but with help, I'm hoping to slay the remainder of the demons behind that closed door.

After I arrive at her office, I relay to Dr. Grayson the entire story of seeing Ian, my weekend meeting his family, and Susan's uninvited arrival. She sits there with her mouth open, listening to my tale. When I get to the orgasm part, she looks surprised and pleased.

"Why do you think that happened, Rachel?"

It doesn't take me long to figure it out. "Because I opened my heart to him. I believed what he told me, that he loved me, and I didn't doubt it." I paused for a moment. "I trusted."

"Do you have any fears that it won't last?"

"Some," I admit, fiddling with the corner of the pillow on the divan. "But, I trust Ian. He's a different kind of man, and I know he'll treat me respectfully no matter what happens in the future."

"So you met his family? How did that go?"

"Ian didn't tell me that it was coming, so I didn't have much of a chance to balk over the idea." I shake my head, thinking of his sneaky trick. "They were exceptionally nice. Oh, and you won't believe this."

"What?"

"His brother is a shrink—I mean a psychiatrist."

"Really, well, I'll be damned," she spouts an unprofessional utterance. "How did that go over?"

"We had a really good conversation. I hope you don't mind, but Ian had told him about my background, and of course, he had concerns. It was crucial for me to let him know about my progression in therapy."

"Did he give you any advice you found worthy?"

"Well, he confirmed a lot of what we've talked about here. He gave a good analogy about wiping the hard drive of my brain clean and reinstalling new software."

"That's one way of putting it," Dr. Grayson smirks.

"Yeah. And he was right about one thing."

"What's that?"

"That I, in time, would respond to love and not abuse. I think that's what happened when Ian told me how he felt."

"So, tell me, Rachel, what are your plans now?"

"To stay in this office as long as I need to, frankly. Is that okay with you?"

"Of course, it is. There are still some areas we need to work through."

"I know."

"Why don't you make a note of those this week, and come back with a list of the challenges you think remain in your life. We'll tackle those in the months ahead."

"Okay."

"I'm assuming that you're going to continue seeing Ian?"

"Yes, of course."

She jots a few more notes. We talk a little more, and then I'm out the door and back to life. For the first time in years, I actually feel deep joy in my heart.

— · ❈ · —

The months pass. Work is work. Ian is tied to his law firm desk. I'm still making my appointments with Dr. Grayson. We spend the weekends together at his beach house.

Ian and I let our relationship grow as it should. My propensity for bondage and torture in bed is nearly non-existent now, as I allow him to love me and receive my love in return. However, I've noticed that Ian has loosened up a bit in the sack, too, which makes me happy. He's learning new tricks that he finds pleasure in.

The only place he never forces me to go is oral sex. I've been entirely honest with him that I can't handle it, and I don't know if I ever will. The male penis, as much pleasure as it gives when inserted into my body, makes me gag at the thought of it in my mouth. It's still hard for me to look at one with any desire—it's only the touch and feel it brings to me inwardly that I like.

I've talked extensively to Dr. Grayson about my aversion, and she thinks it's because my abuser forced it upon me as a child. My innocent eyes saw a part of a man's body that I was not mature enough to handle. Though I don't remember him bringing it to my mouth, the revulsion remains in my subconscious. Each time I saw him brandish his erection, it deeply affected the way I relate to the male appendage, even today.

Ian, however, understands totally. He's not that crazed about oral sex either, which confirms to me that we're a pretty good match. He doesn't feel slighted because I don't suck on him, and I don't feel bad he's not doing me either. I'm learning to please him in other ways, as he teaches me some of his pleasure points that I can handle and the fun new positions we're trying.

Jack and Karen have moved to Portland and purchased a house in the swanky neighborhood of Lake Oswego. We helped them get settled into their new lives. Karen has become a close friend. We talk often on the phone and have an occasional lunch out. She is the first woman I've ever met that I don't feel threatened by, and I know that's part of my healing.

Three months after Jack and Karen move, Ian's parents fly up from San Francisco to see the boys. To celebrate, we all have dinner at the Portland City Grill downtown. It's my first time there, and the view is spectacular from the thirtieth floor in the US Bancorp Tower.

As we ascend in the elevator, Ian has his arm around my waist. He looks handsome, as usual, dressed in a dark suit. I'm in the tight black dress that he likes, wearing a real gold necklace and earrings, which he gave to me as a gift a month earlier.

We step off the elevator, and I sense that he's nervous about the evening ahead. His hand around my waist is cold like ice, which is unusual. I wonder why the anxiety on his part.

When we arrive, I find out that we're eating in a small, private dining room. As soon as we walk in, Jack, Karen, Bill, and Grace all brandish a welcoming smile over our arrival.

"Rachel, it's so good to see you." Grace comes over and gives me a hug. Ian shakes his dad's hand. Everybody is grinning from ear to ear. I'm beginning to wonder if Jack and Karen are going to announce she's pregnant tonight, which would be nice, because I know they've been trying for some time. I'm surprised we're cloistered away like one big happy family behind closed doors. I don't get it, but on the other hand, I like the privacy.

As I sit at the table and sip my few allotted dribbles of white wine, I'm overwhelmed. I feel so much a part of everyone here now that I cannot imagine being anywhere else.

Ian keeps grabbing my hand under the table. Occasionally, he gives me a knee squeeze, and I glare at him to stop it. He flashes a teasing grin. It's not the place to get me riled up thinking of sex. Jack will probably see it all over my face, and I'll blush red.

After dinner, we're all filled and relaxed. Suddenly, everyone quits talking, and all eyes shift to Ian. The moment is awkward, and I don't get what's going on, until he rises to his feet. When I look up at him, he reaches into his pocket and pulls out a black velvet case. A second later, he's on one knee in front of me. All eyes are upon us, because apparently they know exactly what shenanigans he's up to. I gasp anticipating what is about to transpire.

"Ian, what are you doing?" I whisper, glowering at him with wide eyes.

"What do you think, Rachel?"

"I asked you first."

He looks at me with a sweet face and sexy smile. "Rachel Ann Hayward, would you marry me?"

My heart stops beating for a brief moment. I bring my hands to my mouth. Tears sting my eyes. Kind and handsome Ian Richards wants to marry *me*. Not once have we talked about marriage the entire time we have been together, and now he's on his knee asking me to spend the remainder of my life with him. I stare at him dumbfounded.

"You better not say no," he says, breaking the silence. "Because my family is watching."

Everyone laughs aloud as they wait for me to answer. How can I turn down my Prince Charming? I'm living my dream. *Do it, Rachel, this is your chance for happiness,* I hear my inner child encourage me with a joyful voice. I know it is, too, and I'm not going to let anyone steal happiness from me again.

"Yes, Ian Alexander Richards, I'll marry you."

He takes out the most beautiful ring and slips it on my finger. I'm dazzled over the sparkling diamond. The little girl inside of me smiles, and at that moment, I see her grow into a confident woman. My tormentors behind the dark door have left, because they have lost their bid for my soul.

Ian stands up and brings me to my feet with his cold, nervous hands.

"Come on, kiss her," Jack encourages him loudly.

Gently, he places his palms on the sides of my face. As I gaze into his beautiful blue eyes, I am lost in the love and adoration that he shows me. His mouth comes down over mine, and his sweetness fills my soul. When he pulls away, a tear rolls down my cheek.

"I love you, Ian."

"I love you too, sweets."

Now I know that men really do love, because the evidence is holding me in his arms.

All of a sudden, I believe in fairy godmothers, angels, and heaven above. It feels glorious to be loved and to love someone I can trust. My worth has returned, and my redemption is complete.

Epilogue

The last box is finally unpacked. I can't believe the move is over. As I survey the work that's still ahead to get everything in order, I feel a bit overwhelmed. Nevertheless, I can't complain. How could I complain when I'm living my dream life?

After pouring myself a much-needed cup of coffee, I walk over to the French doors that lead out to the back deck. The view is breathtaking, but part of me misses the old. Though we're only another mile south of where Ian's former house in Cannon Beach stood, it still contains so many memories. Yet, as I look around at our new home, with the much-needed extra space, I know that we have a lifetime to build memories together here.

Whiskers wraps himself around my legs a few times, then goes over and lays in the sun. He's a happy cat. I sip my coffee and then shade my eyes with my left hand. The afternoon sun is lowering to the water, and my husband is off in the distance playing with our toddler, now entering her terrible twos. She's in no way terrible and looks a lot like me when I was her age.

Ian and I married three years ago in a beautiful wedding. My brother gave me away. After a long, hard road to forgiveness, we mended our relationship. I knew if I were to heal totally, I had to pardon whatever wrongs I harbored against him.

To my surprise, Bob swears he never knew what happened to me in that upstairs bedroom. At first, I didn't believe him; but when I see the clueless look in his eyes, I know it to be true. He had always been sort of a naïve dork, and he was only eleven or twelve. Of course, it wasn't his fault, either, that I kept returning for another candy bar until the abuse finally ended.

As far as Bob's inability to keep in touch, that was a characteristic he never possessed. I accepted the way he was and released him to be the man he had become. The gap between us had been mended at the wedding, but I knew in my heart he'd probably drift away again in the future, and he did.

Jack and Karen had their first child, a boy, a year after we wed. Then Ian, surprised me one day by announcing he had been hired by a small firm in Seaside, Oregon, about twelve miles north of our new home. I was thrilled to think living on the coast would be my fulltime job, as well as being a mother to a darling little girl.

As I continue to watch Ian and Rebecca play together, I'm thankful that she is still an innocent child. Each day I pray to God that she remains innocent and untouched until she is a young woman and meets the right man who will give her love. I never want my tender baby to endure what I endured. Ian is diligent, as well, to see that she grows up unscathed. He is a wonderful, loving, and gentle father.

Ian picks up Rebecca in his arms and walks back toward our home. The sun is setting, and it's getting chilly outdoors. As he arrives at the deck and climbs the few steps, my heart warms at the sight of him. I love him more than I can express in words and am so thankful that he gave me the unconditional love and patience that I needed to heal from my past.

"Hey sweets," he says, coming up and giving me a peck on the cheek. His endearing term remains.

Rebecca reaches out her arms to me, and I take her from Ian. Her brown hair is blowing in her eyes, so I carefully brush it away until her beautiful face is no longer hidden.

"You know what, Rebecca?" I give her a kiss on the cheek. "Fairy godmothers, angels, and heaven do exist. Don't ever doubt it."

Ian smiles, knowing exactly what I mean. I look at him lovingly, thankful to God for the gracious gift that came into my life.

The End

Conflicting Hearts Now Available

on Audio

About the Author

J. D. Burrows is a pen name for the author's contemporary romance novels. She also writes under the name of Vicki Hopkins in the historical fiction and historical romance genre. Her works include:

The Phantom of Valletta
(Historical Fiction/Gothic Romance)
A continuation of Gaston Leroux's Phantom of the Opera; Released July 2010
Received Recognition from
The Sunday Times, Malta

The Price of Innocence
Book One – The Legacy Series
(Historical Fiction/Family Sagas)
Released February 2010

The Price of Deception
Book Two – The Legacy Series
(Historical Fiction/Family Sagas)
Released October 2011

The Price of Love
Book Three – The Legacy Series
(Historical Fiction/Family Sagas)
Released October 2013

Dark Persuasion
(Historical Romance)
Released August 2012; *Five Star Top Pick
Award and Award-Winning Finalist in the
'Fiction: Romance' category of The 2012
USA Best Book Awards, sponsored by USA
Book News*

For more information visit the following
websites:

http://vickihopkins.com

http://conflictinghearts.com